Belles' Letters

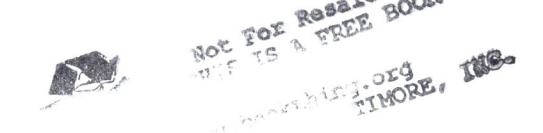

Belles' Letters

Contemporary Fiction
by Alabama Women

edited by

Joe Taylor
&
Tina N. Jones

ISBN 0-942979-57-5, paper
ISBN 0-942979-58-3, cloth

Library of Congress Catalog Card Number # 98-89360

Foreword copyright Tina N. Jones © 1999

All other copyrights belong to individual authors

Judith Richards copyright ©1978 *Summer Lightning*

Cover photo of editor: Jana Heatherly
Cover illustration: Ronnie Maddox

Printed in the United States of America
by
Gilliland Printing

Printed on acid-free paper

Thanks to the following for their typing & proofreading: Anne Briggs, Rebecca Chandler, Nicole Green, Geoffrey Hodge, Lee Holland, Stephanie Parnell, Michal Shar, Kathy Truelove, Wanda Jones, and Jill Wallace

Typesetting and layout: Jill Wallace

Cover design: Tina N. Jones & Joe Taylor

"Specializing in offbeat & Southern literature"
Livingston Press
at The University of West Alabama
Station 22
Livingston, Alabama 35470

Table of Contents

Tina N. Jones	*Foreword*	iv
Robyn Allers	"Alva Beth Sings the Blues"	1
Emma Bolden	"Dead Lands"	14
Wendy Reed Bruce	"Harold Washburn"	20
Marian Carcache	"The Other"	29
Loretta Cobb	"Seeing It Through"	36
Sandra King Conroy	"Fig Picking"	47
Linda Elliott	"Mrs. McCammock"	56
Anita Miller Garner	"Julian Carol Finds the Pine Cones"	58
Anne George	"Where Have You Gone, Shirley Temple?"	61
Aileen Kilgore Henderson	"Leetha's Own"	65
Laura Hunter	"Fishtales Told to a Crow, Mid-spring"	75
Cindy Jones	"Imp-Dancing in the Heart of Dixie"	82
Janet Mauney	excerpted from *Tattoo*	89
Patricia Mayer	excerpted from *Terminal Bend*	93
Julia Oliver	"A Touch of the Spirit"	101
Ann Vaughan Richards	excerpted from *Miss Woman*	107
Judith Richards	excerpted from *Summer Lightning*	112
Michelle Richmond	"The Last Bad Thing"	118
Mary Louise Robison	"Baby in the Cold Frame"	127
Scarlett Robinson Saavedra	excerpted from *Living in the River*	135
Carolynne Scott	"Dancing in the Basement"	141
Millie Anton Skinner	"A Bully and His Victim"	148
B. K. Smith	"Calling Up the Moon"	153
Patricia Lou Taylor	"Sex on the Beach"	161
Tammy Townsend	"Piano Lessons"	168
Betty Jean Tucker	"The Dog That Wasn't a Dog"	175

Foreword

The screen flickers to life, and the theatre grows immediately silent. Vivian Leigh in the role of Scarlet O'Hara sits in a garden surrounded by men openly courting her. Her white dress, trimmed vividly in emerald green, accents her dark hair and white skin. A wide-brimmed hat with oversized green bow frames her face. I, at the age of six, sit in my squeaking theatre chair mesmerized. Smiling to myself, I think I have discovered what it means to be a Southern Belle. In my six-year-old imagination a Southern Belle was demanding attention as a result of her dress, her manners, and her ability to hold everyone at bay with her witty conversation. A Southern Belle knew not to wear white after Labor Day, black patent before Easter; and she knew pearls were always appropriate no matter the occasion or the time.

Imagine my surprise as I grew older and discovered that ScarletO'Hara is not the epitome of Southern womanhood. She's not even representative. Scarlet O' Hara represents what historians call "the stuff of legend." The legend is a planter aristocracy of the Old South symbolized by large white-columned homes, beautifully dressed women, acres and acres of cotton, and slavery. These images are hard to deny as one travels through Alabama towns such as Demopolis, Eutaw, and Gainesville and sees still-standing Greek Revival homes with names such as Gaineswood, Kirkwood, and the Magnolias.

But these are images of the Old South and have nothing to do with the collection of stories presented in this text. *Belles' Letters* represents contemporary stories of Alabama women writers, right? Well, whether the story of Scarlet O'Hara is accurate or not, her image cannot be dismissed easily. No matter one's race or class, stereotypes are the initial tools children often use to define their places in the world. These stereotypes of the Old South are ones writers continue to struggle with as their South changes constantly, though the images which appeared distinctly Southern, such as old-fashioned homes with big front porches, occasionally succumb to the latest strip mall, a new McDonalds or Burger King, and yet another gas station.

So Scarlet O'Hara becomes the first step many little girls take to discover their worlds aren't portrayed by Hollywood. They know the Old South existed, and in that world it was legal for one man to own another man. They understand that writers of the late nineteenth century like William Gilmore Simms sentimentalized plantation life, portraying it as an ordered paternalistic society governed by a strong code of ethics and chivalry. The Plantation myth provided a society—both North and South—which was trying to understand repeated stories in daily newspapers telling of industrialization and ostentatious displays of wealth counter-pointing images of desperate poverty, with an alternate image of a slower lifestyle.

Obvious romantic images of the above sort create an injustice when the Southern image narrows to include only the two races of black and white, and when historical portrayals include only the Civil War and Civil Rights. Southern people and writers, especially those of Alabama, are as varied as the geography that they call home. Whether they choose to place their stories in the foothills of the Appalachians in North Alabama, the golden beaches of the Gulf of Mexico, or in the rich black earth of the Black Belt, the women writers represented in *Belles' Letters* are much too complex to accept misleading stereotypes which trivialize their own identities as women and writers. They know, just as I came to learn, that beyond stereotypes are individuals; and in this volume of short stories women authors of Alabama reveal the humanity of individuals—their hopes, their dreams, their fears, and their heartaches.

Southern writer Doris Betts says, "these days you don't have aristocratic plantation writers like Faulkner. You have people who have come out of the beauty shops and the trailer parks . . . the usual literary motifs historically classified as 'Southern' are being modified by contemporary male and female, black and white. . . ." The Depression, two world wars, Vietnam, Civil Rights, and AIDS have all left their footprints on the stories now coming out of the South. The Alabama women writers of this collection embrace their Native American, African American, Scot, Japanese, Irish, and Spanish cultures. They acknowledge C. Vann Woodward's warning in which he cautioned against placing too much emphasis on the unity of the South, and they depict a South that is unified only by a knowledge of a shared past, not necessarily a shared interpretation of that past.

For me, *Belles' Letters* is important because Alabama women are allowed a voice all their own. They do not have to share their pages with anyone but themselves. They are free to tell their stories. After two years of reading, editing , and sorting through the work of over 120 authors, all of whom claim to be Alabama writers, my co-editor and I have found a rich literary world where past, present, future, and sometimes the imaginary weave to form a place like no other. Long after the covers of *Belles' Letters* have been closed and the book has been laid aside, we are certain the experiences and stories shared by these authors will be recalled because of a song, a house, or even a voice encountered while traveling through the worlds of Alabama's contemporary women writers.

As with any work there are many people who need to be thanked for its completion. *Belles' Letters* is no different. Joe Taylor and I owe much gratitude first to the Sumter County Fine Arts Council for agreeing with us that the writing of Alabama Women deserves to be recognized. Mostly, we want to thank the authors: ours is a small, non-profit press, so we "paid" in contributors' copies. We would also like to thank Jake Reiss of Highland Booksmith for his zealous promotion of this work.

—Tina Naremore Jones, Livingston

Dedicated to

our familes

Robyn Allers

Alva Beth Sings the Blues

*I*n her early morning dream, Alva Beth sits in a dark, smoky bar with Bessie Smith, who talks to her about love. "Honey, what I know about love could fill this room," Bessie says. Her sable-colored fingers wave away a thin blue layer of cigarette smoke and through the paisley it makes around her face, she whispers, "Love is like smoke. In the morning, child, ain't nothing left but the stink."

Bessie Smith throws her head back and laughs, her laughter the sound of a trumpet wailing a single note, high and long, like something stuck. Alva Beth covers her ears, but the sound only gets louder and sharper, piercing right through her until she wakes. And gradually, as the vividness of the dream recedes, Alva Beth realizes that what she hears is neither music nor laughter, but machinery.

"Jesus Christ," she mutters. She throws off the sheet and clomps down the upstairs hallway, following the grinding hum into her parents' empty bedroom. She stands, naked and grumpy, at the French doors that lead onto the balcony. The tree surgeon stands in a little bucket not fifty yards away taking a chain saw to the limb of a live oak. She watches as the saw slices clean through and the branch crashes with a thud to the ground. The tree surgeon cuts off the chain saw motor and looks down, yelling something to someone Alva Beth can't see. He lifts the chain saw easily, as if it were a toy, and braces it on the edge of the bucket. Sunlight, filtered through the branches, dapples his body with shadows that dance over the muscular curve of chest like a strobe. His torso seems to waver, and Alva Beth fears for a moment that his weight will propel him over the side. He lifts his safety goggles high on his forehead and rubs his cheekbones with broad fingers. As he reaches again for the goggles, he looks at the window where Alva Beth stands behind sheer curtains. He nods as though he were being introduced, and then slides the goggles over his eyes and turns away. He grips the side of the bucket as it descends out of sight.

*

In her junior year at Furman, Alva Beth went through what her mother describes as a "very social phase" and as a result is spending the summer back in Alabama, attending a state university to make up the credits she failed while she was being more social than studious. She tells her friends, when she calls them at their summer homes in Gulf Shores, that she is a prisoner in her own house.

"Help me, Merideth, I'm climbing the goddamn walls!"

Merideth understands and invites Alva Beth up for the weekend.

Alva Beth does not go. Because the truth is Alva Beth is not so much a prisoner this summer as a captor. She guards a feeling so new and tenuous that she wants to hang on to it simply because it is so strange and in its strangeness somehow promising. The sensation is powerful, like love, but has no focus outside itself. She goes to class, watches television, talks to her parents—but everything seems to go on from a distance, like a dream you're aware of even as you sleep. Her father thinks she's pouting, her mother fears it's drugs. Her friends believe she must be in love; only a man could keep Alva Beth away from the beach in the summer.

Alva Beth pulls on last year's bikini, hot pink with black polka dots, and a T-shirt. In the kitchen she warms a cup of yesterday's coffee in the microwave. Leaning against the counter she sees, as if it had suddenly appeared, her mother's note posted to the freezer door with a strawberry magnet: TREE MAN TUES.

Another whine of the chain saw shoots up Alva Beth's spine. The sound in her dream. What was it Bessie Smith said to her? Something about love. Alva Beth takes her coffee into the den and sits among the dozens of record albums she listened to the night before, as though the source of her dream will revive it. In the dream, Bessie's words seemed like a revelation. Life stinks, that was it. Alva Beth begins collecting the records, strewn in their wax-paper casings across the carpet. Or was it love? Love stinks, Bessie told her. Well, tell me something new, Alva Beth thinks, although at 20, she has yet to experience the heartbreak that normally produces such cynical generalizations.

The records are part of her daddy's treasured jazz collection which he keeps locked in a mahogany cabinet. Before last night, Alva Beth had seen his collection only once, at a party at which, with a ceremony inspired by gin and lust, he unlocked the cabinet for a select audience that included the wife of his firm's newest accountant, a petite blond with freckled shoulders. Watching from the doorway, Alva Beth frowned as her father, like a game show host revealing a valuable prize, pulled out a rare ten-inch LP and balanced it delicately between his palms. "Sippie Wallace—" he said, gazing directly at the blonde wife, "—one of the greatest blues singers ever." The wife nodded, as if this were a eulogy, and bit a bright coral lip. Alva Beth's father said, "Now those people knew the blues. Knew them clear down to their bones." As he ushered his audience into the dining room, Alva Beth noticed her father's hand against the small of the woman's back.

Alva Beth herself had no particular interest in Sippie Wallace or anyone else in her father's collection until last night. That's when, alone and looking for some small offense to relieve her boredom, she located the key to the cabinet and started playing all the records, one by one, in the chronological order of her father's arrangement. At first the tunes seemed funny, the sound tinny and thin, and Alva Beth giggled at the way the singers repeated lines as if they couldn't quite believe their own troubles. *Everybody is cryin' they can't get a break.* Troubles with lovers and bosses and booze and money. Real trouble. Inevitable, interminable trouble. *Everybody is cryin' they can't get a break.* Rich, black, mama-please voices and fuck-you voices, wailing, shouting, sliding up to a high-pitched whine and then sliding back down to a moan, voices wrapping themselves around a note, mourning it, hanging onto it until it hurt—or stopped the hurting. *Tell me what's the matter? Everything seems to ache.* Alva Beth played them all—Bukka and Blind Lemon and Bessie and Ma Rainey— "Oh, mama, sing those blues away," Alva Beth whispered in the dark, finally hearing the insistent, monotonous rhythm as just the echo of her own heartbeat. Alva Beth, sitting cross-legged on the floor in the dark of her daddy's paneled den, rocked back and forth, played the piano on her knees, fingered a trumpet in the air, waiting, wishing something would touch her, make her feel something clear down to her bones.

From the patio door, Alva Beth sips the last of her coffee and watches the tree surgeon. He is tying thick ropes around the base of the diseased live oak. Huge branches cover the back yard. A younger man, short and wiry, drags these off into piles. He grins at Alva Beth as she steps out onto the pool patio. Tufts of brown hair poke out like chewed feathers from beneath his red cap. "Did we wake you up, ma'am?"

Alva Beth shrugs. The tree surgeon barks at his partner. "Bobby, get over here and help me with this thing!" Alva Beth watches the tree surgeon as he begins slicing into the trunk of the tree, taking out little wedges all the way around. She doesn't see that Bobby is helping much at all.

The pool is still, like a solid sheet of cellophane, its clear surface flecked with a fine film of sawdust. She sits on the edge of the pool and eases her right foot into the water. Slowly, very slowly. She wants to see how far she can sink her leg without creating any movement in the water. But it's colder than she's used to; it tickles her leg and she kicks involuntarily, creating a tiny wake. "Damn," says Alva Beth, and then pulls off her T-shirt, gives a little push with her hands, and plunges in.

As she crouches on the pool's bottom, the water vibrates against her skin in rhythm with the dull hum of the chain saw. It's a strange, hypnotic sensation, like the reverberation of her own voice when she lies across her bed and sings into the mattress. Alva Beth decides she will try to stay under water until the chain saw stops. If she makes it, she will skip class today. She will have earned it. But the chain saw goes on and on, and Alva Beth begins to feel her heart pound as though it's grown too large for her chest. She will count to five and then come up, she decides, but by the time she gets to four she has to shoot up, gasping and angry. She turns toward the tree surgeon just at the moment he cuts off the chain saw and stands back, and they both watch the big tree fall to the ground. The vibration when the tree hits sends the water in the pool bouncing up along Alva Beth's ribs. The tree surgeon pushes his goggles up and turns to look at her.

"Thought you'd drowned," he says. "You want us to chop this into firewood?"

Alva Beth is still trying to catch her breath. "I guess." She pulls herself back up to the edge of the pool and squeezes the water out of her long brown hair. She notices the black polka dots of her bikini top pulsing in rhythm with her heart. She wonders if the tree surgeon notices. "What else would you do with it?"

"Cart it away." He rests a dusty boot on the log. "In my opinion, wood this dead would not last long beside the curb. This here was a helluva tree."

Alva Beth has not thought one way or the other about the tree since she was ten years old. "I used to swing in it when I was a kid."

The tree surgeon looks up again. It seems to Alva Beth that he looks beyond her, not directly at her. "I figured. We cut the swing down. Put it over yonder." He points in the direction of the bathhouse. "Rope was rotten, of course. But the swing itself was solid. A very solid piece of wood." He reaches down for the saw.

"You got any kids?"

The tree surgeon halts mid-bend. He does not look up. "Beg your pardon?"

"Do you have any children? I mean, I haven't used that swing in years, and I just thought if you have kids—and, you know, a tree—you could take the swing."

He stands upright, but his eyes remain fixed on the log beneath his gaze. "Yes. As a matter of fact I do have a tree suitable for swinging." He pauses and does something with the side of his mouth—Alva Beth isn't sure if it's a smile or a sneer. "I also have a baby girl," he says.

These are not the words Alva Beth expects, though she's not sure why. But she suddenly feels ashamed for exposing herself so blatantly—now, in her polka dot bikini, and upstairs where she and the tree surgeon first saw one another.

"Well, feel free to take it. If you want it."

The tree surgeon nods and sweeps his arm across his forehead. Then, with a swift tug of the chain, he starts the motor whirring again and bends into his task.

Alva Beth suns herself in a lounge chair while the tree surgeon and his helper finish their work. She lies on her stomach with her arms wrapped around her head, peering out over her shoulder. The tree surgeon's helper—Bobby—glances at her occasionally, and at one point he removes the blue work shirt he wears over a T-shirt and tosses it up to the patio, a few feet from her chair.

The tree surgeon ignores her. Alva Beth watches the muscles in his broad back flex and relax as he works the saw through the wood. A damp triangle darkens his T-shirt. His arms are tanned and shiny with sweat. They look like buttered toast.

Intoxicated by the scent of her own skin, Alva Beth has almost drifted into sleep when she hears footsteps on the patio. She raises her head and looks across the pool to see the tree surgeon standing by the edge, at the deep end. He's holding a sheet of paper in his hand, and when she looks at him, he stares down at the water.

"We'll be taking off now. Stacked your wood up over next to the fence." The tree surgeon glances back, as if to make sure the wood is still there.

Alva Beth sits up and rubs at the crisscross indentations the lounge chair has made on her thighs. "It's awfully hot, you and your partner want to take a dip?"

The tree surgeon looks startled. His mouth twitches, like it did before, finally shaping itself into a smile. He looks past Alva Beth. "No, ma'am. It's kind of you to offer, but we got to get going."

Alva Beth smiles, stands and stretches. She likes to be called "ma'am." She thinks she might be making the tree surgeon nervous, thinks he's trying not to stare at her polka dots. She likes that too. "Well, come on in the kitchen and I'll get you your check." The tree surgeon hesitates, runs his fingers through his wet hair, and heads around the pool to the kitchen door. He doesn't come inside.

The kitchen tiles are cool under Alva Beth's feet. As she leans against the counter, pen in hand, she rubs the sole of her left foot along her right calf. "Who do I make this out to?"

"Denny Buzbee Tree Service. Here. Here's your invoice." He opens the screen door and holds out the paper. "Pink copy's yours." Alva Beth walks over to the door and takes the invoice out of his hands. Sawdust clings like dew to the dark hair on his arms. This close, she can see the thin creases all around his eyes, tiny rivulets filled with dust, and a dark smudge on his forehead where he has wiped the sweat and dirt.

"Are you Denny Buzbee?"

"I am. I take it you're Mrs. Payne's daughter."

"Alva Beth."

The tree surgeon nods, as he did when he first saw her from his cherry picker bucket. "Nice name," he says. "Different."

Alva Beth takes a pitcher of water from the refrigerator and fills a tall glass. "I was named after my grandmothers—Alva on my mom's side, Beth on my daddy's." She holds out the glass of water in one hand, the check in the other. Denny Buzbee contemplates the offerings, as if he senses there's a choice to be made here. Then he looks directly at Alva Beth for the first time. She sees thin red lines running through the whites of his eyes, but the irises are clear and blue, like the water in her pool.

Denny reaches for the glass. Alva Beth watches his Adam's apple move up and down, takes in the fine musty odor of sweat and sawdust. "Thanks," he says. "That hit the spot."

*

Indigo Road is a hard-packed, red clay road off Highway 137 about fifteen miles outside city limits. In high school, Alva Beth and her friends used to go skinny dipping in Indigo Lake before the sheriff started staking it out for drug pushers. Denny Buzbee's Tree Service is located on Indigo Road, according to the bill he left with her, and as she drives down the highway in her mother's Oldsmobile, the wooden tree swing in the back seat, she thinks this is an out-of-the-way address for a business.

At first, Alva Beth thought the tree surgeon had left the swing on purpose. Maybe it wasn't such a good swing after all; maybe Denny Buzbee was just being polite. But the more she thought about it, the more Alva Beth wanted Denny Buzbee to have that swing, wanted to be the one to put it in his hands. She wanted to watch him hang it in a big tree and wanted to sit in it while he pushed her with his strong, dark arms, pushed her higher and higher until the rope buckled and she shrieked in pleasure. For several days after his visit, she thought of this scene: while she was sitting in class, while she was lounging by her pool, while she was listening to her daddy's records in the dark. She laughed it off at first, called Merideth and said, "I'm so bored I flirted with the damn tree surgeon." She left out the part about the tree surgeon seeing her naked. Merideth asked her the difference between a tree surgeon and some guy who just chopped them down. Alva Beth said she wasn't sure, but she figured a tree surgeon had to have some special knowledge since she had seen the words "Specializing in Tree Surgery" on the invoice.

As Alva Beth turns down Indigo Road, she thinks about the special knowledge a tree surgeon might possess, if Denny Buzbee could cut out disease and bring a tree back to life. She wonders what she'll say when she sees him. She turns up the cassette tape of Billie Holiday that she made from one of her daddy's records. *I don't know why, but I'm feeling so sad, I long to try something I've never had.* Her daddy says Billie Holiday didn't really sing blues, *per se*, but Alva Beth likes her raspy, baby-talk voice and the toe-tapping rhythm of what Alva Beth thinks of as her back-up bands.

About fifty yards ahead, Alva Beth sees a green truck with white lettering on the door: Denny Buzbee's Tree Service. She slows down a little and lowers the volume on the cassette player. The truck is parked alongside a mobile home, white, with a wide tan stripe running around it. And parked on the other side of Denny Buzbee's truck is a big white car with a sizeable rusty dent in the right rear fender. "Double damn." Alva Beth speeds up and drives past the trailer. She hasn't counted on the address on Denny Buzbee's bill to be his own house, for crying out loud. She thought he'd have an office. She pictured it as a little concrete building with "Denny Buzbee's Tree

Service" painted in a half moon on the window. She could walk right in, like she had a legitimate reason to be there. But his house. She can't just go walking up to the door of his trailer and present him with this swing. What if his wife is there?

Alva Beth pulls into a driveway to turn her car around and get the hell back home. Suddenly, she can't believe she has driven over fifteen miles to a tree surgeon's home. She drives past Denny's trailer again, but this time she notices that the white car is gone, and there's Denny Buzbee reaching into the bed of his truck. He looks up as she drives by, and she can tell by the way he just stares after her, kind of puzzled, that he has recognized her. She feels the indignity of getting caught in a forbidden act—necking in the boys' dorm, drinking at football games. Disclosure ruins everything. Now she has to go back.

"You forgot the take the swing with you," Alva Beth says as she gets out of the car. She pulls the piece of wood from the back seat and holds it up, as proof of her good intentions. "Course, then I thought maybe you didn't want it."

The tree surgeon squints his eyes as though trying to bring her into focus, and for one humiliating moment Alva Beth thinks maybe he doesn't remember her at all. Then he says, "To tell you the truth, I forgot about it. Cutting that wood and all. But you didn't have to drive all the way out here."

"Well. I thought it was your office, you know, the address. I got it from your bill." The tree surgeon is looking right at Alva Beth, not past her like he did at her house. She feels her power over him slipping.

"I get most of my jobs over the phone. An office would be unnecessary overhead."

"Right." The swing is getting heavier in her hand. She considers tossing it on the ground and making a swift getaway.

They both jump when the phone rings, and Denny lets it ring once more before he makes a move for the door. "You wanna come in?" he says before he disappears into the trailer.

Alva Beth has never been in a mobile home before. Everything seems so compressed and not quite real, like those period rooms they have roped off in museums. Except that it is clear people live here, eat here, leave their cigarette butts in ashtrays, their dishes in the sink. She's standing in a kitchen about a tenth the size of her mother's. An oak veneer dinette table takes up one corner. On it are two vinyl place mats, a book of crossword puzzles, an orange plastic ashtray containing three cigarette butts, and an AM/FM clock radio tuned to a country station. Alva Beth can't quite place the song or the male voice singing, but it sounds familiar—something about a heart as empty as a whiskey bottle.

Denny is hunched over a counter that separates the living room from the kitchen scribbling some notes on an envelope. Occasionally he mumbles an "uh-huh" or an "ok, sure" into the phone and once he looks up at Alva Beth and rolls his eyes. This makes her feel comfortable enough to take a few steps into the living room. The furniture reminds Alva Beth of the Travelodge in Atlanta where she and the Theta Chi rush chairman stayed one fraternity week-end—a sort of Mediterranean look in black vinyl. The shag carpeting, black and blood-red, has been worn down to form intersecting pathways from the sofa to the television and from the kitchen to the hallway.

Alva Beth takes all this in with fascination. When she was nine, she went with her mother to their housekeeper's home to deliver a Christmas basket. Alva Beth was shocked at how tiny and run-down the house was. She could look straight through the floorboards to the ground four feet below. But Alva Beth's mother didn't seem to notice, didn't once look down. Instead she moved directly to the front window, framed by peach-colored draperies and a valance trimmed in lace. "Sukie," she said, "these draperies are lovely. Did you make them yourself?"

Sukie smiled, holding the Christmas basket with both hands. "Yes'm, sure did." Later Alva Beth noticed it was the only window whose panes were all intact, unmarred by strips of duct tape and Visquine.

Now Alva Beth has seen enough not to be shocked by how little other people have, although, standing here in Denny Buzbee's trailer, she marvels at how well they manage. Everything fits so snugly in this small space. There is nothing unessential here. Even the wall hanging—an autumn farm scene decoupaged onto a block of charred wood—seems to have a purpose that Alva Beth believes she will learn if only she can stay awhile.

"It's not much," says Denny Buzbee, hanging up the phone. "My wife keeps saying we need more room. She wants a doublewide."

"It seems comfortable," says Alva Beth, trying to sound like her mother.

"I own the land free and clear. My daddy left me his three acres and I bought another two at auction. Talk about luck, that was the one time I had it. Reckon I used up my allotment. Five acres run from here all the way to the creek, thataway." He nods his head toward the north kitchen window. Alva Beth stares out across a deep, summer-faded pasture sloping upwards in the distance. "See that hill?" He stands beside Alva Beth and raises his arm alongside her face to point. Alva Beth nods and feels the hairs on his arm graze her cheek. "I'm going to build me a house right up there someday. Lived in trailers too long. Feels like I'm pacing all the time, you know?"

"You could build a house by yourself?"

"Sure. All but the wiring. That's tricky."

Alva Beth pictures the tree surgeon taking his chain saw to trees that will become his home.

Denny looks at her with that unwilling smile, as though he's amused, but not sure he should be. "You want a beer or something?"

Alva Beth thinks it's a little early in the day to be drinking beer. It's after two, but she has only been up for a couple of hours. "Sure, if you're going to have one."

They sit at the kitchen table and, for a moment, Alva Beth wonders how she will talk to this man through a whole beer. She stares at the plastic ashtray, the way the colors are swirled in a simulated marble pattern. The cigarettes have been snuffed delicately, crushing the ashes. "Do you smoke?"

"My wife does," Denny says. "She quit for awhile, when she was pregnant. You know smoking can make the baby come premature."

"That's what I've heard."

"Well, the baby came early anyway, so she figures she quit for nothing. I think she's making up for lost time."

"I saw another car here when I passed by. I wasn't sure if I should stop, I guess you figured that."

The tree surgeon smiles at her. It's an easy, comfortable smile, not at all like those he forced when he was taking down her tree. "My wife works at Woolworth's. Three till closing."

"I guess maybe she'd be upset if she knew I was here."

"I guess." He takes a long sip of beer. "She's a little on edge lately, what with the baby and all. It's tough on her."

"Where's the baby?"

Denny frowns, and for a second Alva Beth thinks maybe she should know the answer. "Still in the hospital," he says. "She was born six weeks early. With a bad heart. That was two months ago."

Alva Beth stifles a belch rising from her belly and when she opens her mouth to speak, she can taste sour saliva at the back of her throat. "I'm sorry."

"Weighed three pounds when she was born. She coulda fit in my hand." He opens his palm, all calluses and crooked lines, like a dried river bed, and Alva Beth tries to imagine it cradling something crying and kicking. "Didn't even look like a baby. I kept thinking, Jesus, it's deformed or retarded or something. She looked like a newborn puppy, her skin all shiny, kinda greasy looking, this purplish-blue color. They call 'em blue babies."

"Why are they blue?"

"Don't get enough oxygen in their blood." Denny leans forward and makes a loose fist, pointing to the hole in the center. "See, there's this valve, this hole, that goes into the lungs, and the blood goes through there before it goes to the heart. In my kid, that hole's all blocked up." He squeezes his fist tight. "They can operate, but they've gotta wait till she's older, maybe another week or so."

"But she'll be all right, I mean after the operation and everything?"

"She's got a ways to go." Denny pushes back his chair. "You ready for another beer?"

"No, I'm fine." Alva Beth realizes she hasn't touched her beer since Denny mentioned the baby, and now she takes two gulps and lets the second fill out her cheeks before she swallows. She hears the pop of a beer tab.

"You wanna hear something terrible?" Denny says. "You wanna know the first thing I thought when I saw her?" Alva Beth still can't see him, and she doesn't want to turn around, doesn't want to look at him when he tells her this terrible thing. "I thought, I hope she dies. Do you believe that? I didn't think I could stand it for even a day. You know why?"

Alva Beth takes another gulp of beer. "Why?"

She hears a tapping sound, metal, Denny's beer can on the counter. He says, "Because I couldn't touch her. They kept her in an incubator in this special room—isolation they call it—all hooked up to tubes and monitors. And they wouldn't let either one of us in the room, not at first. Couldn't even get a good look at her to see did she have much hair, or . . ." The tapping stops. "You know, you think you can fix anything if you can just get your hands on it."

Alva Beth feels like Robert Johnson is plucking his pitiful guitar in the pit of her stomach. "I don't think you're terrible," she says. "Besides, you can't help what goes through your mind, can you?"

"Well, I guess it's a good thing you never seem to get what you hope for, isn't it, Alva Beth?" It's the first time she has heard him say her name. It feels like an embrace.

Alva Beth has to go the bathroom. "Second door to your left," Denny says.

In the bathroom, she realizes she's a little drunk. She's had no breakfast so the beer has gone right to her head. The quiet is surreal, like at the bottom of her pool; every movement seems to reverberate off the tin walls of the trailer. She turns on the water before sitting on the toilet. Looking down at the floor, she sees that the linoleum around the toilet has buckled and pulled away from the plywood flooring. She flushes the toilet and while the water is still running in circles around the bowl, she peeks in a flowered make-up bag beside the sink. Her fingers sort delicately through containers of drugstore eye shadow, a tube of mascara, a plastic compact of mauve blush. She runs her fingers under hot water. Beside a tube of toothpaste is a razor and a small plastic compact. Alva Beth dries her hands, opens the compact, and counts a dozen tiny white pills. She turns to leave and hears voices in the living room. For a moment, she panics, afraid that the tree surgeon's wife has returned home and will know that Alva Beth has learned all her secrets, has learned all about the tough time she is having with the baby in the hospital, possibly dying, and her smoking, and her birth control. Alva Beth doesn't think she has a right to know all these things about someone she's never seen, and she fears the repercussions. She has read newspaper articles about wives who shoot their husbands when they catch them cheating. She doesn't think drinking a beer with someone could be called cheating, but then, she doesn't know where Denny Buzbee's wife might draw the line.

She cracks the door and listens, hears laughter, and realizes the voices are coming from the television. She steps into the hall. To her left, maybe a yard away, is a bedroom. Alva Beth spots a laundry basket just inside the door, a pair of dirty jeans—Denny's work jeans?—heaped on top. The television voices cover the creaking of the plywood beneath the carpet as Alva Beth steals her way toward Denny's bedroom.

It is the smallest bedroom Alva Beth has ever seen. There is barely a foot between the louvered closet doors and the unmade double bed. Alva Beth takes three steps to the dresser and looks in the mirror. A few strands of hair have fallen loose from her ponytail and she tucks them behind her ear. Her face is flushed. On the dresser beside an ashtray is a small stack of Polaroid snapshots. Pictures of the tree surgeon's baby. Alva Beth looks at each one, quickly, like a detective, like she's looking for evidence of a life outside her own. She glances at the door, frightened that Denny will catch her. The pictures seem obscenely private. She takes one from the bottom of the pile and slides it in the back pocket of her shorts.

Denny Buzbee is sitting on the edge of the vinyl sofa leaning forward toward the television. "You OK?" he says.

"Yeah, I'm fine." Alva Beth sits down beside him, her knees buckling as she bends them, so that she almost collapses.

"You want another beer?"

Alva Beth shakes her head. "Beer makes me tired."

Denny Buzbee smiles at her, then smiles at his beer can which he holds like a prize. "Not me. I have one rule—no drinking around heavy machinery. But I don't reckon I'll kill myself turning on the TV, so what the hell." He takes another sip and leans back against the sofa.

Alva Beth stares out the window across a brown pasture at a horse nibbling at the grass, his tail now and then sweeping up to slap his flanks. Denny leans forward and follows her eyes. "Belongs to the folks down the road," he says. "My wife used to ride him every chance she got. They were real nice about it, the owners. Sometimes she wouldn't even saddle him up, just throw a blanket over his back, hook a bit in his mouth and ride away like there was no tomorrow. They were a sight, her and old Dodger."

Alva Beth leans back and tries to picture the grazing horse galloping across the pasture with the tree surgeon's wife leaning forward across his neck, but the picture she formed when she was in the bathroom waiting to hear the blast of a shotgun—the picture of someone big and angry and jealous—just doesn't fit, so she imagines it is her, Alva Beth, riding like there's no tomorrow, her long hair flying and her thighs hugging the horse, whispering, Go, Dodger, giddyup.

She says, "Why doesn't she ride him anymore?"

"Quit when she got pregnant. Now she's either at work or the hospital. I'm meeting her there at six. That's when she gets her break and we go see the baby. You ever watch this show?"

Alva Beth turns to the black and white picture on the screen. Sheriff Andy Taylor is having a heart-to-heart talk with Opie in his office. Barney stands nearby pretending he's sweeping. Denny laughs. Alva Beth thinks he probably laughs like this even when he's alone. She settles back and her shoulder presses against his thick arm, solid and warm. She smells a sweet mustiness, the faintness of soap and sweat. She moves her arm closer to Denny's until she feels the tickle of his thick hairs. Denny keeps his eye on the television screen. "Old Barney just has to get his two cents in," he says.

Alva Beth feels herself getting sleepy. She thinks she should probably leave, but she doesn't want to pull herself away. She feels a certain sadness that she has never felt before. She knows it must be a sadness for Denny and his premature baby, but it feels more general, and not altogether unpleasant. It seems as though she's in hiding from everything she's ever known. "What's her name?"

"What?"

"The baby. What's her name?"

"Claire," Denny says. "After my mother."

Alva Beth repeats the name, whispers it: "Claire."

Denny lifts his arm, the one that Alva Beth has been leaning against, and places it gently around her shoulder. With his other hand he gently presses her head against his chest. He strokes the length of her arm with his whole hand, encloses her wrist, probes the veins that run along the top of her hand. His hand moves across her stomach, and Alva Beth sucks in her breath, a reflex. "I just want to hold you," Denny says. "That's all." Alva Beth feels the warmth of his big hand through her cotton shirt. She closes her eyes. She hears Sheriff Taylor telling Opie that he can't go play football until he finishes his homework. Opie says, "Yessir." After a few moments, or maybe longer, she feels Denny's fingers slipping under her shirt. She opens her mouth, but then decides to pretend she's asleep. It seems so much easier than moving or talking. And then she feels the flat of his palm against her belly, making small circular motions, like her mother used to do when Alva Beth was a child and had a stomachache.

Denny Buzbee whispers against her hair, "Your belly's hard. So smooth. After you have a baby, Alva Beth, it'll be all soft and round. That's what happens, you know." Alva Beth doesn't answer. She thinks she has stopped breathing, stopped feeling anything except the tree surgeon's callused hand making circles on her belly.

*

When Alva Beth opens her eyes, she is alone on the sofa. A television voice is describing a recreational vehicle. She stands, and the late afternoon sun casts her long shadow across the matted carpeting. Alva Beth slips her hands in her back pockets and peers down the hall looking for Denny. She remembers feeling him move away from her, hearing the door open and close, but it's like remembering a dream. Her fingertips catch the stiff edge of the Polaroid. She pulls it out and studies it in the sunlight coming through the window. The tree surgeon's baby is blue, just as he said, a splotchy, almost purple color, and shiny, as though she has been smeared with Vaseline. Her skin looks like rubber. A tube runs from her nostrils, taped at her nose and on her cheek. Her tiny face is puffy, and her swollen tongue protrudes from her mouth. A wire-like tube is attached to a small white disc pressed to her chest. Another tube is taped to a fingertip. She wears a pink knitted cap.

"Claire," Alva Beth says, the sound vibrating in her chest like a chord. She starts to put the snapshot on the coffee table when she notices Denny through the window. He's leaning against the fence like a cowboy, one boot resting on the bottom slat in the fence, staring out at Dodger standing beneath a big oak. His arm is wrapped around the slab of wood that was her tree swing, and he holds it tightly, as if, at any moment, someone might snatch it away.

Emma Bolden

Dead Lands

The desert swallows us whole. Dryness creeps in through the air conditioner, fights its way into our lungs, eats us from the inside. We struggle against the heat with opened windows that help the desert consume us. I know what it's like to be consumed. Allan doesn't. He silently steers into the desert's stomach, sometimes humming to the radio's buzz.

We can't talk. That's why we're out here. He called it a reunification mission, said his therapist suggested it. Our therapist suggested it. Something about building bridges. It seems easier to burn than to build. But Allan always hopes. The desert sun floats high above, a locus of the landscape. Everything glimmers the color of fire.

I don't think a desert is the place for us. I didn't when Allan suggested it, but I sat quietly. He twisted his tie, like he does when he's nervous, spilling the details out on the table. He said in the desert, we'd be away from everything: trains, blood, our bedroom. His therapist—our therapist—thought there was something we needed. He thought we could find it away, together, with me completely protected. But I don't want to be protected. And I think there's nothing in the desert but heat and cacti. No life, no breath.

I don't believe in therapy. It was Allan who started that, because of another dead baby. I don't need to create anymore. But he does. And each death affects him more than the last. Last time he sat on the bed, shaking, covering his eyes with his hands. I couldn't bring myself to touch him. I couldn't even talk to him. He said that he needed to find a way to bring us together. And so we drive on.

I thought Vietnam would be dry like this, when Edward was drafted to go. When his draft number came on the screen I screamed. Allan says I always got hysterical, imagining life without Edward. But what I really imagined was Edward shot, his blood painting the sand. I saw that he'd never fit in such a dry world. Now I know Vietnam was wet, too wet. Like the dead babies, a secession of seven, dead, red, wet. All that fluid makes you want something dry. But not this dry, this hostile. As hostile as Vietnam must have been. This is what I thought Edward would describe, had he made it there, had he not died with me watching, his car smashed by a train. I never thought he'd stay in the car. I thought he'd escape after me. I screamed his name as I ran to him. His warm and pulsing body lay scattered across the train tracks. I touched his severed face. Blood painted my hands red, brighter even than life.

Sometimes I just don't want to talk about life. My life with Allan especially. I like to pretend that none of it happened. That I could run out of the car at any moment and be back before Edward was killed. That he would run after me, and we'd both still be alive. I just want to sit in silence. But Allan keeps asking questions, digging and digging for answers. Like today. "Why did you marry me?" he had asked, staring out to the ash black road.

I wanted to say nothing. I needed to say that I loved him, that Edward's death made me realize this. But I couldn't. There was something about the air. It pressed like a clear hot iron. I said, "There was nothing else for me to do." His face folded. Tears welled to his eyes. The only water here is tears. That's all we have left.

That's what caused the silence. It was complete at first, as encompassing as the heat, holding us still as sandstone. Then he began to move again, then to hum. He has a ritual for getting over anger. Soon he'll ask for a cigarette, something to burn. He won't apologize because he never thinks he has to. I know this. I know what I said shocked him, because it was the truth.

The car reeks of burnt coffee. It was too hot for coffee this morning, and too hot for it to cool off. I threw it out of the window, watching the liquid stripe elongate. Allan yelled about the paint job. I ignored him. I still hold my cup, gas station coffee crystallized into brown rust at the bottom. On the mouth of the cup is an imprint of my mouth, pink, just enough color to cover the white. My lips weren't always so pale. "Your lips are the color of strawberries," Edward said, his hands in my hair, his legs hot beside mine. That was the week before he died.

Allan clears his throat. "Do you have any cigarettes?"

I shake my head. "None."

He shifts, his sweaty legs sticking to the leather car seat. "I think we should talk." His voice is thick, like syrup. "What you said back there," he says, as if our words were part of the road, "Was that true?" I nod. He draws in air, then coughs. "So it's just been a game, then."

"What?"

"The last twenty years. A game."

"I wouldn't call it that," I say. This is far more dangerous than any game.

Out in the woods behind our houses we called Edward "Eddy" and always played in the dirt. Allan built a ditch one time and Eddy and I got inside. Allan said let's play war and Eddy said she's a girl, she can't play war. Allan picked at his scab and said she's not a girl, she can play. Then Eddy got out of the ditch, his white shirt smeared brown with dirt. He and Allan were fighting. Allan punched Eddy and Eddy punched back. I was screaming but I couldn't get out of the ditch. Then Allan pushed Eddy into the ditch And Eddy was crunched up beside me, bleeding. His eyes looked up but he didn't blink. His tongue hung out. I told Allan you hurt him, he's dead. Allan's face got white as a fish and he ran away. And I fell on top of Eddy and said you'll be okay like my mother did when I fell. There was blood on his cheek. His leg bent under him, and there was blood on his pants, too. Everything was warm and sticky as a cat that's just been run over. I held Eddy's hand because he was whimpering and I said Eddy don't cry. He said Helen I hurt I love you and then his eyes went away again.

Allan and I are out of the car. We sit in a booth, facing each other. Overhead, a shaded lamp sheds its flowery light. Classical music slides out through the radio. His face shines lavender grey. Dying beams of day stretch out from the window behind him, grazing the top of his balding head. He's always had thin hair, even when we were children. Edward's hair was thick as an animal's. The sun is huge behind Allan, its face red and furious.

The meal is over. We each ate sparingly. Something about all of that sand makes me want to starve. We struggle over coffee and conversation. He keeps asking questions. I don't want him to know their answers. Silence spreads like sand over the table. Allan hasn't said much. Now he warms to words again, his throat muscles tensing.

"How do you feel?"

"Fine."

"Not weak at all?"

"No."

He looks down, eyes tracing his bald reflection in the over-polished table top. "I'm so sorry this keeps happening." I refuse to look at him. "You need to let out your feelings. I can only imagine how horrible this feels."

"How horrible what feels?"

"Losing a life like that."

I look out of the window. Darkness covers the landscape. Everything is dim, uncertain. I couldn't feel anything, after so much blood, so much death. Birth and burial blend together. In each half-formed face I see remnants of Edward. In each pulsing body I feel what I felt in him, not life exactly, but urgency.

"What should we do now?"

Above Allan's head, darkness consumes the sun. Street lamps throw false flames over the sand. In this light the desert is a rotting mouth. I'm sick of this conversation. After the last dead baby he'd pushed out the same words. I told him I thought I should stop. He asked if I meant trying to conceive. I said trying anything, that I thought I should just stop. He kept on crying, and I left. I couldn't watch him fall apart like that.

"Helen." His voice breaks through. "You've got to talk to me."

"Why?"

"Dr. Earhart says so. I say so. You have to talk about these things."

"I don't have to talk about anything." Allan's mouth moves to speak again. I don't want to hear him. It's his fault anyway, this string of death. It's he who keeps returning to the bed, where death always begins.

I don't have to listen to him. I rise, walk out of the restaurant and into the desert. A chill descends. I think I hear a siren sighing in the distance and shudder. There can't be trains so far from the city. I look up to the night-drenched sky. Blackness falls over the stars like thick, heavy dirt.

I was digging holes. I was looking for something and forgetting what exactly I was looking for, but I still kept on digging. There was something in the sun and the way it shone. I thought that if I dug far enough I'd get to Edward and find him again. And when I did he wouldn't be full of slugs and worms and holes. So I kept on digging into the dirt and the holes got bigger and bigger until I could fit inside one. I lay down in the dirt with my face up to the sky. The sky was so blue it looked painted on. I hated the sky for being so alive. I lay there and hated the sky until I felt that I wasn't alone anymore. I was buried and there were bodies all around and they were all pressing close to me. My heart was beating and I knew that I couldn't be dead, so I jumped out of the grave and onto the ground. The bodies went away. I was still looking for something. I kept on digging. Allan's car hummed into the driveway, but I kept on digging. He came into the backyard and said what are you doing, you're covered in dirt and I said I'm looking for something. I wanted him to go away but he kept coming and saying my name and it was almost like a different voice each time, becoming flatter and more distant. But I knew it was always him and then he was saying come in Helen, Helen what are you doing, Helen, darling, talk to me, you're scaring me. I kept saying I'm looking for something until there weren't any words and I was screaming. Allan came and picked me up and carried me inside. He was crying and I was too, but I didn't know why. The door closed and the sun went away. The dark earth still clung to my body.

We drive into the desert's darkness. Headlights flow in opaque strips into the night. Allan has the news station turned down low. A male voice murmurs about war. The names and places are blurred, as they always are in wartime. Allan glances downward. He likes to protect me from radio voices and the heated facts they spill. But he doesn't turn it off. I am glad for the diversion. Allan taps his fingers on the steering wheel. We've been riding without words for the past thirty minutes, neon lights looming as we drive closer to the city. Our headlights catch on rusted train tracks, nearly covered with dead cacti. My heart pounds.

"Where do those tracks lead?" I ask.

"I don't know. They look too old to be used anymore." His voice sounds thicker than quicksand. "What are you thinking?"

I am thinking that the desert is a monster's mouth, that the landscape is digesting us. I am thinking about Vietnam. About what color sand they have there. I think it's the color of Edward's blood. Allan said they had to close the coffin, that he was all in pieces. I am thinking of pieces of muscle and blood, how I would be in pieces if I hadn't left him there, to die.

"Nothing," I say. Street lamps whirl by like miniature suns.

"I'm thinking about when we were in high school." He turns the radio down lower. He always thinks about high school, the three of us as friends. I never told him I loved Edward. Things are simpler this way. "You and Edward always skipped lunch. What did you do?"

I look down at my hands, cast hot orange by fluorescence. "Whatever we felt like doing."

"Like what?"

"I don't know. Talking."

"Anything more?"

I look out of my window. The moon stands high in the sky, its face grayed by craters. Fragments of sandstone line the freeway. "Yes. A lot more."

Your lips taste like strawberries, Edward said. I told him it was my lip gloss and he smiled. He smelled like earth moistened by rain. I moved in closer to inhale more of his scent. He drew back and ran his hand through his hair. He said I have to talk to you Helen and I said I'm listening. He said I've been drafted and I said I know. I fell back against the grass and looked into the sky. I couldn't look at his face anymore. I pictured his blood against elephant grass, splintered pieces of him dripping from desert trees. There were no clouds in the sky. The sun was a bomb in its brightness. Edward said I'm leaving for training in a week and I closed my eyes to shut out the words. I said you can't go and he said I have to. I kept seeing the trees painted red, his fingers blown off and scattered into bushes. Then he said we'll get married before I go I promise and I said who'll be here while you're gone. He said well there's Allan and I laughed for a while. The sun was so bright that it burned my eyes. I turned my cheek against the grass and laughed. Edward said you know he loves you and I said poor guy he doesn't realize and then I laughed some more. I tasted the grass. The taste of grass was like the taste of blood. I stopped laughing. Edward leaned over saying God I love you. He lay against me again. I kissed him and we lay there on the grass. I thought about blood and the war and how Edward would only be postcards soon. I closed my eyes to shut out the light.

The lights of the railroad crossing flash, echoing city lights springing up in the distance. A screeching sound flows through shadowed trees. I sit up in my seat. Allan stops the car and glances at me. He shifts. "There aren't any trains out here, are there?" I ask.

"I don't think so." A siren blares. "I thought those tracks were too old."

"Oh God." I finger my seat belt. I don't want to be strapped into the car. I need to escape. "Can't you turn around?"

He looks over his shoulder. "No. Christ, Helen, I'm sorry about this."

"I have to get away from here."

"Calm down. It's just a train."

"Just a train!" Light douses the tracks. Like a ghost. I grab the dashboard. I have to get out.

"You need to learn how to face these things. You have to live in the present."

"You said there wouldn't be trains here."

Dust rises around the car. "I didn't think there were."

"You lied to me."

"So did you."

The train thunders closer. "I have to get out of here."

When they found Edward's body it was tangled like a fetus. All they could salvage was nothing at all, so they closed his coffin. I couldn't believe he was in it. I placed my hands on the black wood. It was cold as dirt. I thought it was impossible, his death. The train zooms closer. Now I know it was possible. I have faced it. I face it with each death. I face it every time I look at Allan. His face is always serious, like he's hiding things from me, to protect me. Like Edward's mother, after he died. She stood behind me with a group of women who whispered poor Helen, she loved him so much. His mother's voice floated over their wrinkled white faces, saying we don't think he parked on those train tracks. She said he wouldn't leave his mother like that, but he did. Like I left him in the car. I never thought that he'd do it. His blood covered the ground, my hands, my legs. Like blood coats my thighs with each baby's death.

The train thunders closer and closer. I cannot take this. I unhook my seat belt. The train's light is bright like the sun. Its siren screams like a baby's cry, like Edward's voice the last time I saw him. He screamed that he was afraid of war. That he'd rather die by his own means. He was hysterical. The train flies closer. Like it came closer then. And all I could do was run and watch as it rammed into his body. I couldn't close my eyes. I should have closed my eyes. Pieces of car and body flew through the air. He was ripped apart. I ran to him but he wasn't whole anymore. The train rushed into the darkness.

Allan is screaming about something. In the darkness I see Edward's car on the tracks. Don't Eddy, I scream, it's not worth it. And it isn't worth it, anymore. There's nothing but sand and desert and death. And Allan. Who should be dead instead. Who should be splattered across the tracks. Shoved in some hole with dirt sealing him in. Sealing me out. I hate him for being alive. I run out of the car. Into the desert. Thunder roars over the tracks. The train screams by. I am running. It's too dark for me to find Eddy. I cannot imagine him whole. Only severed. Body broken and bleeding and black. My hands are black in the darkness. Not painted with slime and death. I always smell like death. Like salt and sweat and water. Now the smell is leaving. Eddy's car disappears. All I can do is run. Away from Allan. Away from the train.

Wendy Reed Bruce

Harold Washburn

*E*ven after the cool of the night's darkness, the shop's temperature was still stifling. Most people would be sickened by the day-old diesel fumes that circled through the air, but Harold was used to it. The four windowless walls seemed to stand guard, blank, except for the black metal lunch box and white button-down that dangled from the nails. "You can't fire me for what you don't know, you son-of-a-bitch," Harold had said when he removed his shirt, glad that Junior would be out of town all week. "If he worked just eight good August hours with the oven roaring at 1500 degrees, I bet he'd change his tune about presenting a good image.

"Hell," Harold continued, "nobody worth impressing comes by anyway." It was no use to try and change things now. Come December he would retire. He would just do his job and keep his mouth shut until then. Then he wouldn't have to put up with any of this shit anymore.

In one corner a large pie-shaped fiberglass hutch was wedged. Its exterior offered no clues about its refrigerant capabilities. The opening, to what Harold called the oven and Junior insisted be properly called the retort, was perfectly square. Two substantial steel hinges hinted of its weight. Behind the door lay the grate looking like a large piece of scorched honeycomb. A long formica-topped table separated the room in half. It was littered, not with scientific tools such as microscopes and chemicals, but with hammers and nails of varying sizes. Harold breathed in the familiarity. He felt at ease. The phone disturbed his momentary peace.

"Washburn."

"Harold. It's Joe. We've got a body that the next of kin authorized us to dispose of. She's been here almost a week and we need her slab."

Harold glanced toward Mrs. Walker in the cooler and thought of Mr. Carlisle's cremains in the oven. The State Pen had one arriving any minute.

"Can you wait until tomorrow? I'm swamped."

"We really need to empty a slab today."

"All right. I'll take her, but wait until around two."

"Deal! Thanks. I owe you one."

"Can you assholes not count? You owe me three."

Harold twisted the silver key into the lock of the cooler. He pulled up on the doorknob while turning the handle and the door came open. He'd told Junior somebody needed to be hired to help out part-time. Harold was good but lately he'd been backed up three of four times and he didn't like having bodies wait in the cooler for more than a day or two. Even after cremating thousands of bodies, he could get the creeps if he felt outnumbered.

"I'm working on it," was all Junior would say when pushed about hiring extra help.

"Good morning, Mrs. Walker. Sorry to have kept you waiting." He spoke loudly to the corpse, as though she were just sleeping. "Time now for the defrost cycle," he enjoyed his own joke. He laid her on his work table and unzipped her body bag. Bodies combusted slightly faster if they were at room temperature he'd discovered early in his vocation. Much of what he knew about his job had come from trial and error. When he'd started the job twenty-two years earlier as a favor to Lloyd, Sr., he was only going to help him out part-time until someone could be hired who was licensed. Harold had been a carpenter then and didn't care to spend his days burning bodies. What the two of them found out was that the state department didn't really care about licenses as long as they could dump a few bodies every now and then with no questions asked. In fact, the nearby penitentiary had been a steady source of clientele from the beginning. Within 6 weeks Harold had gone from 20 hours a week to 50, and found himself enjoying the autonomy Lloyd allowed him, not to mention the money.

"Doesn't it ever get to you?" Ellen, the only girl he'd ever dated, asked.

"I'm paid enough not to let it get to me. I do my job and that's it."

The relationship with Ellen had ended abruptly. He'd relived that evening over and over, night after night as he drifted off to sleep. Over dinner he'd planned on asking her to marry him but things had not gone as he expected.

"Harold, this ring is exquisite. I didn't know any jeweler around here carried a piece so unusual."

"Do you really like it?"

"It's perfect . . . well, almost," she said as she tried to force the ring onto her finger. "It'll just need to be re-sized. Which jeweler did it come from?"

Harold had not anticipated this. "I'm sure any jeweler can size it for you."

She had stared at him, shrinking her green almond-shaped eyes into narrow slits. Her mouth had slowly opened, stretching a thin string of saliva until it popped. "Where did you get it, Harold? Tell me. I need to know."

The hum of the restaurant had seemed to cease. The fat, white candle that sat between the two vases of fake pink carnations had flickered and gone out.

"I took it off a body, okay, Ellen? Jesus, there was no use melting such a nice ring. The fiancé had wanted her cremated with it, but I didn't see the point. He never knew any different and she sure as hell didn't. She was dead for Christ's sake." And that had been the last he'd seen of Ellen.

"Aw, she was a cunt. She was a snobby little cunt. I'm just glad I realized it before it was too late," he'd explained to himself. "I guess I'm lucky. To luck," he said as he raised a bottle of Wild Turkey and drank until it was empty. Harold had passed out right on the very table where he had taken the ring from the body and where he now unzipped Mrs. Walker's black, vinyl body bag.

He slid the back of the bag out from underneath her and let out a whistle.

"Well, well, well Mrs. Walker. I had no idea silicone was part of your chemical composition."

Atmore was mostly rural and breast augmentation was almost nonexistent. Harold had only cremated two other bodies with silicone implants and he was surprised by the almost non-effect death had on them. They remained firm, but not hard, even when the rest of the body began to stiffen. Beneath the cold, dead skin Harold had discovered by accident the packs still bounced. As he was placing the first body he'd ever handled with them in its container, he'd flipped it from her side to her back when they'd jiggled up and down like bobbing apples. Harold had felt guilty that it had excited him. He'd placed her in the box and shoved her into the oven even before he had opened the gas valves. That was probably the only time he'd put a body in before the flames had been ignited. He'd heard most other furnace operators always did it this way—body first, then flames—but Harold liked to see the flames darting about before feeding the body to them. The second body had only aroused pity. He'd hardly noticed her breasts for the bruises which had formed spirograph-like designs over her entire body. A deep, narrow slit had separated her right thigh into two separate halves. Small, circular scabs had created a symmetrical path from one shoulder to the other almost as if someone was creating a connect-the-dot puzzle. He'd seen lots of damaged corpses, after all this was tractor country, but they were always men. Seeing a woman, and a tiny one at that, so badly abused had made him feel a little sick in the pit of his stomach.

"Who the hell tapes the ID and DC to the body?" He tugged at the pink forms but the taped resisted. He yanked harder and her breasts bobbled slightly. "Must have been the new guy," Harold thought. Mrs. Walker's eyes stared at the ceiling. "Do you want to go into this thing with your eyes open or not?" he asked, snickering at his own humor. Most of the time he closed them and the mouth, too, if necessary. For some reason he didn't want to close Mrs. Walker's eyes just yet. He leaned closer trying to find where the pupil ended and the chocolate iris began. There was something in the shape that intrigued him. The corners drooped slightly at the outside where her lashes clustered in long thick clumps. A trace of smudged mascara led back to her ear. Harold studied her face. It appeared older than the body. The cheeks had grown puffy with fluid and then sagged, setting like concrete as rigor mortis had set in. Death had obviously come prematurely but something in the eyes looked different. He could not put his finger on it but the blank look of death, that which Harold thought of as a peaceful void, was not there. Harold thought he felt a draft. The body still looked alive, especially her breasts. Normally he would cover the body with a white sheet while it warmed, but he could not bring himself to cover Mrs. Walker's.

Collecting the ashes was Harold's least favorite part of his job. Sifting the bone pieces out and then grinding them was tedious. If he thought he could get away with it, he skipped the grinding and inurned it all, bone chunks included. If he was running behind on time and he knew the gray concrete-like dust would be examined, he just tossed the chunks in the garbage. Most people had no idea what the weight of the cremains should be anyway.

"They've probably been trying to lose a pound or two all their lives anyway. I just lost it for them," he reasoned. One time he had put the bone chunks to good use. An older couple from Mobile had stopped by investigating burial alternatives for her terminally ill mother. Harold had been delighted to give them a tour, complete with a hands-on demonstration. "Feel this," he'd told them, offering a bone remnant rescued from the industrial size black garbage can. They did. "This is how we hand-grind the leftover pieces of bone to match the consistency of the other ashes," he'd said and proceeded to demonstrate, exaggerating the difficulty of turning the crank. The husband had reacted as if someone had dragged their fingernails down a chalkboard.

"Is that an artificial material used for demonstration purposes?" the wife had asked, her red-enameled lips slightly quivering, her emerald eyes struggling to look calm.

"No ma'am. This here's the real thing. In fact it was probably Eloise Turner's elbow. The elbow always has to be pulverized. It's no good for burning."

The couple had suddenly remembered an appointment they were forgetting and left. "That was for you, Junior, and your fucking new pay scale," he'd thought.

Mostly, in Harold's opinion, cleaning the retort between bodies was unnecessary. "What does it matter if an ash or two of Mr. Smith's gets reburned with Mrs. Lowell?" he argued with Junior. "No one's gonna know it anyway." Occasionally, he did vacuum the oven out. Tiny particles of grayish-white ash would swirl about, air-dancing with the tempo of the sucking roar. When the vacuum was turned off and the remaining flakes settled, Harold would emerge looking like his chest hair had dandruff.

Harold remembered Mr. Carlisle's cremains were waiting. They'd cooled all night and were ready. He quickly packed them in the translucent plastic bag, bone pieces and all. The instructions Mr. Carlisle had left in his living will were to send his cremains to the NEA and allow them whatever artistic license they needed to utilize his ashes for art. As a result Francis A. Carlisle would be Federal Expressed that very afternoon and possibly be part of an exhibit by the end of the month.

"Probably some fruitcake actor," thought Harold. "I hope he winds up in a mason jar full of piss."

As he labeled the box, he stole a glance at Mrs. Walker. He blushed as he felt himself stiffen against his zipper. Next he would need to assemble a container for her. Stapling the cardboard to the plywood frame never took very long. He could have that finished and the furnace going by lunch time, he reasoned. "What a shame to burn that body," he couldn't help thinking. He had seen hundreds of bodies, young and old, large and small, but never had he found himself so drawn to one. He removed her death certificate from his file. Rebecca Ann Walker DOB-9-05-59 Cause of death-internal organ failure induced by drug overdose. "Suicide?" Harold wondered as he looked for the instructions. Maybe that was the reason for the expression still in her eyes. He was certain she'd been lonely, too. The instruction page was missing. "Dammit!" He'd have to call Joe.

"Joe? This is Harold. The body that you sent over yesterday came without instructions. What the hell am I supposed to do with her cremains?"

"It figures. A new kid brought her over and I heard him throwing up after he zipped the bag. Did he even attach the death certificate and ID?"

"Yeah, he attached them, but you're not gonna believe how."

"He didn't put them in the window?"

"Hell, no, he didn't put them in the window. He taped them above her bush. With masking tape."

"Masking tape?"

"Damnedest thing I've ever seen. It stuck too. Must be some industrial strength masking tape you guys use. Don't say anything to this kid yet. I want to see where he tapes the next one."

"Harold Washburn. You're one sick son-of-a-bitch." Joe laughed. "I'll bring the instructions by after work . . . as long as there's beer."

Good Ole Joe. Always ready for a beer. Harold had rarely seen him without one. It was beginning to show in his gut, too.

"Tell you what. You bring me a couple rolls of that tape and I'll see what I can do."

"Like I said, you're a sick son-of-a-bitch, Washburn."

"Well, Mrs. Walker, it must be your lucky day. You've just won an extra night with me." Harold could actually get started on her without the instructions. He rarely paid much attention to them anyway. The families never knew if the bodies were cremated with their favorite book or clutching the Bible. Mostly there weren't a lot of instructions, but this time it was a good excuse to wait.

Harold heard the beeping of the State van as it began to back up to the door. He pulled his shirt on and fumbled with the buttons. Junior was friends with some of the guys at the Pen, so Harold thought it best not to take any chances. He started to open the door but walked back over to Mrs. Walker.

He pulled the white sheet just over her head.

"Morning, Harold." It was Zeke. Harold had put his shirt on for nothing. "Got a big one for you."

"A big one, huh? Is that the line you feed your whores?"

Zeke's mole-like face twisted into a grin. He was beginning to gray prematurely.

"What women? You know Betty won't put up with none of that shit."

Harold had only seen Betty twice and both times he couldn't keep his eyes off her. It wasn't that she was pretty or sexy or even ugly. She was just big. Much bigger than Zeke. Harold couldn't help but imagine how they looked when they fucked. "Hell," he'd joked with Joe, "I bet it takes Zeke all day to satisfy that much woman."

"Ain't no way one of Zeke could take care of a woman Betty's size. I'm not even sure if two of him would be enough."

These raw references fueled each other's laughter. It had sustained them for years. Being in the body business for as long as they had been had a way of affecting one's entire physical perspective in a way few could appreciate. One night when Joe stopped in to pick up some cremains, he crossed their imaginary boundary of black humor. He ventured into the sober. For September, it had been unseasonably chilly. The moon had been low and slightly yellowed around its edges as it began its ritual ascent.

"Does it ever get to you?" Joe had asked gazing up at the deepening blue.

"The moon?" Harold asked. He had been caught off guard by the philosophical tone in the question.

"No, the burning?" He was silent for a moment. "And the bodies?"

With anybody else Harold would've instantly said no, or cracked a smart-ass joke, but there was a naked flatness in Joe's voice that seemed too sincere to make light of it.

"I don't know, Joe. I don't know." And that was all Harold could say because he really didn't know. Joe had taken the thick plastic package and left.

"Who you got over there?" Zeke asked pointing to Mrs. Walker. Harold's first impulse was to pull the sheet back and let him look. Zeke probably would like to see an average size body. Something held Harold back, though.

"Number 3124."

"Female?" Zeke asked walking toward the table.

"Look, I'm too busy to play show and tell right now." Zeke shrugged his shoulders, slightly taken aback.

"This one's anonymous." To the penitentiary guys, that meant there were no nosy family members to ask questions. To Harold it meant he could do what he wanted with the body. They wrestled the bag into the cooler and placed Mr. Anonymous right beside the two six packs.

"Which one's next?" Zeke asked. He was walking directly toward Mrs. Walker.

"I don't know yet. I've still got cremains to collect in the oven."

"You need some help putting her back in the cooler?"

"No," Harold said. "I've still got to measure her and get her box built."

"Mind if I take a look at her?" For some reason Harold did, but he couldn't say so. It would sound odd. It even felt odd to him. Normally, Harold would have shown Zeke her breasts and tried to deliberately embarrass him. For some reason, though, he didn't want to share Mrs. Walker with Zeke.

"I don't mind. Go ahead." Then he paused. "Let me warn you though, she has hair as red as Betty's." Zeke stopped in his tracks. For all the joking they did, Harold knew Zeke really loved Betty. Harold envied it in a way. He knew it was something he probably wouldn't ever have. He had counted on Zeke not wanting to ogle someone who reminded him of Betty.

"You know, I probably better get a move on after all. I didn't realize it's already after ten."

Harold lit up a Pall Mall and wished for a drink. The furnace wasn't even on, but the temperature was increasing with the climbing of the August sun. He sat on his round three-legged stool that he'd built himself and took a long drag. He flicked the ashes onto the floor. A thin mustache of perspiration began to form on his upper lip.

"Rebecca," he said out loud. "Re-bec-ca Wal-ker." He whispered her name in syllables tasting each with his tongue. "And how would you like to be cooked? Medium? Rare? Well-done?" He grinned again. It was an old joke but he still enjoyed it. He let himself look over at her again. *She would have liked me*, he thought and took another drag from the cigarette. "I guess I'll get started on your container, Mrs. Walker. I'll fix it up especially nice for you."

There had been occasions when the body was small enough and he would just put it directly into the oven. The box was really just to make the body manageable, and normally he didn't mind building them. He rather liked it. He'd always been good with a hammer, after all.

Harold never volunteered to explain the whole cremation process to anyone unless he was forced to. Most people couldn't take the knowledge that he crawled on his belly with a lit broom stick held at his side under the oven until he reached the gas valves. He would slowly aim the lit end of the broomstick at the diesel gas opening and Boom! the furnace would be lit. Next he would inch back out and insert the container with the body through the square door. During the first hour a thick, black smoke would rise from the chimney gradually turning into the pale gray of a hearth fire. If the person had been extremely fat the smoke would stay black for hours as the fatty tissue burned slower than all other parts except for the brain. Most people didn't want to know the details at all. They didn't want to know that cardboard and plywood ash made up about half of a pound of the cremains. They just wanted to avoid a burial for whatever reasons.

"Don't look so sad, Mrs. Walker. I'm going to have to close your eyes if you keep looking so sad." He brushed a hair off of her forehead and picked up the claw-backed hammer lying beside her wrist. He quickly finished up the box and went out beneath the shade of the pecan tree to eat his bologna sandwich.

He kept thinking about Mrs. Walker and her breasts. He tried to fight it, but it was as if there was a magnetic force he could not resist. He was sure she had been sad when she died. Not scared or shocked or hurt. Just sad. Harold wondered if she had been lonely when she died. It seemed impossible that such a beautiful woman could be lonely. Sure, he spent most of his time alone but he liked it that way. He liked knowing he played a part in spinning life's circle. The Bible even said "Ashes to ashes, dust to dust. . . . " He just helped speed up the process. And this way didn't waste a good six feet of ground.

High white clouds floated overhead interrupting the expanse of cerulean blue. He closed his eyes and imagined how her voice had sounded. It was smooth and low he was sure, not squeaky and high. She had enjoyed cigarettes, he imagined, by the breathiness in her words.

"Don't worry, Re-bec-ca Wal-ker. I'll take good care of you." He decided no one had ever taken good enough care of her. Today he would take care of her.

Harold wadded up the foil from his sandwich and stuck it in the lunchbox next to his uneaten Little Debbie cake. Mrs. Walker shouldn't be kept waiting any longer.

Harold removed his shirt from the nail and carried it to Mrs. Walker. He rolled her onto her side and placed her arms in one at the time. He pushed each button through the button hole except for the top one. Her round, pink nipples showed through the thin material, as though eyes, veiled, but watching. He had no brush or comb so he ran a screwdriver through the sides of her syrup-colored hair, separating the strands into smooth lines.

"Now that's much better, Mrs. Wal-ker," he said. "You really are quite lovely." He studied the gentle curve of her chin as it lead to her thin neck. He leaned down and let his lips brush the little mole that jutted out just below her ear. The chill from the cooler was gone.

Harold placed one hand beneath her neck and his forearm behind her knees. He lifted her off of the formica and placed her into the box. It smelled of plywood and was rough with splinters.

"Now this just won't do. Wait right here. I'll be back, Rebecca." He grabbed an old quilt that he used to cover the ripped cloth on the passenger's side of his truck and worked it beneath her body a little at the time. He rolled her shoulders to one side and pulled the quilt. He rolled her to the other side and did the same. It was just after two when he was satisfied with his job.

He knew it was early but he wanted a beer. "Did you like to drink, Rebecca?" he asked her. He pulled her chin down parting her lips. He rubbed his fingers along the bottom of the top teeth. She'd worn braces he thought. They were too perfect to have happened naturally. Her incisors were noticeably whiter than the rest of her teeth. "I bet you liked coffee too?" Mouths were so different after death. No warmth. No wetness. The tongue felt similar to a snake. Harold almost never touched either. They both looked as though they should be slippery and warm but a touch always revealed them to be dry and cold. He poured some beer onto his fingertip and let it drip onto her lips. The drops lay still as if congealed. Still her eyes stared upward. "What was your last drink, Becca? Did you eat good before you died?"

Harold knew it was time to get her started. He wanted to be finished by the time Joe arrived. He removed the broom but then put it back. He didn't want to see the flames spiraling through her white shirt seeking her flesh for fuel. The thought stirred him emotionally, physically. It would be a release from whatever had haunted her he knew, but he didn't want to give her up yet. What else could he do, though? He knew he really had no choice. He lifted up the box and was surprised at its light weight, but then he put it back down. He took her face in both hands and looked again at her pitiful eyes. He wanted to hold her just once before he freed her to the fire. He unbuttoned the white shirt and spread it open. He lifted her up by her underarms and pressed her to his bare chest. Her coolness felt soothing. He braced her lower back and held her head to his shoulder. She fit perfectly against his body.

"Oh, Becca, it's such a shame we didn't get to know each other sooner." He rocked from side to side dragging her feet against the floor.

"One . . . two . . . three . . . four," he whispered heavily, beginning to move his feet up and back doing what he thought was the waltz. The only sounds were the scratching of her toenails against the concrete and his breathing. He closed his eyes and kept moving, swirling in larger and larger circles until his arms burned from her weight. And then as though the song had ended, he stopped.

"Thank you," he whispered and he placed her back into the box on top of the quilt. He buttoned each button and pulled the shirt hem to below her knees. He wiped the mascara from the corner of her eye and closed both lids.

"You're free now, Mrs. Walker," he said and he closed the box.

Marian Carcache

The Other

I tried to tell all this to Dr. Carmichael, but he says it's not his area. He knows me in some ways better than anybody. He vaccinated me when I started to the first grade and then he fit me with a diaphragm when I married Dudley. He says I need to talk to someone else, that he's not equipped for this. He says a therapist, but I'm not crazy. Or a preacher, but I could never tell a preacher. Plus therapists cost like rip, and what if it was a man. I could never tell a man, except Dr. Carmichael. You can tell him some of the details and he can figure out the rest. But a therapist would want more details. I've heard that they want you to tell it all. They watch every eye movement while you're telling it, even when you tighten your lips or shift in your chair. That's how they psychoanalyze you, by watching for hidden signs. I read an article in *Redbook* that says if people kept a journal, they wouldn't need so many therapists. It also implied that most therapists are messed up themselves, hence their interest in other messed-up people. Misery loves company. Plus a journal is free. Here is my journal.

My name is Pamela Perkins. The year I was born the Beatles appeared on Ed Sullivan and Kennedy got shot. Some people tried to connect the two things and said the Beatles were the Four Angels of the Apocalypse from the *Revelations*. There was free love everywhere. My mama met my daddy at a rock concert called "The Big Bam Show" because it was sponsored by a radio station with the call letters WBAM. I was their big Bam. Mama was only nineteen when I was born and even though she loved *me* a lot, she turned against my daddy and free love forever. She said, "love definitely is not free." I've never lacked for anything. My grandparents saw to that. As soon as my daddy was out of the picture–Mama even cut him out of all the photographs—my grandma provided me with the best of everything: velvet-trimmed hats and gloves with tiny pearls, things that other little girls would've killed for, piano and dance lessons, even calling cards with my name, "Miss Pamela Perkins," engraved on them in script. Everybody used to say when I grew up I'd marry money, or at least class, and that's where the problem starts. The man I love does have class. For example: he is from England and wears suits, even hats. He is very educated, a college professor. And he calls down there a *pubis*. Nobody in my family ever called it that. When I was real little Mama would say "don't forget to wash your *teenky-wank*," or sometimes she'd say "*rosebud.*" My grandmother called it a "*biscuit.*" Granddaddy didn't call it. When I was married to Dudley, he didn't call it either, and if he referred to it at all, it was just as "*it.*" At school I heard it called all sorts of things, especially on the bus, but never "*pubis.*" He calls it "*Mound of Venus*" also. Even Dr. Carmichael doesn't call it "pubis."

He hasn't mentioned marriage yet, but I think the fact that he calls it a pubis is a good sign that he might be the one everybody thought I'd marry. There's just this one thing he always wants to do that is not very gentlemanly. At least not in my book. He says I should just relax, but who could? I don't use the same wash rag on it and my face, two separate bath cloths. I never touch my face with its, and I never touch it with my face's. The two don't mix, but he thinks I should relax. To me, that is not a thing a man with a lot of class would ask to do. Maybe he is tainted way back and doesn't even know it. He also eats oysters which is a socially acceptable thing to do but is proven to cause hepatitis and has killed many people. It has become a kind of Russian roulette to even eat an oyster and here he is wanting to do the other, which to my way of seeing things, is not even a socially acceptable thing. I mean I can imagine being at a rich hotel and ordering Oysters Rockefeller but not talking about the other over martinis with socialites like the Astors or the Vanderbilts. My grandmother always called me Miss Astor when I wanted something nice or expensive. I guess it pleased her so much because of Mama's hippie stage. It seems she was wearing a miniskirt and army boots when she met my daddy. Grandma said I have champagne taste and I do. He buys champagne at least once a week. We drink it and everything's all very romantic in front of the fire until he starts wanting to do the other. That spoils the mood. Plus I know as good as I know my name what will follow if I would give in, which I won't. What would follow is he would want *the reverse.* I knew a girl once who would only do that, the reverse. She got a lot of dates. We had PE together for four days and she told me about doing the reverse all the time. My PE teacher had a moustache and real short hair with a ducktail in the back, and she walked like a man. She punished anyone who didn't shower after class by making them take a shower with her. I didn't do either. I dropped PE and took Latin, for which I am thankful. Otherwise, I wouldn't have known what he was talking about when he said *pubis.* The Latin teacher was cross-eyed and I never knew if she was talking to me, but at least I had my clothes on. I think hepatitis is a real threat either way. You don't put your mouth on things where it doesn't belong, and you don't kiss people who do. That would be a good rule of thumb and would probably wipe out hepatitis. When I was in high school people just got herpes or syphilis at worst. Now there's AIDS, but I was allergic to penicillin so I couldn't afford to take chances even then. When Mama was young, they got trench mouth. A girl at her school could drink water from the fountain and it would go through the hole in the roof of her mouth and come out her nose. The reason I don't put my mouth on public water fountains or sit on public commodes has nothing to do with integration and never has. People just want somebody to lay blame on so they don't have to admit the human race is filthy, putting its mouth on everything and spreading all kinds of disease that you wouldn't mention in polite conversation with the Vanderbilts over oysters. Why are people so driven to put their mouths where they don't belong? It is obvious that the cost of not keeping a clean mouth is high.

Dudley never suggested putting his mouth there, although he did like to do weird things that nobody who ever met Dudley would believe he'd think of. Mama called him "Dudley Do-right." Little did she know.

***

His name is Blaine S. Windsor, which is a classy name. Like I said he's from England and that name over there is like Vanderbilt over here. He won't tell me what the "S" is for which is a bad sign because a man would tell a woman he planned to marry, knowing she'd find out anyway from important papers. If he doesn't think highly enough of me to tell me what the "S" stands for why should he think we're familiar enough to do the other? What if I let him and then we quit dating and I saw him on the street or in a restaurant. How can you face a man on the street who's done that with you in the past, but doesn't anymore?

Lord Byron collected pubic hairs of women he slept with. I wonder if they knew. Did he pull them or just collect them from the sheets later on? If he did the second, how did he know he wasn't getting his own mixed in? A famous movie director whose name I forgot used to collect underpants of the women he did it with and then have their initials embroidered on, I guess so he'd remember. These are things I've learned at college that were never mentioned in high school. I used to hate when Mama wrote my name in my underpants with indelible ink. She said to cut down on the risk of putting on the wrong underpants by mistake in PE. She believed you could catch disease that way and on toilet seats. I think there's no need to take PE when there's Latin and there's no need to leave a trail of your name on underpants. "Fools' names and fools' faces . . ." I used to hear about college kids having panty raids. The fraternity boys would break into the girls' dorms and steal their underpants and run them up a flagpole or something. Imagine if your name was on your underpants on a flagpole in indelible ink. That's what Dudley called his—"*flagpole.*" He was not very modest about some things. By the time Dudley Do-right did wrong and I nailed him for college money, they didn't do things like panty raids anymore, but I didn't live in the dorm anyway. I was older and divorced and wouldn't have felt comfortable. Blaine says older students make better students. I'm older than Blaine but don't look it. He's had more advantages, but says I have great potential. Dudley is the same age I am, but doesn't act it. Dudley is rule-bound, but rule-bound people often explode. That is exactly what happened to Dudley. He exploded and I ended up with the money to finally go to college which is how I met Blaine Windsor.

***

I've read enough books to know that women love a man who is wounded in some way. Sometimes it is physical, like Lord Byron. He was a cripple with a clubfoot. He also wrote poems and had curly hair which is now called *Byronic Locks*. Attractive men who have a limp are said to have a Byronic limp, but unattractive ones are just said to be crippled. Lord Byron was also wounded in other ways. He couldn't seem to sustain a relationship with a woman. He broke the heart of Shelley's wife's half-sister who had his illegitimate child. It must have been awkward since Byron and Shelley are always lumped together and were friends. Some say the half-sister was weak-minded, and it figures that a handsome famous poet would choose a woman who would be no competition in the intelligence arena. Men do that often. It helps their ego. It makes me admire Shelley more. His wife was very intelligent. She wrote *Frankenstein*, but then he died; some say he killed himself, and she pulled his heart out when they burned his dead body on a pyre. It makes you wonder if *Frankenstein* was her way of saying in code that there are two sides to every man. Maybe he couldn't take the pressure of a smart wife either.

The other kind of wounded man that women go for is the emotionally wounded, like Edgar Allan Poe. Blaine doesn't teach Poe because he came here specifically to teach English writers. But he says he likes Poe above all other American writers before Faulkner. Poe was definitely emotionally wounded, the way he seemed to seek out mother-figures after his mama died when he was so young. He went for other men's wives, his friends' mothers, his old aunt. Sometimes they would serve as mothers to him, but it's almost certain some were lovers. Then he married the 14 year old cousin. "Prepubescent," Blaine says. Some think he might have married her mainly to get her mother, who was his aunt, to be a mother to him. Some say they never had sex. Some say he picked a dying girl because his mother died young. It makes you wonder. He covered her with his tattered coat and she died. TB just like his mother. From every angle, the story is sad. First a man wanting a mother, then trying to take care of a sickly child-bride, and never ever suggesting that she let him put his mouth where it didn't belong. I'm sure *he* didn't do that. Lord Byron probably did that all the time, but not Poe. Another side people never think of with Poe is how the older women who adored him must have felt when he took up with the fourteen-year-old girl.

***

Eve is the name of the woman Blaine Windsor was dating when I first met him. Eve is a doctor, a psychologist. She teaches classes at the university and has a clinic of her own in the afternoons—another good reason for me to keep a journal instead of going to therapy. No matter what creeds they take, you know doctors talk to each other. Preachers, too, but probably not priests. Preachers tell their wives, which in my opinion is why the Pope won't let priests start marrying. He can't say it, but he knows they'd tell their wives.

Then who could you tell? Not that I would anyway. You don't want to put something like this in the mind of a priest if he hasn't heard of it. It would be like contributing to the delinquency of a minor at best, a mortal sin at worst. And with doctors, it's like this: even if doctors didn't talk, nurses and receptionists do. I know some. I've heard them. They have access to records. Imagine me telling a therapist about Blaine and the business about the mouth and the pubis and all, and then that therapist's secretary telling it over lunch and eventually it getting all the way back to Eve who would: number one, gloat (I feel sure she let him) and number two, probably tell Blaine I was off talking about it just to spite me and embarrass him (she is probably bitter). Eve is very pretty, but she is also aggressive which hardens her look. That's probably how she got so far in life so young—the aggressive, not the pretty. She is very intelligent, too. She has degrees from good universities. Sometimes I feel stupid when I think about them talking about things I've never even heard of over champagne, and us watching *Lifestyles of the Rich and Famous*. Blaine says I'm just as smart as he is (I want to ask "But am I as smart as Eve?," but I don't mention Eve). He says that I just haven't had the opportunity, until now, to tap into my *native intelligence*. He says I'm intuitive and that knowledge can be learned, but that you can't be taught to be intuitive. That's a gift. Eve could probably even get him fired and sent back to England for wanting to do that with a student, never mind that I'm older and divorced. She might just turn him in and say "righteous retribution." A woman scorned.

When I married Dudley I didn't think it mattered if he was smart as long as he could be attractive and show decent manners in public and make a good living, all of which he could. I don't mean to say that Dudley is stupid. He is not. He is not the missing link between man and monkey, only not interested in things like art and literature. Dudley prefers machines. Only once did he want me to do the reverse, and that was after he started running around on me with other women. He learned it from them. I told him flat "No," that I wasn't about to catch some whore of Babylon's venereal disease in my mouth. Then he said if he got a blood test, would I? I said "Never mind" and he dropped it. I've read plenty of women in magazines who say they lost their man because they refused to do the reverse. That is not what happened to my marriage with Dudley. What happened is that I got bored, not with sex but with conversation, or lack of it. Then Dudley got determined to show who was boss and went over the line with sex which I got on videotape, without his knowledge until I had the original in my safety deposit box and a copy to show him. We settled out of court and now I'm in college and dating Blaine Windsor, my professor and a doctor from England, until after midnight every night of the week and solid weekends, overnight and all. Dudley calls sometimes and wants me back. It makes me sad because I still feel something for him, but don't want him back at all. Plenty of women do. He'll be alright. It's probably his pride more than anything else.

He calls drunk a lot, not on champagne I'm sure. I can hear Dwight Yoakam in the background. I know he's sitting in the dark with a six-pack watching Country Music Television all by himself. It does pull on my heartstrings. When he calls and Blaine is there, Blaine gets real protective and wants to get a restraining order, but what's to restrain? Blaine plays Chopin on disc.

***

When I was in the sixth grade a neighbor lent my mother a dirty book to read, *Fanny Hill*. My mother didn't like dirty books. She put it in the recipe drawer so no one would see it before she could return it to its owner. I read it every afternoon, bent over the kitchen drawer, watching out the window by the stove for mama to come up the walk so I wouldn't get caught. I wasn't as worried about being punished as I was about her giving the book back—or even throwing it out—before I could finish it. She wouldn't have let the sun set on that dirty book in the recipe drawer if she'd known I was reading it. The things I got Dudley trying to do on videotape were not even included in *Fanny Hill*. Neither, though, is the thing Blaine wants to do. They don't say "*pubis*" in that book. I don't remember what they called it, if anything. Only for men. For them, they said "*machine*" and "*instrument*," but not "*flagpole*." I wonder if people like the Vanderbilts read books like that. I wonder what *they* call it.

***

Last night Blaine Windsor mentioned marriage. I should be happy and I am. I still have not given in, but maybe I will—after the ceremony which will be civil since I'm divorced. There is no point in another walk down the aisle.

One thing that worries me is this: why did Blaine leave Eve for me? She is just as pretty and smarter. I am beginning to be offended. Am I to him what Shelley's retarded half-sister-in-law was to Byron? Someone who can't compete? When I finish school and get to be as smart as Blaine, will he go off and die like Shelley? And look at Arthur in *The Scarlet Letter*. Just when everything is going to be fixed and he can leave for England with Hester, he dies on the scaffold in front of the whole town. She's left standing there with his illegitimate child and a Scarlet A, and him dead. No telling who Poe left waiting when he died on the street in Baltimore. Plus I learned today that James Joyce's wife never read *Ulysses*. Who can blame her, but still. Isn't it strange that he would pick a woman who wouldn't read her own husband's book? There must have been plenty of women who were pretty and smart around somewhere, even back then when women didn't go to college. The whole thing makes me worry, makes me even mad.

He wants to take me to England on our honeymoon which he can afford. Plus my tuition would be cut in half if I were the wife of a faculty member. Lately, he hasn't mentioned "the other." Maybe he has seen it my way, or maybe he is using reverse psychology. Maybe Eve gave him a crash course in it—psychology, not "the other." Maybe he thinks if he doesn't bring it up again, I will. Maybe James Joyce didn't *want* his wife to read his books. Maybe he knew if he wrote plain, and shorter, she'd be more inclined to pick them up and skim them. I wonder if the girl in PE who did the reverse didn't take showers sometimes because maybe she *wanted* to get caught and have to bathe with the teacher. It would make sense.

***

Today is Saturday. Blaine had to go to the library this morning when it opened to work on an article he is writing and will publish in a journal. I got bored and started looking through the books on the night stand. I found one called *The Hite Report on Male Sexuality* which I picked up out of curiosity. Who is this Hite? Where does he/she get the information? A feeling came over me when I touched it like the way the exorcists at Amityville described feeling when they walked into certain rooms. I should have left it alone, but I opened it and inside the front cover it said "Happy Valentine's, Love *Biscuit*." I knew it was Eve. Could we have had the same grandmother and not know it? The chapter on "the other" went on and on and was worn. One man said he liked it because he could hear the woman's pulse in her *thighs* on his ears. My own ears started to ring. I felt dizzy and sweaty, and vomit tied a knot in my throat just to think about him listening to her *pulse* on his *ears* in her *thighs*.

Then Blaine came home with a bag of *biscuits* from Hardees. I was crying and shaking and he couldn't understand. He said the same thing Dr. Carmichael did, that I needed therapy, that the divorce had been traumatic. I said "So Eve and her friends can get a big laugh at her Christmas party?" and he said Eve was nice, a friend, and wouldn't know anyway, that doctors had ethics and didn't talk among themselves about their clients. That shows how naive he can be. He sat there with a Hardee Biscuit in his hand and called the woman whose pulse he listened to God knows how many times in front of the same fire as me over champagne a *"friend."*

He is being very sweet to me. Unlike Mrs. James Joyce, I will read every word of every article he ever writes. He says I am talented but just need guidance. I am supposed to take my journal, which he has not seen, and go to a therapist in another town that doesn't know Eve and her group of friends. He will pay for all this although his insurance won't cover it because we are not married yet. He will go with me. Sometimes I'll go in alone and other times we both will. He still hasn't mentioned the unspeakable again. I think he thinks I'll go into another fit, but I wouldn't. I think he really loves me now, and maybe will even stay when I am as smart as he is, or smarter. I hope he'll be able to stand the pressure of it.

LORETTA COBB

Seeing It Through

I've always been a good natured, easy-going woman, but I don't take no crap either. As long as things are rocking along smoothly, I'm easy to get along with, but my friends and my husband Hooty know better than to cross me.

At first I laughed about the doctor's office not being able to find a pot for a woman to pee in. My doctor is one of those fools that are moving into the north end of the county, more interested in them prissy horses they raise than anything else. In fact, ever since I've been seeing him for my rheumatism, I've noticed that he talks about his horses more than my problems. I figured it was my good-natured way that made him do it, so I smiled and listened good and secretly started keeping score, tallying his comments. Right now it's me: 11, horses: 32.

But lately, I haven't had time to keep score. One day last February Dr. Alvarez was talking away and I was trying to tell him about these strange little spells I'd been having, I get so hot it feels like my hair is on fire, which I know sounds like the change, but I also get so cold, I mean so cooooooooold it feels like all the heat is going right out the top of my head or the tips of my toes.

That's how come I started wearin' these hats. Most of 'em are baseball caps, the Birmingham Barons and such, but my favorite one come from a little man who died over at the nursing home where I work as a cleanup woman. His wife give it to me along with several pairs of his flannel pj's that I'm crazy about, but that hat is the stuff. It's bright blue, almost purple. She said it come from Paris, France. It's the style like they used to wear back in the first world war days. I don't know what you call it, but I like to wear it cocked to one side. Hooty says I wear all my hats like a French whore.

So, I'm sitting in the doctor's office explainin' to him, wrapped up in a wool scarf and got that hat cocked just right. He said real casually while he was writing in the folder like he could care less, "There's a test we could run, might tell us a little more."

The girl out at the desk, the one with all that gook on her eyes and dressed fit to kill like she's goin' somewhere else in about two minutes, told me it was a 24-hour urine test. She told me just when to start, gave me a little diet and all.

The nurse was a boy or at least partly boy if you know what I mean, kinda prissy. He brought me a thing out that looked like a urinal and told me to urinate in that thing every time I had to for 24 hours. I asked him how he thought I could, and he started stammering around. Then the made-up girl started giggling.

"See, she knows what I mean," I said. But he still looked blank.

"Use your imagination, Kevin," she said ducking her head and looking up at him all cute like.

I could hear myself gettin' loud. "Dearie," I said to him, "some of us have to squat to pee. I can't stand up and fit myself into that thang. I need one of those little round containers that fits under the toilet seat."

His little pale face just got pinker and those long eyelashes actually started fluttering. I felt a little sorry for him being so stupid. So just to help him figure it out I said, "I can't sit down on the toilet and hold this thang up under me; there's not enough room in the toilet even if I did want to make such a mess."

He finally got it, and she assured me she would find the right receptacle as she called it and call me. A couple of weeks passed and the spells had let up some, so I just plain forgot about it.

Then it got to be summer, and Hooty had started swearin', like he always does, how we couldn't live in this oven of a trailer another year while I'd be settin' there freezin, with three sweaters on and my hat. I decided it was time I called the make-up queen. She said she hadn't been able to locate a receptacle, that I should call their office in Birmingham.

When I did the girl there told me to call the horsey office, but I told her, "Hold on here, girl. You the one gettin' paid; you call them and take care of this, and I mean business."

It was along about then that Hooty started to get that mean look on his face when the subject of my doctor came up. In September when the time came for my follow-up appointment, I realized that in all the excitement about the receptacle, both the girl and I had forgot to set up an appointment, which was already overdue. At that point, the first time I could see the horse's rear: December 5.

"Well," I sneered, "at least this oughtta give y'all enough time to get that test done."

It hurt me to look in her eyes with all that mascara caked on them, so heavy. Looks like she couldda seen her eyes were red as road maps, probably allergic to all that gook. But I fixed her with my gaze: "I came up here in person to set up my appointment so I could pick up that pee pot." (By now I enjoyed watching their shock, they felt sorry for me, thought I didn't know any better . . . like I couldn't learn to say "receptacle.")

"I'm sorry, Ms. Sims," she said, putting her claws—painted a dark Satanic looking color—out to pat me on the shoulder. I can't stand that little old lady treatment, so I brushed her hand away. She went on, her voice act-ing like her hand was still patting me on the shoulder, "I have ordered it from a special lab and it should be here soon."

Well, then to top it off, finally in November when I called to see what was holding her up she said, "Oh, it's been here for weeks. I thought you'd come to pick it up."

"What's wrong with the US Mail?" I asked. "Or Alexander Graham Bell's invention, the plain simple telephone that doctors used to use to call their patients?"

Then she said, "Could you please hold?" and snapped the connection, never gave me a chance to answer. Of course, she assumed the answer was yes I can wait all day. She came back on all cheery, like it was good news: "Doc said maybe you should just wait till he sees you again, maybe you don't need this test, after all since it's been so long already."

I said, "You tell him that the symptoms we talked about are a whole lot worse and I don't need to go to medical school to know that something's wrong and I still need whatever it was he wanted to test." So they did the test, naturally.

Who do you think had to see to the pot's delivery! Yours truly. Since I couldn't get up there during the week, they had to hide the pot in the bushes for me one Saturday when me and Hooty were going into town.

Then, when I saw the horse doctor, a full ten months after my last visit, he said very casually, "The test came back normal, but you could still have a carcinoid tumor. There's another test that goes into more detail."

My heart stopped, but I tried not to show it. Tumor. I was not about to admit that I wasn't sure what carcinoid meant, but I knew what carcinoma meant and carcinogenic. Well I sorta knew.

I had Mama with me. I couldn't think about all that right then. Hooty had said we could take Mama to her favorite restaurant, a "joint" that makes good greens and fried okra. The food used to be better till they moved up to this end of the county to serve all them Yankees and yuppies who don't really know how to appreciate good food.

I didn't mention anything to Mama and Hooty at first. We just went on to dinner, and then I told them I had to go to a specialist, but I didn't mention tumor in front of Mama. That night after Hooty was asleep I got up and went to the front of the trailer and looked up carcinoid in the dictionary, but it wasn't in there. I found carcinogenic and carcinoma and had myself a good cry. Ten months wasted from sheer stupidity. I was just numb, but I didn't know nothing yet. I had just begun to jump through the hoops.

Dr. Alvarez could call himself South American if he wanted to, but he looked Mexican to me. He was big and fat and sloppy and his skin glistened like he'd just rubbed Crisco all over himself. I was always saying I wouldn't buy a used car from this man, but there I was, letting him see after the best engine I had—me. To give him credit, he could be nice and gentle once I started pushing for information. He said he couldn't say for sure what the problem was, but that carcinoid tumors were not malignant. I sighed, relieved. Then he said he wanted to do the urine test over and do it a little differently, wanted me to come downtown to the big office. I tried to tell Hooty how nice Dr. Alvarez could be when he took the time, but he didn't seem to hear me.

Hooty took a day of sick leave, insisted on it. He put on them snakeskin boots and strapped his pistol to his holster like he was going to war. When we got off the elevator, he set off the beeper and the security guards searched him.

"Wait just a minute, buddy," the elderly man in uniform said when the beeper went off.

Hooty reddened, but he wasn't about to tell them about the gun, so they frisked him. He enjoyed making them find it, started grinning all over himself.

The elderly man said, "You got a permit for this thing, friend?"

Hooty showed him the little card he carried around, showing that he was a volunteer deputy. Then he swaggered a little and said, "There's been so much trouble downtown lately, all them drive-by shootins, we couldn't believe it. Wadn't no way we was coming downtown without some protection. We watch the 10 o'clock news ever night, by damn."

The guard was looking sorta funny by then because Hooty had started to get that mean look. "Well," he said, "you're welcome to protect yourself and this lovely little lady all you want to once your bidness in the hospital's over, but we have a policy here that nobody can take a weapon into the hospital."

"We ain't goin' to no hospital, she's got a appointment with the doctor, that's all," Hooty explained, grinning now.

"Yessir, I see," said the guard, "but since the hospital is connected to the research wing, we just hold weapons here. It's the same difference as leaving your car keys for valet parking."

"Yeah, but see, I don't use valet parking, buddy, never have," Hooty said.

"Hooty," I interrupted. "Give him the gun. We gonna be late."

"Aw hell," he said, "ahhhiiight."

We made our way through the lobby of what Hooty called the country club and finally found Dr. Alvarez's office. Hooty kept grumbling all through the hallways about how they musta thought he was Dr. Kevorkian or something or maybe one of these guys bent on shootin' abortionists. "Hey, that's a way to show 'em some excitement, ain't it?" he said, jabbing me in the side too hard. "Ask 'em where the abortion clinic is and flash this holster." He was patting the empty holster, laughing strange.

I tried to distract him. I had read in the paper that some famous Chinese man with a name like I Am Pee had designed the building. It had a big huge fountain in the front that I thought looked just like a man peeing, without a receptacle, of course. Sorta like the way men like to pee in the yard I figured.

Hooty just gaped at it, craning his neck over the railing.

"What you call this thang, a atrium?" he asked. "Reckon how much money they waste a month on the water bill?"

I was troubled over the length of time it took Dr. Alvarez's staff to locate a lab that could do this different kind of test, making calls all over the country. I was in his office a total of 3 and a half hours, watching this nurse look up in what looked like a little catalog all the details. She changed her mind maybe ten times. She asked several people how much acid to put in, but nobody seemed to know what was going on. Finally, she settled all the details and told me to keep the urine on ice and bring it back. Hooty thought it was funny I had to keep his beer cooler in the bathtub and close the little container up extra careful every time.

By now, it was close to Christmas, and I waited ever day for a week to hear from the test. After a week I started calling the office. Naturally, they had one of them little "trees" I hate: If you're dying, press 1, if you need an appointment, press 2, if you need lab results 3, etc. Then the lab would come on and give you a bunch of choices. I was usually pretty tired of that by the time I got to my choice, so I'd say, "This is Thelma Sims and I wanna know what's going on with my lab test. Call this number."

By the end of the 3rd week, Hooty took to calling and he wouldn't use that tree. He'd just punch 0 without listening to them choices and say, "Let me speak to that boy in the lab."

The boy finally agreed to call the Mayo clinic where they'd sent the test to see what the trouble was. The next day, the whole office just disappeared over the telephone. The fools took a whole week off for Christmas without warning us.

The first day they opened, me and Hooty was waitin' for 'em. "We don't want to be put off no more," I told the girl at the desk who looked like she might faint when she saw Hooty's mean look and the little strip of leather from the holster that he flashed when he opened his jacket. He give her that look where his eyes look like pieces of coal just about to flame up, that lump in his throat moving all around. The way he'd started balding and then let that bottom hair grow long made him look like some kinda outlaw, but it was that far away look in them eyes that made folks nervous.

Hooty told the receptionist we wanted to see that lab boy. Her lips trembled a little when she said, "I'll see." But she was back in a minute with him. Hooty had on his boots that make him almost as tall as me, but still about half as big around. It just felt like he was standing on his tip toes or something.

The downtown lab boy looked kinda like Hollywood: tall, dark and handsome. He wasn't prissy like the other boy, but he didn't look like much of a fighter either. He looked scared when he saw how mad Hooty was. Usually Hooty just grinned at everything, but he was hot now. The boy promised to call us later in the day. Don't be surprised when I say that it was a whole bloomin' week before we actually talked to a human instead of a recording again. On Friday morning, the boy called me and said that the urine sample had never left Birmingham. I said, "Why on earth did they do that? Was they keeping it for theirselves for a little Christmas present?"

He said, real sheepishly, "They said they didn't know what to do with it." He added half-heartedly, "It is a real unusual test. Dr. Alvarez is the only one here who ever heard of it."

"Son," I said slyly, "let's get this down in writin', ever name and ever detail just as clear as we can because I just might let a lawyer friend of mine take a look at it."

He sounded real nervous then, but he wrote it all out and had it ready for me the next day when I came back with the third collection of my urine. I had got to be pretty expert by now, I probably coulda used one of them urinals by that time. The boy guaranteed me this specimen would get to the Mayo Clinic.

I got real busy workin' in the yard then. I had some fruit trees to fertilize, and I had the pine bark I'd been getting a little along at Wal-Mart piled up behind the trailer. See, we have the front lot, and we have appearances to keep up. When my cousin Robert first rented that spot to us at Riff Raft Acres, he told me that being along the highway wouldn't be too bad. He showed me how we could build us a little deck at the back where we could see down to the water. That sunset on the water was mighty important to me, but the lots right on the water was way too expensive, and Robert wanted somebody on the front who'd keep up the yard and everything. We had some good weather for about a week and I stayed busy every afternoon.

One morning out at the nursing home, I saw Dr. Meriweather. He'd been my doctor for years and years before he retired. Though he was nearly old enough to be a patient himself, he came out and visited some of the old folks every now and then out of the goodness of his heart. He said he knew his favorites that had always perked up when he saw them before would still perk up some now and make him and them feel better. And he could have all the favorites he wanted now that he'd retired and it was free of charge. I cornered him in the coffee room and started pumping him for information.

"Dr. Meriweather," I began, "did you ever have a patient with a carcinoid tumor?"

He scratched his head and his eyes rolled up like they were trying to remember. "That's a pretty unusual ailment, Thelma, and I don't think I ever had the honor."

"They tell me they're not malignant," I said, "but I thought carcinoid meant cancer. You ever hear of a cancer that wasn't malignant?" I asked.

"Best I can remember those little buggers are hard to track down, real slow growers, but always malignant." Then he stopped and looked at me sideways, "You goin' to medical school, Thelma, or you worrying about this for a reason?"

"I might be," I said, not answering either way.

He motioned for me to sit down and fixed me a cup of coffee. He always was the sweetest thing on earth. So I told him about the crazy things that had been happening.

"Thank God I'm beyond it," he said. "When I practiced medicine we didn't have all these wonders of modern science, but we could take the time to tell a patient what she needs to know."

Before I knew it, he was drawing those little pictures on a napkin like he used to in his office on the back of prescription pads. We talked awhile, and then he was scooting his chair back and standing up to go, saying "I tell you what you could do. You can make Robert get on the internet and find all kinds of information, keep you just as up-to-date as any of the doctors nowadays. His boy's always carrying on through the e-mail with my grandson who can find me anything I want to know about a whole bunch of subjects, some of which I can't discuss with a lady. You stay after it Thelma, make 'em give you satisfaction. It's such a rat race today it's not even like the same profession. I'm surprised the patients don't start a revolution."

Then I started calling everyday again to see about the test, and finally I got a nurse who told me that the Mayo clinic said it could take them anywhere from 1 to 3 months to get the test done. I just busted into tears right in the middle of her talking. I said, my voice just screaming, crazy sounding, like somebody else talking, "Them carcinoids are always cancer and cancer is always malignant. There ain't no such thing as benign cancer."

"Yes, ma'am," she said, "I'm just relaying the message I was given. Dr. Alvarez thought you'd want to know." I told her I figured that fool Mexican just had a language problem. He ought to learn to speak English, that's what. She just got real quiet. I said, "I know it ain't your fault, it's just that I feel like beating the crap outta somebody, and I can't figure out who."

"Yes, ma'am," she answered.

That's when I started calling the cancer society. Once I got them nice ladies on the phone who didn't treat me like a fool, and I read all that stuff they mailed me. I felt like I was getting somewhere. I could at least figure out some things I didn't have to worry about. That's what gave me the confidence to ask Robert about the computer. He said Dwayne C., his boy, was the expert, but he couldn't use it these days because he'd been grounded.

Robert scratched his head and tugged on his T shirt that wasn't quite covering his belly, "Tell you the truth. It would save me a lot of grief if we could just move it up to your place for awhile."

"No, sir, I'm not letting you . . ." I started.

He wouldn't hear of it though, seemed too eager to get rid of it. By late afternoon Robert had showed me how to use it, set it up for me and all. He told me, when I tried to thank him, "Us riff-raff has to stick together, hang on to the same raft." Then he gave me one his bear hugs and shuffled barefoot back down to his boat that he was always fixing.

Truth was his wife was the wickedest, fattest stepmother I ever seen, made him take that computer away from his boy cause she thought all that stuff he read on there would turn him into a gang member. She'd been looking over his shoulder watching him on those chat groups, saying they was ruining the English language, talking like colored folks, all that. Me and Hooty just started lettin' Dwayne C. come over here after school and use the thing all he wanted to till they got home from their jobs. Tickled us really.

Hooty even got us on America Online after I seen him in there with Dwayne C. giggling over them naked lady pictures on them chat groups. Besides they had a free 30-day trial thing I could use. Dwayne C. told Hooty the only gangs he was studying was gang banging. They laughed like two children, and only one of 'em spose to be one.

I started using everything I could to find out for myself. I started going to the computer every morning. I couldn't believe how much stuff you could learn about cancer just pushing them buttons. Some of it was written for them little medical students. I could tell by the way they made it sound so hard and used big long words and sentences you'd have to read 10 times before you knew for sure it didn't make a bit of sense. But some of it was written just for patients, put out by the cancer society. Tell you the truth, I was about ready to open a practice. Hooty said, "Hell, you could do a whole lot better than them guys you paying a fortune to for nothing."

It seemed like doing my investigation kinda took my mind off the worry. It also helped me quit worrying so much to realize that even the experts don't always agree on stuff. Hooty didn't have any use for reading though and he just got madder. I started going online some at night while Hooty turned into a baseball game in front of that television.

What I liked the most was the cancer chat group. One night I got up my nerve to try to talk on that thing since these little boxes would flash on automatically. I think they were trying to sell memberships or something. These kids would all be talking about how much they drank, how much they liked sex, stuff like that. I kinda liked listening in, kinda like when I was a girl and Mama n' 'em would listen in on the party line. I never did that though. It seemed wrong to me.

This was different. The people wanted you to listen. They had funny names like *surfer* and *sexad* and *GVMESMHD*. They'd say stuff like: "ssssup?"

"So how old is everybody in here?"

They didn't want to tell how old they were; all of 'em wanted to be older than they were. One guy said, "I'm sure I'm the oldest person in the room; I'm 26."

So I just spoke up and I told him I was exactly twice his age, 52, and he said, "No come on, I'm serious."

They couldn't believe there was anybody that old. I loosened up a little, but I didn't say much for awhile.

Then I asked casually, "Anybody in here can tell me how to get to the cancer chat group?" I was amazed at how hard that was to ask. My palms were sweaty and my throat felt tight, like I needed to clear it but I couldn't.

It was a minute before somebody answered me and told me what keyword to use and how to try it. Then four or five of the kids said stuff like:

"Hang in there."

"I hope you find it."

But by the time I left the "room," they were already back to praising Jack Daniels and talking about how big their bosoms were.

The talk on the cancer chat was different. There would still be two or three conversations going at once, but people would be talking about how long they'd been in chemo, how long it took their hair to grow back, stuff like that. One lady was about to scream because she had gone in for chemo and they put the wrong stuff in her veins. Several people suggested she shoot something poisonous in the veins of some lab technicians. That seemed like a pretty good idea to me, too. Then some guy came on the screen, saying, "Ooooooooooooooooooo, help me I am dying of cancer."

A lady named *ur4given* answered, "We're right here, how can we help." But the guy never said anything else, and most folks figured he was a fake. I didn't know what to think, but it gave me the creeps. I just signed off then and went to bed, but I couldn't get that scream, that "Oooooooooooooooooooo" out of my mind. I also started thinking horrible things about kidnapping that lab boy and torturing him. Or maybe the makeup queen and scrubbing her for about an hour. I decided all this stuff could make you crazy if you let it. Maybe Dwayne C. was being corrupted by that computer. It was worse than the television to give you crazy ideas because it was real life what all those people were going through. I couldn't let go of the idea that the lady who had the wrong chemicals put in her veins ought to poison some lab technicians. I didn't sleep much at all anymore.

Usually on Saturday mornings when the ballgames hadn't started yet, Hooty would go to Robert's place and watch him make bullets. In his basement, Robert had a little machine where he made his own bullets, hollow points he called them. I never paid them any mind, couldn't stand the sound of a gun when Hoot insisted I need to learn now how to fire one. "Why do I need to learn if I'm gonna sleep with the best crack shot in the county and my cousin's always at home in the daytime down there in his own private arsenal?"

One morning I just got to staring at myself in the mirror after breakfast. I used to pull my hair back in a tight bun every morning, but lately I had just let it straggle, especially since I had to keep putting my hat on and off. Them eyes looking back at me from under that hot blue hat were almost purple, little amethysts stuck in dough. I had lost a lot of weight since all this stuff had started and my neck showed it, all gobbled and flabby at the throat.

I didn't like what I saw. I got the scissors and cut my hair off real short like a boy's. Then I got in the tub and soaked myself for over an hour. I put on lots of perfume and some dangling earbobs since my hair was so short it looked like something was missing. When Hooty woke up, he asked me if I had a boyfriend or something. I told him, "Yeah, Dr. Alvarez."

"You mess with that fool and I'll fix him," Hooty said, and that dark cloud came over his face. It seemed like he just couldn't let go of worrying over me. Hooty just went to work at the plastic factory and came home and drank beer in front of the TV. One night he came in with two Atlanta Braves hats and told me he thought maybe I'd like a new hat to go with my new image. I tried wearing it some, but I still liked my Paris blue one best. Hooty never wore his outside the house, but he'd put it on every night when whatever game he was watching came on.

One Saturday in the spring just when the buds on the trees had started to bust open and make those tiny little baby fists of leaves, I was sitting on the deck, sweat pouring from working some fertilizer in around my azaleas. That's the day the crazy mail came. There it was in the mail without any letter to explain to us or anything except we could see where Dr. Alvarez had written, "Mail to Ms. Sims." The lab report said: *Test canceled by Reference Laboratory. Above test requires that ph of specimen be between 1.0 and 5.0. Please resubmit if desired.*

Hooty jumped the switch and made the old Chevy run somehow. We put them baseball caps on backwards and cut the radio up loud. We looked just like them gangs we'd heard about. We had even bought us some Afro-tique panty hose to put over our faces, so we'd look colored. We stalked that doctor like we'd been doing it all our lives. We saw him come out of that Catholic church, looking all smug and satisfied. We followed him home and just as he got out of the car, we got a good look at him.

I could see his face as he squinted to see what an old car like ours was doing on a hifalutin street like his. Then I saw his face change when he saw the gun, his mouth fall open. His little bug eyes looked like they might pop out. I had to work hard to keep my eyes on the road, drive that car as fast as I could. Hooty fired the pistol. Bull's eye: right between the legs! Blood was spurting everywhere as Alvarez fell to the ground, reaching out as if he thought we would stop and help him. Then I gunned the motor and we were out of that little cul de sac before anybody could have seen us.

We laughed till we cried. "Let that fool see what it's like to be a victim of the medical profession," Hooty said. "Wonder of they'll be able to find him a receptacle to pee in now," I answered in a high-pitched voice that didn't sound like mine. We dumped that old car at the bottom of the heap in his uncle's scrapyard like we'd been doing that kind of stuff every Sunday.

I'm not saying we were right, but I am telling you we felt the sweet taste of revenge, riding home that night with the smell of fresh rain around us. I might be dying and I might not, but I ain't going back to no doctors, and I won't have to die without knowing the satisfaction of revenge. All I had to do to get up my nerve was close my eyes and remember that woman who had the wrong stuff put in her veins or that scream, "oooooooooooooooooh I am dying."

They tell me holding grudges will cause cancer. You have to do something about stuff that makes you angry. They have documented cases of people who "deal with their anger" and then find that tumors disappear.

When we went to bed that night, Hooty took me in his arms, and it was kinda like coming home after a long time away.

"You know what?" I said, just as he was dozing off. "I just might take that GED class at the library and become a LPN."

Hooty never answered, but I knew he heard me. Somehow I also knew I'd be able to count on him to see me through.

Sandra King Conroy

Fig Picking

I came to regret the day I agreed to spend my fourteenth summer with Granny Sweetwater, but never so much as when she made me go with her to Bunch Mosley's yard to pick figs. Ever since I'd arrived, all she wanted me to do was work and I was tired of it. I would've played sick like when she wanted me to milk her stinking goats, except she promised I could go to the picture show Saturday afternoon if I behaved.

Even at that I had to think about it. Granny was smart, give her that. When we went to the clinic last week for her medicine, I saw the new *Gidget* movie advertised on the marquee of The Strand and started begging then. "We'll see," was all she'd say. "Let's wait and see how you behave, whether you keep on being so sassy." So I'd been on my best behavior, not fussing and whining when she drug me with her to the pea patch or peach trees or blackberry bushes, lugging buckets. After the picking, we'd sit on the porch and shell, shuck, peel, chop, whatever, then stew, preserve, or can the stuff in her hot little kitchen. But figs! I didn't even know what they looked like.

"I dreamt about a fig tree last night," Granny told me as we walked the road to Bunch's house. I hated the road; it was paved with oyster shells and hurt my feet, even through my tennis shoes. A big shell flipped up and struck my ankle and I hollered. It stunk out here, too. Granny lived on the river road next to the paper mill and I had yet to get used to the awful stench.

"I ain't even looked in Bunch's yard to see if the figs are ripe yet," she continued, not noticing I wasn't paying no attention to her. "When I dream of a fig tree, I know without looking."

I rolled my eyes. It embarrassed me the way Granny played like she was some kind of medicine woman or something, just because she was part Cherokee Indian. I wasn't about to tell anybody I had Indian blood. She'd proudly told me that some folks was scared of her, that most of the colored people on the St. John place wouldn't even come in her house. I figured it was probably because she looked so funny. When I was a baby I was scared of her and hid behind Mama's skirts. Glancing over, I saw how she could spook a child or a colored person. She wore a long bright-colored dress and a cowboy hat with a silver band, and her trademark was the pipe she smoked, packed with tobacco she raised. From under the hat a long black braid without a trace of gray hung down her back. Her dark eyes were stern and unsmiling, making her look kind of mean.

It was about a mile to Bunch Mosley's house and the sun overhead was so hot I felt like I was about to faint. Sweat poured in my eyes and I squinted. Most of the time we picked early morning or late afternoon, after it'd cooled down some. But today Granny'd got it in her head she wanted to have figs for supper, so we set out right after lunch. I was afraid she'd have a sunstroke in this heat. Granny was old as dirt; she claimed she didn't know but I bet she was almost eighty.

We turned off the oyster-paved road to the dirt path that came up behind Bunch's neat white-frame house, a better-looking place than Granny's tin-roofed shack. At first I couldn't believe that a colored family had a better house than my own grandmother, but since Bunch was the housekeeper for the St. John family, the house was provided. Granny was always going to Bunch's, trying to make me go, too, but I wouldn't. I told her Daddy'd beat the living daylights out of me if I went into a colored person's house. Granny'd hooted and said she was glad Mama hadn't lived to see what a drunken fool Daddy'd become. The two of them had never gotten along. Daddy claimed Granny Sweetwater hated him because he and Mama eloped when she was only sixteen years old.

Granny untied the white-washed gate that led into Bunch's backyard. She held it open for me and I hesitated before going in. It was overgrown and snakey-looking, full of bushes and trees and flowers I'd never seen before. I lugged my bucket through the ankle-high grass as I followed after her. "Looks like Miss Bunch'd make Calvin get his lazy butt out here and cut the grass."

"Calvin's her baby so she spoilt him rotten," Granny chucked, then suddenly stopped by the honeysuckle-covered fence. I almost ran into her. "Yep, they're ripe, all right," she said.

She put her hand up to shade her eyes as she looked at two big trees by the fence, and I knew with a sinking heart that these were the fig trees and they were sure ripe. Brown globes of fruit covered the skinny twisted limbs, weighing down the lower ones so that they touched the scrubby Bermuda grass beneath them.

I forgot my efforts to be good and threw my bucket down. "Don't tell me we've got to pick all of them," I cried, wiping the sweat off my face with the back of my hand.

"Now Fern," Granny said reaching for a fig branch and bending it toward her, "don't you think of it that way. Think about how good them fig preserves are gonna be on our biscuits."

"I never had a preserved fig," I snorted, wrinkling my nose, "and I don't intend to start now."

Granny started plucking the figs nearest the ground, throwing them into her bucket where they made soft thudding sounds. "You don't know what's good," was all she said until I kept standing there with my hands on my hips, scowling at her. Then she got mad. "I could walk to town on those lips of yours. Get to picking or I'll wear you out, Miss Priss," she snapped at me.

I sighed loud as I could, then reached for a fat round fig hanging from the branch nearest me. "What is this thing?" I yelped when I pulled it from the stem. The fig I held in my hand looked like a woman's veined breast, leaking some kind of white milky substance. I saw that the pale green leaves were also weird, big and soft and hairy. They gave me the creeps and I stepped back in disgust. I was surprised to see Granny plop a fat brown fig in her mouth, biting it off at the stem and chewing happily. She held another one in her big old hand, as brown and spotted as the fig. "Try one," she said.

The fig was too ripe and the skin had busted to reveal a fleshy-looking pink inside. The over-ripe ones had fallen on the ground like dead things. Wasps and yellow jackets swarmed around them and I shuddered. "How can you eat those nasty things, Granny?"

"Wait till you smell them cooking, you'll see," chuckled. "Not many things on this earth smell that good. Now, hush up or no picture show for you!"

I turned and began grabbing the disgusting things, throwing them in the bucket, trying to touch their soft flesh as little as possible. Nothing to do but fill the buckets and keep my mouth shut. I knew Granny well enough to know she meant what she said.

At least the figs were easy to pick and I used both hands, not looking Granny's way as I flung them in the bucket. "Bucket's full," I was able to tell her finally, straightening up. Seemed like hours but probably hadn't taken half a one. The tree was so full I'd not even had to move, me picking one tree and Granny the other. But when I turned to her tree, Granny was gone.

"Granny? Where—" Before I could get the words out, I saw that she'd gone to Bunch's back porch and was now coming back, carrying an empty fertilizer bucket. Turning my head, I spotted her own bucket, propped against the tree trunk, full.

"I hope you're not bringing that bucket to put more figs in," I cried. I was so sweaty my eyes were stinging and watering. Granny'd tried to get me to wear a hat but I'd refused. In spite of my dark complexion, I'd already burned and peeled a couple of times this summer. Now the top of my head felt like it was on fire, and my arms were red and hot. Granny'd tried to make me wear one of her dresses instead of my shorts and sleeveless shirt, but I wouldn't be caught dead in one of her tacky old dresses.

"Them figs is for us," Granny said, nodding her head toward our buckets. "Now we're gonna pick Bunch some." And she made her way up to the tree, grabbing a branch right above her head. "We about picked this one clean. Shimmy up your tree, girl. We'll have to get to the top to pick another mess."

I looked at the gnarled trees and shook my head. My tree was about a foot taller than Granny's but the trunk wasn't much bigger than my arm. "Shoot, Granny," I protested. "That tree ain't big enough to climb. It'll break."

"Huh! Light as you are, you couldn't break a peach tree. Get your fanny-butt up far enough to reach those top branches." I sighed loud but grabbed a limb over my head and hopped up, pulling upright and positioning myself between two small branches at the top of the tree. I wanted nothing more than to pick those stupid figs and get it over with.

I bent a heavy-laden branch over so she could reach it and, with a frown, she picked it clean, her brown hands moving like the wind. Then I moved to reach another branch, higher up.

"I hate this stupid tree, Granny," I cried when the soft fuzzy leaves brushed my skin like human hands. "It looks like it's alive." The leaves, like the figs, leaked a milk-like substance when broken. I shuddered, averting my eyes.

"All trees is alive," Granny said, shading her eyes with her hands as she watched me pull a branch toward her.

"I mean, like a person. Like something—real!"

"This tree is real, Fern," Granny said, squinting as she stripped the branch of its fruit. "It has feelings just like me or you. It's proud of itself for giving so many figs today. Your fussing'll make it feel bad."

"Oh, sure," I laughed. "I believe being out in the sun has made your brain soft."

Before I realized what was happening, Granny grabbed my arm, jerking me down from my perch. I reached for a low-hanging branch frantically as she pulled me down beside her. I fell on my feet but she jerked me up.

"I don't know where you got that smart mouth of yours, Fern Cooper," she growled at me, giving me a shake, "but it weren't from your mama!"

I glared back at her, trying to think of something to say. Her big rough hand on my arm was hurting because of the sunburn, but I wasn't about to say so, give her satisfaction of telling me I should've covered myself like she said.

"I bet you made Mama pick these stupid old figs when she was my age and that's how come she ran off and married Daddy, to get away from you," I cried, my eyes suddenly smarting with tears.

Tightening her grip on my arm, Granny reached to break off a switch as I tried to pull away from her. Looking over her shoulder, I saw Bunch Mosley coming through the tall grass toward us. An enormously fat colored woman, she was dressed in a black uniform of a silky material, except for the white apron, which stuck out from her big body like one of those skirts ballerinas wear. I had an idea that she'd been watching us fuss from the porch and showed herself at a critical moment.

"Here comes Bunch Mosley," I hissed at Granny, and she dropped my arm.

"Well, Lord-a-mercy me," Bunch said, laughing her loud laugh, throwing her head back. I'd never seen her without bright red lipstick on, her mouth so wide it was like a pink cave splitting her face in two, showing the wide gap between her front teeth. "Look who done come picked my figs! I can near about taste them preserves of yours, Posey Sweetwater."

"I dreamt of a fig tree last night," Granny told her, thankfully forgetting me and my sassiness. "So I knowed it was time to make preserves for supper."

I relaxed, rubbing my arm and taking a deep breath. I knew I'd barely escaped getting a whipping. Granny'd never hit me, but I'd seen her switch my brothers good for sassing her.

Bunch bent and looked at the full buckets as she smacked her fleshly red lips. "I want you to look at all them figs!" she declared. There was something different about her, and I blinked in surprise. Today was the first time I'd ever seen her without her hair tied up, a scarf turbaned around it. I was astonished that her kinky salt-and-pepper hair was as short as a man's. It made her look funny and I giggled. Big and fat with so little hair, she looked like the plump brown figs with the small stems on top.

"Posey Sweetwater, get on and get them figs going," Bunch laughed again in her jolly way, rolling her big brown eyes at Granny. "Then fo' dark, I'm gonna come sit on your porch just to smell them cooking!"

Granny shook her head. "No'm. I'm gonna pick you a mess before they get too ripe. I'm fixing to get Fern to shimmy back up the tree—"

"Uh uh, you ain't no such thing," Bunch interrupted. "I told Calvin to pick them figs and I'd pay him. He be mad if y'all get 'em first."

Granny looked at Bunch skeptically, narrowing her eyes, but Bunch ignored her, turning to me and smiling. "Besides, I need Miss Fern to help me do somethin', if you'll let her."

I drew my breath in. "Oh, PLEASE, Granny—"

"Huh! Reckon I might be too soft in the noggin to decide whether you can or not," she grunted, but there was a twinkle in her dark eyes.

I wanted to hug her neck, hot and sweaty as we both were, but Granny wasn't affectionate. She'd not hugged me since I'd been here. "Granny, I'm sorry I sassed you. Please—"

"Aw, you ain't helping no how," she sighed. "Go on with Bunch and behave yourself."

Bunch shook her head as she stood watching us, hands on her huge hips. "You forgot what it's like to be a young girl and have to work in the sun, Posey. 'Sides, I'm gonna trade you this girl for Calvin. I'll send his sorry black fanny out to carry them figs home."

I was so glad to get away from Granny and the figs that I practically ran after Bunch Mosley as she started back toward her house. Only after I stumbled up the back porch steps I realized I'd actually be entering a colored person's house, something I never thought I'd do.

We went into the kitchen and I looked around me in amazement. It was as fine as any white person's house I'd ever been in. Bunch's kitchen was painted butter yellow and had starched white curtains in the windows. Both windows had fans in them, going full blast, making it much cooler than Granny's. It was so clean that the appliances and stovetop gleamed like new.

I couldn't help but feel even more ashamed that Granny's house—and my own, too, for that matter—was so much worse than a colored family's.

I could see part of their living room, drapes pulled tight against the hot sun, with a small television, gray-and-white images flickering in the semi-darkness. Neither Granny nor my family had a television set yet. I'd only watched the programs a couple of times, at my teacher's house. "Calvin Mosley, turn that thing off and go help Miz Posey Sweetwater carry two buckets of figs to her house," Bunch hollered.

"Yes'm, but I sho' ain't going in!" Calvin yelled back, and I giggled.

Bunch turned to me, rolled her eyes, then nodded her small round head toward a hallway leading off the kitchen. "Come on, sugar-baby. You gonna help me make yo' Granny a batch of yeast rolls for y'alls supper, but let's get you cleaned up before you blister any worse. You a sight if I ever seen one!"

I couldn't believe the green tiled bathroom she led me to. It was twice as big as Granny's and she had it fixed up real nice, with a green crocheted thing on the commode and a ruffled skirt under the sink, matching the flowered curtains at the window. Even the tub was green.

"You've fixed your house up real pretty, Miss Bunch," I told her, breathing deeply of the sweet talcum powder, a scent that I'd first smelled on her.

She seemed pleased as she nodded toward the sink. "There's you a washrag and some soap. Let's see if we can git you looking better."

I couldn't believe my eyes when I looked in the medicine-cabinet mirror, and I turned to Bunch, horrified. "Oh, Lord, Miss Bunch—look at me!" My hair was matted and tangled, wet with sweat and sticking to my head. My face was not only blood-red but filthy, my nose peeling in strips. My arms were covered with welts from insect bites and tree scratches. The white milky stuff from the figs made me feel sticky all over.

"You a mess, that's for sho'. Get yourself washed up then come across the hall to my room," Bunch said, going out and closing the door after her.

After washing myself gingerly, wincing as the soap stung my burnt skin, I left the green bathroom and peeked in the bedroom across the hall. It was big and sunny, with flowery wallpaper and heavy brown-painted furniture. Standing by a mirrored dresser, Bunch motioned for me to sit down on the cushioned bench there. "Least you clean. Now let's see what we can do with that mess of hair."

I was too surprised to yell when Bunch grabbed my hair and started brushing the tangles out, hard. Our eyes met in the mirror and she threw her head back and laughed, her brown eyes bright. "Now don't you worry none, baby. This here brush ain't never been used. No colored hairs in it."

My face flamed red, making the sunburn even brighter. Bunch nodded toward a blue Vick Salve jar on the dresser. "Rub some of that stuff on your face."

I opened the jar and stuck my fingers in, then looked up at her, shuddering in disgust. "It looks like snot, Miss Bunch."

"Your Granny fixed it for me, so no telling what it be. Might be gator boogers." She threw back her head and laughed at the expression on my face. "Old Bunch be teasing you, baby. Ain't nothin' but aloe juice, but it'll make your face quit burning."

I patted the green slimy stuff on as Bunch began pulling even harder on my hair with the brush, jerking my head back. When I realized she was plaiting my hair I swallowed and squirmed nervously, not daring to meet her eyes. I hoped I didn't turn out looking like a pickaninny. When she finished, I was surprised. Instead of cornrows she'd made a tightly-braided plait which encircled my head like a wreath, high off my neck, and cool. She leaned over and gave me a sweet-smelling hug when she saw my smile in the mirror. "I had me a baby girl once, but she didn't live no time, hardly. She would have been about your age now."

I didn't know what to say to that. I looked up and saw her watching me. "Did you know my Mama, Miss Bunch?"

She nodded. "Sho' did. You the spitting image of her. I know it hurts Posey to see how much you look like her. I thought she was gon' grieve herself to death when that girl died! She's been so happy you finally come to stay with her she can hardly stand it."

"She don't act like it. She's mean to me and makes me work all the time," I sniffed.

Bunch chuckled. "Don't you pay no mind to Posey's talk. She do that to hide how happy she is that you here. After all these years your daddy let you come, and now she scared it's been too long, that you won't come back. Come on now, baby. Let's go fix them rolls."

I spent most of the afternoon with Bunch in her bright yellow kitchen, helping her mix up yeast rolls and roll them out, folding them into pocketbook shapes and brushing them with melted butter. I was actually enjoying myself, though we didn't do anything but work all afternoon, just like at Granny's. But Bunch was jolly and fun and didn't fuss like Granny did when I made a mess. I didn't sass her like I did Granny, either. I almost hated to see the sun going down. Bunch'd already told me we wouldn't cook the rolls; we'd take them all risen and ready to pop in the oven so they'd be fresh baked for our supper tonight.

Me and Bunch didn't talk as we walked the oyster-shell road to Granny's house, each with a pan of rolls in hand, the pans covered with a dish cloth, bleached-white and soft as a baby diaper. The rolls gave off a rich yeasty smell and as we climbed the cement blocks leading up to the front porch of Granny's house, I realized I was starving. Something else was in the air besides the yeasty aroma of the rolls. The awful river smell had been replaced by the most heavenly fragrance I've ever breathed, like all the spices of the world had been thrown together to simmer over a fire of burning flowers. I turned to Bunch wide-eyed as she waddled up the steps behind me, turning her huge hips sideways to navigate the narrow blocks. "What on earth is that smell?" I asked her.

Bunch laughed. "Baby, that's them figs your Granny's cooking. You just in time for supper."

We went through the cluttered living room into the steaming little kitchen. Sure enough, Granny was stooped over the tiny stove, stirring a big washpan full of syrupy caramel-brown figs, looking and smelling completely different than they did on the tree.

Granny nodded approval when we came in. "They done," she announced solemnly. She held out a lard bucket toward Bunch. "I got y'all some preserves cooled off to tote back, Bunch."

Bunch put her pan of rolls down on the cabinet. "Much obliged, Posey. And we made you some yeast rolls," she told her. "They ready to go straight in the oven."

Granny nodded her head toward the stove. "It's on. I was about to make some biscuits, but I'd ruther have them rolls. Stick 'em in the oven, girl, and give Bunch her dishrags back."

I did as she told me, jerking my head back at the heat from the oven. "Did y'all have a big time this afternoon?" Granny asked me. She was still dressed in her long dress and sweat covered her shiny broad face, dripping from her chin. With the rolls cooking in the oven, it was so hot in the cramped little kitchen that it was hard to breathe.

"Yes'm, we sure did," I nodded. "Miss Bunch has the nicest house, and she showed me how to make rolls. When we eat all these, I'll make us some more."

"I gotta git on back now, git our supper," Bunch smiled, moving toward the door with her lard bucket of fig preserves. She had to turn sideways to get out the narrow kitchen door.

"You welcome to stay and eat with us," Granny told her, but Bunch was shaking her head before she could finish. "I hope you didn't let this girl pester you too much this afternoon," Granny added, cutting her dark eyes toward me.

"Lord-a-mercy, no. We had us a big time," Bunch said.

Granny poked me in the ribs with her elbow. "What you say to Miz Bunch, Fern Cooper?"

I turned toward her and smiled. "I appreciate it, Miss Bunch. I want you to show me how to do my hair like this sometimes."

Bunch reached back in to hug me before she went out the door. The kitchen was so little the three of us could barely stand in there together, especially with Bunch taking up so much room. It was a little better after she left, but still unbearably hot.

"We can't eat in the house tonight, Granny," I groaned. "Let's take our plates out on the front porch and eat our supper."

Granny looked at me slyly. "Reckon you'll have to fry you some eggs, since you don't want to eat no figs."

I shrugged as I grabbed the big wooden spoon sticking up from the cooked figs and stirred them slowly. "I might eat a few."

Granny chuckled and shook her head. "You're about the stubbornest girl I ever saw in my life," she said.

"Reckon I take after my granny, then." I raised a spoonful of thick caramel figs to my mouth and blew on them before touching my tongue to the edge. It was so good I ate the whole thing, burning my mouth. Then I licked the spoon.

"You wash that before putting it back in those preserves," Granny snapped. "And I smell them rolls. Git them out before they burn, you hear me?"

I ate so much supper I like to have made myself sick. I left Granny sitting on the porch in her rocking chair and went to bed, so full I was miserable. Before I went in, I stopped by the rocker and put my hand on her big brown arm hesitantly, then quickly removed it.

"Goodnight, Granny Sweetwater. I'm going on to bed now," I said to her. It was hot and airless, but thunder was rumbling in the distance, so maybe it would rain.

"Goodnight, Mary Fern," I thought Granny said. She was smoking her pipe and she didn't take it out of her mouth.

"That was Mama," I told her, "not me. I'm just plain Fern." I didn't think she heard me because she didn't move, not even to rock. I shrugged and went inside.

When I went to bed I lay on the cot by the window and listened to the night sounds, the frogs from the river and the crickets and mosquitoes. I heard the thunder again, and then I heard the sound I'd been listening for: Granny's rocker, creaking as she rocked and smoked her pipe, looking out over the black starless night. The sweet-smelling pipe smoke floated like angel wings through the front window and hung over my bed.

In spite of the heat, I fell off to sleep. Like Granny, I dreamed of fig trees, but my dream-trees were shaped like people, with twisted limbs that reached out deformed arms to me. I saw bent tree-people standing in a circle, except their feet were roots, buried in the ground. I walked among them and they touched my braided hair with soft green leaf-hands. Then I saw why they stood in a circle. In the center was an old fig tree, bent and brown and gnarled with age. Underneath it was Granny Sweetwater, laid out in death, her big brown arms folded over her chest. The tree dropped figs all over her body, so ripe they fell like tears.

Linda Elliott

Mrs. McCammock

The dirt was tramped smooth over the red clay with its spongy smooth places that felt cool and familiar. Weeds and grass made an intermittent pattern across the path and she felt every variation in texture and wondered that her tired rough soles could know each one. At 26, life in these woods, life with a brood of seven young 'uns, so far, was a load on those feet and they were old before their time. Sara Littleton is who she was before. A woman who laughed, sang, thought things through, and knew what had to be said when it needed to be said. A woman sharp as a tack, and pretty as a picture. All that was lost and didn't matter anymore now. It had been a long time since she felt like that woman, looked like her, or sounded like her.

A big pot of field peas for supper brought her out often on this path behind the cabin. It ran next to the woods on one side with the garden on the other side. Picking peas for supper and getting away from him brought her out today. Supper better be on time, better be on time, better be on time she scolded in her head. "Ain't no excuse, ain't no excuse, ain't no excuse," she recalled before she shuddered thinking about the blows she took the last time it wasn't. Today was heating up for more of it. It didn't seem right. She shuddered again, this time from a dark feeling coming over her as she gazed toward the woods. She stood with her arms wrapped around her shoulders, her rough hands stroking at the faded flowers on her dress.

A fear, a sort of dread came on her when she heard some kind of noise, like there's a devil in them woods, she nodded to herself. A devil in the dogtrot, a devil in the woods and nowhere to go. Run out the door to get away but she couldn't get away at all.

Everybody would say she was sorry, a sorry, no-good woman to leave a good man. A good man worked hard. He worked hard, he was a good man. That was the way it was. Didn't matter about what went on behind his doors. No one wanted to know, no one wanted to hear about it, no one wanted to help. A man could seem all right and then turn on somebody like a wild animal. And it didn't get no better. Wouldn't get no better with so many of 'em doing it. They took their cues and their comfort with it from one another. Now he was leaning out the back door, his face red and angry blending right into his red hair, cussin' and hollerin' her name as she turned to the green rows at her side. Stayin' with him was gonna be the death of her one of these days, she knew. A sudden rustling, grunting, and fast thudding steps made her heart pound. She had to get back to the cabin flashed across her mind, and she swung around losing her balance as the raging beast charged, knocking her over in an instant, her head violently slamming the ground. Tears formed and she struggled to rise up, to scream, to do the impossible— to run. To run to her young 'uns down at the creek and pull them close, to gather them close against the pain, the terror. But the attack was on and all his savage rage was concentrated in his lunging, snorting head that the crazed monster thrust at the stunned form. A cry passed her lips when the sharp teeth stabbed into her flesh again and again in the instant she lifted herself. Only a few seconds had passed, seconds that weren't long enough for him to snap out of his temper fit and get to her in time. As she fell back, her soft wavy hair lay matted around her pale freckled face, and her eyes froze in horror and agony.

"What in the hell!" he yelled as he stomped and kicked at the crazed swine, grabbing with a terrific pull for a pea vine stake to beat it to death, only to have it turn squealing into the woods.

A big male pig, same as on any farm, gone wild. A feral killer when he reverted to primal instincts, nurtured and honed by the pack. Her marker said: *Mrs. McCammock 1870-1896 Killed by a wild boar.*

***

This story is dedicated to the memory of an ancestor, a woman who, it was recorded, was "killed by a wild boar."

Anita Miller Garner

Julian Carol Finds the Pine Cones

Julian Carol would not like the way you say his name. He grunts it out like this: JEW yun Carl, in a matter of fact way. He has lived in this county, in these woods, all of his life. His family has been here longer than mine, which is a feat in itself considering that mine had been sitting over in Georgia with their bags packed for three or four years just waiting for Andrew Jackson to run the Indians out before they raced their wagons over here to claim these pine hills of Alabama. Julian Carol's ancestors had already been hanging out with the Indians. They were clever folks, but mean.

Julian Carol is sitting in his truck waiting for us to arrive. We are on a pine cone mission. We stopped killing deer and wild turkey a couple of generations ago since none of us could really stand the taste of wild game. Now what we like is just the fruits of the land itself, the flora, and we don't even want to hurt it or dig it up. Mostly we just like to see it, but it is getting on towards Christmas, and what Mama suddenly craves are those giant pine cones that grow somewhere on the land that goes with the first home place. Mama will probably spray them with gold paint that will get all over everything around it. She may or may not get around to wiring them to the front door.

Mama opens her car door and swings out her legs and her giant purse, then reaches into the back seat and pulls out her .22 rifle, a ladylike piece. Julian Carol's shotgun looks big enough to dislocate my shoulder if I had to use it. Mama and I put on bright orange caps. Julian Carol is already wearing his.

Julian Carol starts leading us off through a deer trail, and Mama starts talking.

"This is sure not the way that Busby took me the other day."

Busby, our alcoholic cousin, is a smart mouth who always knows everything. Mama told Busby she wanted pine cones, so Busby volunteered to take her right to them. Mama walked around in circles for an hour and a half with a drunk man carrying a loaded rifle. When she found herself back at the car, she said, out of sorts, "Busby, where were the pine cones?"

Busby stared at her with his bloodshot, flat blue eyes. "You didn't see 'em? We passed 'em bout half hour ago."

JULIAN CAROL FINDS THE PINE CONES

Mama had spun red mud all the way back to the paved road. The car was a mess and had to be sprayed down underneath with the water hose before all that clay turned hard. Mama called up Julian Carol, who knows everything about his own land and everyone else's, too.

So here he is, walking us with precision by my childhood memories. Here is where I gathered moss for my first terrarium. Here is the field of blueberried cedar where we used to cut our Christmas trees.

The reason I am along on this trip is because it wouldn't look right, Mama says, for her to be all alone out in the woods with a strange man, meaning "stranger," meaning not blood kin. Mama is only twenty years older than Julian Carol. She has known him since he was born, knew his mama, knew his grandmama. He lived for a while in our second home place when he and his daddy weren't speaking. He worked with my father for fourteen years. He burned our barn down. Is he a stranger? Is he strange? Why are we wearing these stupid orange caps if we are alone out in these woods?

Julian Carol leads us up a short rise and there, behind a short wall of crimson sumac, the ground is strewn with pine cones the size of footballs. Julian Carol says he'll be back in a few minutes and walks off into the woods as quietly as a ghost, the woods just folding around him. Mama pulls out of her purse the two cotton-picking bags, tow sacks she brought along for this gathering part, one for her and one for me. The tow sacks have been sitting on the shelf of her linen press so long that they have dry-rotted on the folds. My sack holds together better than hers (I am not throwing the cones in with reckless greedy gusto). It is quick work. The ground beneath the pine tree now clean, I lean back onto the clean-smelling brown needles and look up at the sky as vacant as Busby's blue eyes, I think. I stare at it, and it stares right back.

I hear in the distance back out on the road a log truck with a bad muffler, then I hear a single shot off in the other direction, deeper in the woods. *Crack-pow.* It makes a crisp sound like a twig snapping.

I doze five minutes, maybe ten, maybe longer. Julian Carol carrying a large dead wild turkey quietly walks back through the curtain of crimson sumac. I look up at a strange angle out of my nap and instantly see this: my mother has found a needle and thread in her purse and sits stabbing the needle in and out of the rips in the tow sacks; Julian Carol stands holding the turkey by its legs, its large mangled head almost touching the ground, a single drop of its blood falling to the pine needles.

We walk back through fields so overgrown it is hard to imagine these tow sacks were used for anything but pine cones. Mama tries hard to juggle her load of pine cones, purse, and a .22. I am glad to walk behind her, but Julian Carol is walking in front of her. The .22 is not loaded, I am sure. I remember something.

Julian Carol shot and killed his son. It was at night. They were living at our second home place, my mother's home place. His son went out by moonlight to saddle his pony. Julian Carol had told him not to. Julian Carol believed he heard prowlers, aimed and shot. A jury of his peers in this county wouldn't find him guilty.

Julian Carol's father died of sorrow.

Julian Carol moved back to his own family's home place. Two summers later, the barn my mother's great-grandfather built burned to the ground. My mother cried silently as she walked through the ashes, sifting, sifting, searching for nails. Of course we could find no nails in the ashes. The barn was built in the time before nails.

I look at Mama's .22 and it is loaded, pointing right at Julian Carol's back.

Julian Carol is my father's best friend. He is an honorable man.

Anne George

Where Have You Gone, Shirley Temple?

Mary Alice said she never thought she would die under a Duncan Phyfe table at Judy's Antiques, that the idea had just never occurred to her and why on God's earth hadn't I turned on the TV and checked the radar. Lord knows it felt like tornado weather and if I had just bothered to turn on the weather channel we wouldn't be under that table on all fours with our butts in the air like those trucks you see going to those tractor pull things.

"You could have looked yourself," I said, listening to the wind slamming against the old warehouse that housed Judy's Antiques.

"You're the weather freak. You're the one always running outside holding up a finger to see which way the wind's blowing and checking your rain gauge."

I held up a finger under the table but it was too dark for Mary Alice to see. "I'm not a weather freak."

"Nobody else in this whole town has a barometer and a rain gauge."

"They were a door prize at the Home Show."

"Y'all okay?" Judy's voice was muffled by whatever antique she had chosen to take refuge under.

"Fine and dandy," Mary Alice called back. "Sixty-five years old, two hundred twenty pounds, and ass up to meet my Maker."

"What?" Judy said. "What?"

"We're okay," I yelled.

"We are not!" Mary Alice shifted her weight and bumped into the drop leaf of the table which banged back against her head. "I want you to know, Patricia Anne, that I hold you completely responsible for this."

I didn't bother to answer that. She's been holding me responsible for everything that has gone wrong in the sixty years we have been sisters including an earthquake that hit Los Angeles twenty years ago while we were there at a convention. Compared to that, what's a little tornado warning.

"That Shirley Temple doll better still be here, too," she continued, "with the white dress with red polka dots."

"And the red shoes and socks with lace on them," I said.

Mary Alice tried to elbow me and banged the drop leaf again.

"You're going to hurt yourself." I moved as far away from her as the table allowed. "You called Judy, didn't you? That was the way she described it, wasn't it?"

"She could just have been wanting to sell it."

"Judy!" I yelled. " Does the Shirley Temple doll have on a white dress with red polka dots?"

"What?" Judy's voice was barely audible. She must have had half her merchandise piled on top of her.

"Never mind!" Mary Alice tried to straighten her back some. "I have got to lose some weight."

This is dangerous territory. The reason Mary Alice is twice my size is because she says I've never eaten like a normal human being and she has always felt compelled to finish the food on my plate. I swear I've heard her say, "If Patricia Anne would eat I wouldn't be fat." Once she informed me it was a moral issue, that she took those starving children in India seriously and I didn't. *Mea culpa*, Patricia Anne.

"I think it's calming down some out there," I lied, changing the subject.

"It is not," Mary Alice said. "You're changing the subject."

"Jenny Craig," I said, "Weight Watchers, Ultra Slim Fast."

"Anorexia."

"I was never anorexic and you know it."

"You would have been if it had been around when we were young."

"And you'd have been a drug addict. Aspirin and Cokes, aspirin and Cokes."

"I always had cramps real bad."

"Yeah. Every day. Aspirin and Cokes."

"Pot calling the kettle black. You were the one drank paregoric."

"Just that once."

"Mama hid it after that. Dear God, you were pie-eyed. Aunt Sally kept saying, 'What's wrong with this child, Della? Are you sure something's not wrong?' and Mama, 'Oh, she's fine, Sally.' I don't know why she didn't tell her the truth."

"Like we tell each other."

"Exactly." Mary Alice has always been oblivious to sarcasm. "Just like I told you when Ray got arrested for growing marijuana."

"I would have read it in the paper, Mary Alice. Four acres in the Bankhead National Forest! That's not your usual little backyard plot."

"He was going to use the money for law school."

"Well, he learned a lot about the law and didn't even have to study." I was sorry the second I said it. Ray is her youngest and her heart. The sweetest child either of us has. Least likely to end up in trouble, you'd think, even if he is sort of dense. Sweet and dense. "I'm sorry," I said. But Mary Alice backed away from me as much as she could. I reached for her hand and she snatched it away.

My knees were beginning to ache. "How long we gonna stay under here?

I think it's quieting down out there."

"You bathed with my Shirley Temple soaps, too," Mary Alice said. "There were two of them in the box, red polka dots and blue and you washed the polka dots right off before I even set a washrag to them. I looked in the cabinet and there they were, white as Ivory and not even looking like Shirley Temple, let alone the polka dots. And you'd put them back in the box like I couldn't tell the difference."

"You left my Charlie McCarthy doll out in the rain."

"Not the same thing. He was ugly. You remember Shirley Temple's tiny red patent shoes? One button. It was easier to slip them on; that button was so tiny." Mary Alice suddenly shoved against the elbow I was propped on. My head came down thunk against the drop leaf. "What did you do with her, Patricia Anne?"

I rubbed my head. "My Lord, it's been fifty-five years. How do you think I can remember?" I held my hand out in the dim light. "Am I bleeding? I better not be bleeding."

"Of course you're not bleeding and I remember that day exactly. You and I were sitting on the steps and I saw June Harper coming down the street and I handed Shirley Temple to you because I didn't want her to see I was still playing with it and June said, 'Mary Alice, come see what I have but Patricia Anne, you can't come because you're too little.' It was a Tangee lipstick and we went to her house and tried it on. And when I got back, you and Shirley Temple were gone. And I didn't think about her until the next day and then you couldn't find her."

I had had enough. I started crawling from under the table.

Mary Alice grabbed my legs. "Where are you going?"

"Out of here. I don't give a damn if this tornado pisses or gets off the pot, I'm not listening to you blame me for your Shirley Temple doll any longer."

"Get back under here!"

"You're not the boss of me!"

Suddenly I had the feeling of everything dropping away. I heard Judy scream and then the roaring sound of the train I had heard described so often on TV.

"My God!" Mary Alice threw herself from under the table and over me. Eighteen seconds, maybe, and it was over. Part of the roof was gone and I was gasping for air from a combination of too much White Linen perfume and pure weight. But we were okay.

Mary Alice sat up and looked around. "Look what you've done now," she said. "I think you broke the leaf on the table, too."

"Y'all all right?" Judy crawled from her hiding place. "Oh, Lord, look at that roof!"

"You got some plastic? My sister and I'll help you cover things up." Mary Alice pointed to the corner where the roof was gone. "The Shirley Temple doll isn't over there, is it?"

"What? That was really a tornado, wasn't it? We could have been killed."

Mary Alice propped the leaf against the Duncan Phyfe table. "You've got insurance, don't you?"

"Sure, but . . ."

"Good."

She and I helped each other up "Now," she said to Judy, who was still sitting on the floor watching the rain pour through the roof. "About that Shirley Temple doll my sister wants to buy. You're sure it has red polka dots?"

AILEEN KILGORE HENDERSON

Leetha's Own

When Leetha Purl Long married Erbie Hite in Old Ruhama Church, folks said there never was a more mismatched pair in the entire county. Their marrying was like an ant joining up with a gadfly, or the dark, still river wedding the fickle Mulberry Creek that ran all over the woods, changing beds after every rain. Leetha Purl took her religion seriously, considering herself a female Nazarite. No wine nor strong drink had ever passed her lips. No scissors nor razor had ever touched the hair bundled against her nape.

Through her mother she came of a dark and strange people who had established themselves in the coves long before the Scots-Irish chopped their way into the foothills. Everything about her bespoke these people—the deep silence, the big eyes of a neutral color and expression, the muddy skin flushed with copper stretched taut over the high cheekbones and disappearing into the hair dull as lignite. Muscles, primed by hard work, layered her big frame. Her brothers had been exacting taskmasters, hitching her to the plow when the mule died and always leaving the drawing of the well water to her. She had hand-over-fisted the streaming bucket out of the depths of the red clay hill since she was big enough to outweigh it.

Erbie was a different matter, gatless as a tomcat but ornamental as a filigreed watch fob with his tune playing and his pretty talk. He blithely took Leetha to live with his Uncle Tipton, not far from the west fork of the river. No matter that Uncle Tipton hadn't spoken to Erbie—nor hardly anyone else—for years. No matter that he lived like a hermit, enforcing his solitude with an ancient double-barreled shotgun kept within easy reach of his front door.

"Aw, that thing won't even shoot," Erbie claimed. At any rate, though an unwilling host in the beginning, Tipton soon recognized what a blue-ribbon prize he had in Leetha. The girl could work from can to can't and make no fuss about it. She eased the routine flow of his days made painful by the arthritis that had seized hold of his old body, drawing it almost full circle.

Gradually the two of them united in focusing their lives on Erbie. They existed that he might be shielded from exertion, provided with food to his liking, and clothes starched and ironed smooth for wearing to the crossroads store. This unspoken partnership shaped their days. As a result Erbie flourished like the biblical green bay tree. Off and on he ranged the countryside cutting firewood for anyone who could pay. Along with the few silver coins, he garnered news and saw sights which he brought back home. The three of them would sit on the front porch—somber Leetha bent over her lap shelling peanuts or peas; Erbie on the floor slouching against a post, one foot dangling off the edge, harmonica in hand; the old uncle tilted against the wall in a straight chair, immersed in Erbie's talk and his tunes, freed for a time from his dimming eyes and aching joints.

The sight of them sitting there was enough to turn the head of a stone prophet twice, should a stone prophet ever pass that way. But only the Widow Gaffney happened by on occasion, and she never raised her eyes from probing the brush, searching out plants for her store of doctoring herbs. So stealthily did she move and with such complete absorption that her small frame was like a gray vapor floating along the ground, basket gripped in a thin brown hand.

Erbie talked without fear of interruption, even when he paused for several minutes to savor a point or dream a bit. He talked about his tobacco patch, the prospects for its harvest and curing. He talked of the pickup with a bed built on the back which he and Tipton would borrow to haul the crop to town. He talked about what he would buy with the money he made from the sale. Sometimes he told about creatures that came out of the deep woods toward the river in the dark of the moon, creatures he had heard lurked about the Widow Gaffney's cabin giving off a wild musk that caused her mule penned in the shed to stamp its feet uneasily and blow its lips. The widow herself had told him when last he was by her place that even her hound dogs hid in silence when the creatures came about.

"She'll disappear one day, you watch," he warned, cutting another chew off the quid of tobacco that bulged his hip pocket. "She's too far back to be alone. A varmint's bound to get her."

When the three became a quartet at the birth of Rob, the focus of Leetha's life and the old man's changed. Rob was a second Erbie, new minted, with hair deep red as galax leaves in the fall of the year, and eyes the lavender blue of chicory blossoms. He laughed Erbie's laugh, his whole face alight, his gold-lashed eyes dancing like the ripples on Mulberry Creek.

"Ain't he a wonder?" Tipton marveled, watching the boy climb over Leetha in the rocker or tumble about on the floor. "How come such a pretty little crawdad would choose to live with us?"

Tipton was his only playmate. The two of them darted round Leetha at her work like flashes of illuminated color dancing about a clouded prism. They made up games as they went along. Rob delighted in the unexpected; when Tipton suddenly imprisoned him in the circle of his knotty arms, Rob struggled and laughed while Tipton exulted, "Leetha's little red bird. Caught in a bear trap!" Sometimes Tipton came up behind the boy soundlessly and clasped his hands over Rob's eyes. Out of his sudden darkness, Rob would exclaim, "Leetha's little red bird. Gone! Gone!" His shouted laugh when Tipton removed his hands, restoring Rob's world, was echoed by the old man. Other times Tipton seized the boy and held him kicking as high off the floor as his stooped back allowed. "Snared Leetha's little red bird! Won't let him go till he sings me a song." Rob would then tilt his bright head, close his eyes as he had seen Erbie do, and warble a wordless tune till his breath gave out and Tipton released him.

Leetha said nothing, her expression unchanging. But she noted her son's every movement with the same intent regard she used to have for Erbie, and she tended his every need as possessively.

Erbie more often strayed from home on wood cutting trips. When at the cabin, he lounged on the fringe of their group, rarely blowing them a tune. But when he did, Rob forgot even his playmate. The rollicking notes made him squeal, convulsing his body with a delight he could not contain. Tipton laughed so hugely every one of his tobacco-stained teeth showed. "Leetha's little red bird. Dance! Dance!" he would chant, clapping his crooked hands.

The only thing that pleased Rob more than Erbie's harp-playing was the bird Tipton brought him the Christmas he turned three. It was life-size, with flecks of silver over the scarlet body and a silver fiber tail inserted in the back.

"I vowed it would be Rob's when first I sighted it at the store," Tipton explained to the cabin in general. "Saw his name on it plain—Rob Hite—and nobody else's. Had to give my jackknife in trade, but a feller who can't hardly bend his fingers anyway got no need for a jackknife." He held the bird before Rob, swinging it from a ribbon threaded through a glass loop in the middle of the fragile back. "Now Leetha's little red bird has got a bird of his own."

The boy accepted the gift with reverence. From the first he handled it with a touch soft as mullein leaves. He wore it round his neck and sang his wordless tunes to it. And at night, falling asleep in Leetha's arms, he watched it sway from a nail above the fireplace. Heat waves rising from the fire made the bird turn gently this way and that. "Little red bird. Fly! Fly!" Rob murmured.

When Rob was five and a half, summer sprang upon the hills with an instant heat that seemed to wither him. He lay in Leetha's lap without moving, while she rocked and fanned him on the porch. Tipton hovered close, studying the boy anxiously. Erbie, just back from a woods trip, leaned against the post and began to blow a tune of his own making. Rob gave no sign he heard. Tipton seized his bare feet. "I feared so! They're cold as frog titties!" His old hands fumbled over the boy's body, then brushed the auburn hair away from the unresponsive face. "But the rest of him's on fire! What we going to do?"

"It's the weather," Erbie drawled, thumping the harmonica against the heel of his palm. Saliva prickled the dust that coated the floorboards. "If the rains don't hurry and come, won't be no use to set out my tobacco."

As the days passed Rob fought against being held. Leetha spread a quilt for him on the floor between the front and back doors, hoping to catch a breeze. He rolled about on the pallet, hands working at his throat. Tipton never left him except to bring more water. Leetha bathed Rob's face and body over and over and held up his resisting head to force small drinks between cracked lips.

"He's like a fired-up cookstove," Tipton whispered, staring.

Erbie dragged the old man away from the house to help him set out and water the tobacco plants. "Ain't no use setting out tobacco! Ain't no use in nothing!" Tipton cried as Erbie herded him toward the field.

Shortly afterwards Leetha came to the tobacco patch and stood until Erbie, crouched in the shade of a persimmon clump watching Tipton bent over a row of wilted plants, acknowledged her.

"Rob's got to have a doctor," she announced, lifting her chin.

Erbie unfolded slowly. He shot a deliberate gob of tobacco spit across the rows. It thudded on the dirt like a lead sinker. A plume of dust rose over it and hung suspended before settling again.

"You know there ain't a doctor for thirty miles, woman. The boy'll be all right soon's there's a break in the weather."

"Uncle Tipton." She had never called him by name before. The old man held a can of water poised over a plant, waiting. "Rob's got to have help."

For a space of time it seemed he hadn't heard. Then he rose, straighter than she'd ever seen him. He drew back his arm and hurled the can toward the far edge of the field. Then he kicked over the galvanized bucket from which he had been dipping water. Without a glance at Erbie he started toward the house. She followed.

At the well he gulped water from the dipper like a mule at the end of a hard day's plowing. Swiping the back of his hand across his mouth he said, "Fix me a bite. I'm going to fetch that herbwoman." Away he hobbled like a three-legged June bug along the path lighted by the sky-high sun. By the time the whippoorwill's call throbbed in the hollow, Leetha heard his slow step shuffling over the porch, returning. He crumpled into a chair and said above the rasp of the boy's breathing, "She's got a granddaughter to look after but promised to come first thing tomorrow."

Leetha and Tipton waited, washing and fanning the boy. He fought, making strangled noises like a thwarted animal. When the Widow Gaffney came she seemed to fill the room. The lamplight magnified her shadow to an enveloping darkness as she leaned over Rob's pallet, prying open his jaws, inspecting his throat.

"Got to have salty grease and a spoon," she said without turning. From her apron pocket she took a handful of dried leaves. "Got to have hot flannel rags to make a poultice for his throat."

Tipton kindled a fire and brought more wood. He filled the crusty iron kettle so full of water it spat, hissing, into the flames. The small woman turned on him like a stepped-on hornet. "Get from underfoot! Menfolks ain't needed!" When Leetha brought the grease from the pantry lean-to, she saw him on the porch straining to look inside.

For the rest of the day she had no thought of him. While the Widow Gaffney slowly massaged the warm grease down Rob's throat, Leetha kept hot rags on the herbs that plastered his neck. They worked in silence on opposite sides of the little body. Their dresses stuck to them with sweat. Not till sundown did they take time to eat. By then the child had stopped struggling, though his breathing came harder than ever.

"Now I've done what I could for the lamb," the herbwoman said, laying him down. "The rest is up to Jesus." She went to sit on the back step, wiping her face on the grease-splotched apron before taking a piece of cornbread from her pocket. "I got to get on home. My granddaughter's a town girl. She's not used to staying by herself in the woods."

"Ain't you afraid some river varmint'll make off with her?" Tipton asked, standing in the yard.

"It's not the river varmints that fret me." She pinched together the crumbs scattered over her lap and placed them carefully in her loose-lipped mouth. "It's the two-legged varmints that make the trouble." She rose, shaking the wrinkles from her long skirt.

"What do I owe you?" Tipton asked.

"I'll take that red play-purty over the fireplace."

"No, no," Leetha spoke from the doorway. "That's Rob's—what he loves best in this world."

The herbwoman gummed the lining of her cheeks and pursed her lips. "Then I'll take the iron kettle."

Leetha brought it, bending from the porch to hand it, still hot from the fire, to the Widow Gaffney.

"Much obliged," Tipton said.

"You welcome." The small woman, tilted from the weight of the kettle, floated off to meet the dark rising like a fog from the hollow.

In the cabin, Leetha lighted the lamp. She and Tipton sat on the floor beside the inert child as though brain dumb. Rob's gasps rose above the night noises that pushed against the cabin from all sides. Darkness slowly slid its feelers deeper and more bindingly into the hollows and over the hills.

Footsteps meandered across the porch and Erbie entered the open door yawning. Without glancing at Rob's attendants he laid his harmonica on the mantel. "No use in everybody staying up, if you ask me. I'm going to bed." He kicked a nub of wood onto the red coals that pulsed like a living heart. An explosion of sparks disappeared up the chimney, then the fire quietened again. A still span of time snaked by. Leetha clasped the boy's hand in both of hers while Tipton stared at the red bird hanging motionless from its nail. The heated silence of the room pressed upon them until Tipton leaped to the door as if summoned. Clutching the jamb he peered outside. Leetha hurried to him.

"What is it?" she whispered.

He stepped backward uncertainly, eyes attentive to the dark. "Old Death's on the prowl tonight. We might as well ready ourselves."

With a panther scream, Leetha slammed the door. She rammed the latch into place and hammered it with her fist. "Rob's not going! He's mine! Mine!"

Tipton sank in a chair with a sigh that came from the depths of his heart. "Old Death don't ask nobody's leave. . . ." His words trailed away.

Leetha scooped the boy in her arms and held him fiercely against her while she rocked. "Not this time, Old Death. Not my Rob! Not my Rob!" Her voice rang out the denial. But by the time Rob died, a while after midnight, the words had faded to a whispered plea.

Tipton helped her bathe the cooling face and limber body. They dressed him in his Sunday clothes. When he was arranged prim and straight on the pallet, in the light from the kerosene lamp, he did not look like Rob. He looked like a miniature city preacher carved out of yellow wood. Even his bright hair was dimmed.

"We got to cover him with something," Leetha whispered. From high on a shelf she took a folded shawl. After spreading it over him and smoothing every wrinkle she lay down, her arm across him waiting for day to come. The old man crept away from the sound of her tearless croon: "Leetha's little red bird. Gone. Gone."

Next morning Tipton prodded Erbie awake. "Help me get a box made for Rob. I'm thinking we'll use that heart cedar, but we'll not make it too stout. So he won't have no trouble busting out on Judgment Day."

Erbie stared around the cabin without understanding. "Lawd Gawd! I thought the old woman cured him."

Tipton didn't live long after Rob's burial in the graveyard behind Ruhama Church. "Seems like the lamp's gone out," he told Leetha one night as he knotted himself together on the hearthstone. "Can't see how to make no sense out o' living." Leetha rolled another chunk of wood on the fire—a dry, sound piece of hickory she had brought out of the woods herself. Under it she inserted a splinter of pine that blazed into immediate flame illuminating the old man's matted beard and pus-steeped eyes.

"Sometimes when I'm laying here I hear the wild horses neighing," he said. "I hear them running, running, down the hill, their hoofs kicking the rocks helter-skelter."

"Where they going?"

"I finally got it figured out." He lowered his voice. "There's a big cave way back in the woods where the creek makes a Y with the river. That's where they come from, rampaging through the woods at night and whinnying." Silence held the room. "My grandpappy spoke of hearing them. They come just on particular nights, he claimed." Tipton's eyes rested on the scarlet bird, lightly turning on the end of its ribbon. "I heard 'em that night."

Leetha sat impassive.

"If you pay close attention," his voice quavered, "I'm of the belief they'll be running tonight."

She waited till he sank into an unstirring sleep. Then she tucked a coverlet around him before going back to the corner mattress where Erbie snored.

In life, the old man had walked far beyond the town, bartering twists of tobacco for the trinkets he arranged on Rob's grave. From among them Leetha selected a milk-glass egg and a handful of marbles to ornament the raw clay of Tipton's grave. He was hardly longer than Rob, once they lay side by side in the ground.

After that, Leetha lived in a state of suspension. She seemed to have forgotten how to work. During the long summer, her garden went untended. Peaches ripened on the tree beside the well, but she did not slice them, nor spread them in the sun to dry. She did not store them in airtight jars in the safe to be made into fried pies, tender of crust and sweet of taste, for Erbie's pleasure. Mostly, she rocked on the porch, in all kinds of weather.

But Erbie stayed away from home more and more, two or three days at a time. When he was about the house he never played his harp. He never lifted it from the place on the mantle where he'd laid it the night Rob died. Even when winter faded and everybody's need for firewood lessened Erbie could hardly stay home long enough to get his tobacco plants set in the ground. After the patch was planted he couldn't pay enough attention to it to keep the weeds chopped nor the worms picked off the felted leaves.

A day came when Leetha realized Erbie had been absent a long time. She stood aimlessly in front of the fireplace, wondering. It was then she noticed the harp missing from the mantleshelf, just above the nail that held Rob's bird. Where the harp had lain for over a year, there was now only an oblong outline in the dust. Erbie and his harp, together somewhere else. He had no intention of coming back. This certainty flicked in and out of her consciousness like a puff-adder tongue. He would not be coming home. Old Tipton's question leaped into her mind: "What we going to do?"

With fierce concentration she rethought the months since Rob died, the details vague at first but gradually sharpening. Erbie had come and gone as he pleased. It had not mattered to her. She was wandering through the days and nights like a person in a puzzle box, going first this way and then the other, only to turn around and head in yet a different direction. That had not mattered to her either. Now Erbie had taken his harp and run off.

She felt like a black bear lumbering out of heavy winter sleep, awakening to life again. Erbie was gone, and she had no idea where. But she knew from what source she could wrest an answer. It took a while to find her Bible. Lately she had spared no time for it. But now she labored through the old tales, finger plodding from word to word, returning now and again to the Psalter as to a refrain. She rocked and she read. A relentless, wordless burning consumed her. As she slowly fingered the fine-printed pages over and over, she felt the answer looming round her like a darkening thunderhead. Sweat oozed from her tense forehead and tightly gripped jaw. With dilated eyes she stared, not at the printed words, not at the blinded, reasonless insects that flew into the walls and the lamp, and not at the light, but into the depths within herself. Out of this darkness she dredged the pieces that locked into one another to make the answer she wanted.

A limpness crept through her body. She brushed a languid hand across her eyes, then rose, blew out the lamp, and stood waiting for the dark to lighten.

By sunrise she was up and moving with a purpose. Taking Erbie's loose-headed chop-axe from where it leaned against the well, she tramped to the tobacco patch past Erbie's plants smothering among the weeds. Straight to the young persimmon trees she went, three coarsely grained black trunks topped by a blended crown of drooping leaves. A few truly aimed whacks brought down the sturdiest. With quick short strokes she trimmed it, savoring the tough, mouth-puckering odor. She hefted it in her hand, then struck the large end against the ground. Trimming the handle a bit more, she tried it again with satisfaction.

Once more at the house, she covered the well after taking a drink. Into a flour sack she gathered what food she could find in the lean-to's safe and closed the back door. From off its nail over the fireplace she took the scarlet bird. Cradling it in her hand, she shut the front door behind her, picked up the persimmon club, and set out on the path downhill. At the logging road, without hesitation, she turned right to the Ruhama churchyard. Singling out Rob's grave, she knelt and placed the bird at the head of it, looping the ribbon about the sandstone marker.

"I might of known I couldn't keep you," she whispered.

Back to the logging road, she paced off the miles to the crossroads. Talk in the shadowed store stopped sudden as an indrawn breath when she strode out of the morning glare. The storekeeper, leaning on the candy counter scrubbing his teeth with a sweetgum brush, blinked at her.

"Hidy, Miz Hite."

"My man been here?"

The storekeeper glanced around at those watching and listening, as if to give them the opportunity to answer. Everyone looked carefully away.

"Well, let's see," he finally said. "Not lately. Yes. I would say not lately."

She turned toward the door.

"Snakes sure must be bad out your way, from the looks of that club. Seen any today?" the storekeeper said.

Closing the screen door soundlessly, she walked away. At the Widow Gaffney's cabin she found the old woman hoeing her Irish potatoes. Leetha stood in the dust till the widow sighted her. Though her wrinkled face quivered, the old woman said nothing.

"Your girl home?" Leetha asked.

"Not right this minute."

"Where she gone?"

"More'n likely to her mammy's across the county line. She'll be sending me word any day now."

"When did she go?" Leetha pressed her.

The old lady smoothed her apron. "I forget." Her voice wavered like an echo in the bottom of a dry well.

Leetha went first to the sawmill shack beyond the cut-over pine woods. She found it leaning behind mildewed humps of sawdust, windows empty, front door hanging by one hinge. A yellow-striped lizard sunning on the porch told her plain as words that nobody was anywhere near.

Next she sought the abandoned coal mine. Years back a cave-in of ceiling timbers had shut off its passages. Dirt daubers had built row after row of long-fingered mud houses on the grayed timbers. Underneath, the dust showed no footprints.

In the shady hollow below the mine she paused to drink at a spring. The persimmon club slipped to the ground while she slapped water over her face, washing away the sweat and heat. As she rose and dried with the flour sack, her eyes followed the water flowing from the spring. Not far down the slope, it trickled into the branch. The branch wound through the fern and sevenbark until it joined Mulberry Creek. She knew the changeable Mulberry frolicked and danced into the hills, finally flowing into the river.

The river.

She had never seen it, but Erbie's stories crowded out of her memory. From the river, bobcats came on the prowl for meat. Those other nameless creatures, more fearful than bobcats, crept from there after dark and roamed the settlements. From the river Old Tipton had said the wild horses galloped on the rampage—from a cave where the creek joined the river. Looking in that direction, she felt a calm certainty possess her. That way she should go.

Taking a fresh grip on the club, she set out along the branch. By nightfall she had reached the place where the Mulberry settled down within age-old banks. It widened and deepened so that she skirted it with care, sensing its wine-colored waters concealed dangers she could put no words to. Soon now, she knew, the creek would slide into the river.

After eating the last of the food, she lay down under a ledge of rock. With her knees drawn up to her chest, she covered herself with the flour sack, a flimsy shield against the damp.

Next day, as she picked her way through the brush, the morning wind wafted a slight fog of wood smoke toward her. She stopped, waiting till the bay leaves stilled. Over and under the fern and laurel there wove a light melody.

A harp.

Erbie's harp.

The tune verved to an end; it was echoed by a girl's laugh and a little squeal. Erbie's lazy laughter drawled through the woods. Leetha eased out where she could see the wooded rise that, rock by gray rock, piled itself skyward from the river's edge. Partway up crouched the dark blot of the cave, mottled by sunlit leaves and pink laurel blossoms.

She took her time finding the way along the slope. Once she stopped to wipe her sweating hands on the flour sack. Then she dried the handle of the persimmon club by grasping the sack tightly around its stem and turning the club against her hard grip, as if unscrewing a tightly sealed jar.

On the lip of the cave mouth a coffee pot squatted in the coals of a dying fire. Scattered around were crumpled papers, sardine cans, and empty bottles.

They did not hear her come. The girl was seated on a quilt spread on the cave floor, a comb poised in her hand. Beside her knelt Erbie, his face buried in her long hair. Next to his knee lay the harmonica. A vagrant sunray struck silver from its polished side.

He did not know Leetha stood watching until the girl cried out and stiffened away from him. He raised his face to see her, stricken gray as an old bone, staring over his shoulder. His head snapped round.

"Leetha!" He leaped to his bare feet.

Without a word she strode past him. Raising the club with both hands, she brought it down with all her strength. The girl made no sound. Her mouth shaped some word, but it was never spoken. Blood ensnared her smooth-combed hair, straggling it across the soft face and rounded white shoulders.

Leetha hit her but once. Dropping the club, she stepped back to wipe her hands on the flour sack. Erbie watched from outside the entrance.

"Let's go home," she said, tossing the sack to the ground.

The raucous call of the rain crow dogged their steps as he led the way back. When they broke out of the woods within far sight of their cabin the sun had paled. Thunder rumbled behind the hills.

"Seems like it might rain," Erbie said, appraising the sky. "First thing tomorrow I got to get my tobacco hoed."

Laura Hunter

Fishtales Told to a Crow, Mid-Spring

May 1953
Lottie Winters

Gary Evans drowned on Easter Sunday, but he didn't rise for thirteen days. When the water's still and the fish are tired, they grow roots to the bottom, long white roots, so they can stay in the same place as long as they want. I knowed this was true when Gary Evans drowned. Right here in Papa Johnson's pond.

Gary Evans stayed in the water almost two weeks growing to the bottom under black tree limbs. When the water started to warm up and move, his roots broke loose, and he come to the top all puffed like an adder and the color of mushrooms. His family kept the box closed to keep kids from poking at him to make the pond water run out.

I was born on Pest Hill, just out from Sandy Grove, where a long time ago they'd bring people with the pox to die in the big open house they called the Pest House. Going up Pest Hill you see right off a fancy white house with a yard pond out by the road. When I's a little girl at the Walker County fair, I threw pennies and won a goldfish that glowed. I took my goldfish there to that yard pond so my brother wouldn't throw him down the toilet, and it growed to match the pond size. I put it there. But the mule pond where we fished ain't got fish that big, only Gary Evans for almost two weeks.

It's the pond in Papa Johnson's pasture where the mule stands against the heat. There's plenty of bream there, so I knowed Gary Evans'd go. He ain't much of a fisherman, so he likes a pond with plenty of fish.

At the pond you can lay on your belly and look over the tall end bank. I still go there and watch the fish grow roots as the days warm up again. Where'd the fish come from, nobody knows, except maybe some science teacher at the school in town. Papa Johnson says he never put none in. No water in, no water out. Maybe crows drop them down from the sky.

The mule don't grow roots because his legs reach to the bottom in places where he shades. When he walks out of the water, his hoofs suck air out of the clay mud and leave bowls that fill up with water so tadpoles can grow legs and become frogs. And the fish eat the tadpoles. I've seen them do it myself.

Nobody knowed Gary Evans drowned on Easter Sunday but me, and I didn't tell. Just like I didn't tell about what happened after the fish fry and the sawmill last May. Jim Crow knowed what happened to Gary Evans, but he won't tell neither. One time when I rode the old mule around in the pasture, I found this little crow, slick and shiny as a lump of coal. It'd fell out of its nest, so I brought it home and called it Jim. Jim Crow. Papa Johnson said he come to Sandy Grove when he was no more than a boy because it was a good Alabama town. A jim crow town. I figured he brought the jim crows with him when he moved from town so's they could live in his own pasture since he liked them so much.

One day when the road workers was working down under the hill, Jim Crow flew over to that oak yonder and set on that bottom limb. I could see it from the front yard. I called him. "Jim! Jim!" And he answered back, whining up through his throat and out his beak, "What? What?" But he never flew back till almost dark. He stayed put, watching the strangers bury the ground under their shiny tar.

Jim Crow was there on the deep side of the pond when Gary Evans drowned. Gary Evans, born July 1930, drowned, 1953'll set long and hard on his headstone. Another month and it'd've been almost a year to the day after Papa Johnson's regular fish fry. When Gary Evans drowned.

Papa Johnson has the best fish frys in Walker County. Everybody's invited. Everybody comes. Bream season he'll set up black wash pots over open fires in the front yard, fill them with lard and set the women to work. The men'll catch bream, some as broad as your hand, specially in May, and the women'll clean them. Scrape off the scales. Lop off the heads. Dip them in dry batter and fry them whole. If the grease's hot enough, they'll crunch up so's you can eat every bit. Fish and fins, fish and tail. All laid out on a loaf bread sandwich.

I knowed I wouldn't go to no more fish frys with Gary Evans there. First it's Christmas. Then winter's gone. Easter's coming round. Bream'd be biting, and the black pots set to be fired. I was ready.

The day he drowned I told Gary Evans I knowed about a pond off the side of the road with trees holding up the rock walls. Bream the size of a three-year-old. I told him I'd growed from last May when he took me from the fish fry to the sawmill to see where he worked. "I'm a woman now. Fourteen," I said.

I told him I had my daddy's liquor where I could get it easy, if he wanted to go to the pond with me. So he went with me, but I took him to the mule pond. He didn't know no different. When we got there, he was so sloppy drunk he wouldn't've cared if there weren't no pond atall. I'd knowed all along he couldn't swim worth a lick, so he was going to be easy.

In the truck, it was the ride to the sawmill all over again. Him biting the inside of his bottom lip to keep back the grin told me he was remembering almost a year before, the same as me, but I didn't say nothing. I kept my face set.

April 1952
Charlotte Winters

Gary Evans watched Lottie play hide and seek with the younger kids, then he followed her out behind the smoke house where she'd squatted behind an old Rose of Sharon. "You're too old now for playing with these kids," he said. "Come on, Lottie girl. Come see my place at the sawmill. I got my own office now. I'll let you shift gears in my truck. Your sister won't care if you go. We're family now, ain't we? There ain't no difference in brother and brother-in-law but two words. Now, ain't that right? Besides we'll be right back. Come on, Lottie girl."

"My mama named me Charlotte, not Lottie."

"Sure. Okay. Whatever you say. Come on, now. That sawmill, it's a wondrous thing." He took Lottie's hand and walked her through the back yard, away from the house.

At the sawmill, he walked her around, showing her this, telling her that, till he'd led her out behind the sawdust pile. She looked up its sides. "Never seen nothing so big," she said. "Taller than the pasture trees," she said. She wanted to climb it, if she hadn't've wore a skirt.

"You just climb right on up," Gary Evans said. "It won't matter none." She started trying to climb up the pile, when he stepped in front of her and slipped his hand under her blouse, grabbing her nipple.

"Good start for thirteen." He grinned.

"No." She kicked herself away and tried to run up the sawdust hill. It was like climbing a ladder with the rungs falling away under you, sliding down and groping around to hold on to something that's not there.

"Feisty little whelp." The satisfaction of her scare struck out through his eyes. He slapped off his belt, grabbed her legs. She was caught. He pulled her back down, then lifted her by the shoulders and stood her up in front of him so's he could look at her.

"I'll show you not to mess with Gary Evans," he said with his teeth in her face.

It was Lottie. It was Charlotte. It was Gary Evans splitting us in two. There on the sawdust pile. All we could hear was her panting. Her hands flat against his chest, her elbows straight as boards, she pushed away. He pulled her back to him. All he saw was her face, her mouth open. Her eyes screamed words that wouldn't come out her mouth. He twisted both arms behind her, reached around in back of her, wrapped her wrists with the belt, and jerked it tight. He bent her head back and tried to prize open her mouth with his tongue and dingy teeth. Lottie's mouth wouldn't open.

"Trashy whore." He hit her hard in the belly with his fist. Her head drooped, then popped back, and she vomited up the bream and bread, fin and tail, out onto his shirt. It stunk. She stunk, like stale fish lard.

"Slut. You little bitch. I'll teach you to puke on me." He looked toward the weeds. He was talking to hisself. "The crew and me, we spent all day poking at a little old chicken snake that come into the mill lot. If it ain't still alive, it's right here where we dropped it. In these weeds. Didn't know he'd be so handy."

It was Lottie what went with Gary Evans to the sawmill last spring, not me. My mama and daddy knows their Charlotte wouldn't go. Not for no man, no matter what he promised. But I can tell about it because I know the snake. The snake comes in my bed ever time I smell dust in the night. My mama says it's just the folds in the covers, it ain't really no chicken snake, I'm the chicken. But he's magic. I know it. He disappears when Mama switches on the light.

And he's at the well. When I try to let the bucket down, gentle so's I won't muddy the water, he's sliding down and down and down inside my hands. I can't bear to hold him no longer. I turn him loose because I can't stand the feel. Then the bucket thuds against the bottom and stirs up the mud that takes all day long to settle.

Lottie watched Gary Evans move toward the weeds. I saw her know what'd happen. She turned her head and saw the snake, brown plaid with a yellow belly. It was the biggest snake she'd ever seen, almost twice as long as she's tall. When she looked at the snake, something squeezed the breath out of her. She thought she might die and rot, her legs fixed there in the sawdust pile.

Gary Evans picked up the snake with both hands and stood in front of her in one move. The snake was spilling out of his hands. With his elbow, he pushed her down, then piled the fresh killed snake on her chest. She could feel the snake quiver as its weight hit her. Her eyes rolled back and she stretched her neck so she wouldn't have to see. She knew it would look at her and know about Gary Evans. The snake sucked out her breath and rooted her in the sawdust. It laid heavier on her than any man. As its ants crawled into her blouse, her shivers made them stumble across her body. She didn't dare move. Snakes don't die till sundown.

"Well, my little wall-eyed catfish, that ought to keep you still." He unzipped his pants.

Lottie squeezed her eyes shut. I looked up past the top of the pile and watched clouds float easy through the sky. Lottie and me we heard him. Grunt. Grunt. Grunt. Then he fell into the sawdust by her feet and moaned. He lay still till his clumsy breathing stopped. Behind her lids, she could see her arms and legs as they laid where she would've put them, stone-still, like parts of a broken statue, separate from her body.

Lottie remembered what Papa Johnson had told her about snakes. Whip snakes put their tail in their mouth and roll after you, even up hills. She opened her eyes and watched Gary Evans roll over on his back and wipe his hands on the grass. He was chanting through his breath, "My love, my love, my Lottie, my love" and staring off into the sky. She wanted to tell him he needed to be quiet so the snake's mate wouldn't come and pay back the killing. But the snake smothered her voice.

Then he stood up, kicked the snake off her, rolled her over with his shoe, and took his belt. She laid still, her face in the sawdust pile. "Just you wait, girl. You'll want old Gair one of these days. You got to get a little riper." He got into his truck and left her there, the snake wadded next to her in the sawdust.

When she heard him drive away, she kicked herself up and away from the snake, her heels sliding into the loose sawdust, her hands pulling her backwards. As she moved, her voice come back. Once it got back to her, it started to scream.

May 1953
Lottie

Fourteen now and old enough. I know about men and boys. I've gone to the high school in town for a whole year since the sawmill and Gary Evans. I hear the girls talk. It's all in the clothes, they say. And how you move when you walk.

So I put on some old tight blue jeans and rolled them up under my knees to show off my legs. I buttoned my brother's big white shirt low and let it hang loose so's Gary Evans could guess what was under there. And I set out early Easter Sunday morning.

I found him in the tool shed sorting fishing tackle. I told him I'd like to go fishing myself. He started to chew the inside of his bottom lip when I lifted my hair up off the back of my neck. I watched his muddy teeth through the crack in his mouth. "It sure's warm this morning," I said. "We could even go swimming. I know a pond with a shallow end."

I got into the truck he kept behind the barn. He slammed his door. I give him my daddy's bottle. He drove off. Down the road I told him, "Leave the truck here behind this pine stand and walk with me. I'll show you a fishing hole and a place with slick rocks that'll take us under for a swim when we walk on them, a hole under the bank where we can take off our clothes and play without nobody knowing, if we want to. It's real shallow there."

He'd drunk most of a whole bottle of Daddy's liquor going down the road, and he was wobbly. "I'm older now and I know what a grown man wants," I told him. "Wouldn't it be too bad if this old shirt got all wet?" I pulled the shirt tight down across my breasts. I remembered to smile and look out from under my eyes, like the girls at school said. He grinned his truck grin again. This time it spread all over his face.

I led him out the pine stand, to the pasture, and under the wire fence. I kept him just a few steps behind my back, pulling him along with one hand to keep him from falling down, unbuttoning my shirt with the other one.

The mule saw us coming and moved back, under a tree where Jim Crow was waiting on a high branch, out of the way. As I'd tugged and he'd stumbled, I'd opened the shirt, one button at a time. When we got to the deep end of the pond where I watch the fish, I turned around and let the shirt fall down my shoulders. A breeze come out of Jim Crow's tree and run ripples across my chest. The air made my breasts stand up in front of Gary Evans. His mouth opened up wide, and greedy words come out of his eyes. He fell at me for a grab.

All I had do was step over one step, and he'd go straight into the pond.

But he didn't fall in. He stumbled against my chest and I fell, my head bouncing up off the ground. I didn't know 'bout the hit till I opened my eyes and thought to breathe again.

"You pushed me. You pushed me." I tried to dig my heels in the dirt to get up.

"Just getting you ready, Lottie girl." He laughed my daddy's liquor out of his mouth.

It was the sawmill all over again. Gary Evans was mashing me in the ground. And it was a snake, there on the ground. It had to be a snake, a firm thick snake, black with splotches all round. There was a snake underneath my right side. I couldn't breathe.

"Charlotte. Charlotte. Come here. Come here and know this for me." My voice was talking out loud in my head.

Jim Crow said "What?"

"Charlotte, you got to be here for me." But Charlotte just stood there watching Gary Evans on top of me, mashing out my air. I looked up into the tree by the deep end of the pond so's I couldn't see his dingy teeth and squeezed my mouth shut to keep his spit from dripping in and choking me. I looked through the branches for Jim Crow. And I held my breath till I heard Charlotte answer me.

"Don't be afraid, Lottie," she said. "Remember the chicken snake. Remember its face. We saw it, you and me. At the sawmill. Look at its eyes. They look like the kitten in the barn. It can't hurt you again. Get up. Push it out of your lap."

"Charlotte?" I turned my head to see where her voice was. She was gone. I picked up the black spotted limb and hit Gary Evans in the ear. I hit and hit till he rolled off'n my belly. I got up kicking and hitting, hitting and kicking, while he tried to wrap his elbows over his face. He didn't say nothing.

He tried to run, haunched over to break the whacks. Blood was all in his face, so he couldn't see what was before him. He run straight for the pond. He went in, a little dirt following him over the edge. In the water, stirring up mud in Papa Johnson's fish pond. He went under, into black trees, stiff near the bottom to hold him down, breaking the fish roots loose with his thrashing.

When he come back up, his mouth was open. His voice'd found its words. Shouting words left over from the sawmill. His hands grabbed at the air, trying to climb up and away from the water. But the air wouldn't take him, so after two tries, he settled down quiet into the pond.

The fish come near the surface to see who'd caused the commotion and swam round and round till the ripples spread out on the bank.

The mule switched its tail to swat the flies. He lowered his head and looked off to one side. Jim Crow said "What? What?" But I didn't answer him. I just pulled the shirt up over my shoulders, turned around, and set my face to go back home.

Cindy Jones

Imp-Dancing in the Heart of Dixie

I finished school, signed a job contract, rented an apartment, bought a Subaru station wagon, adopted a puppy, and witnessed a murder, all within a 72-hour slice of my life. Some consider me impulsive. I like to think that I'm just always prepared and, perhaps, a little eager. I can be quite practical, at times. For instance, I promised myself I'd get a rubber stamp with *Lindsay Hayes* imprinted on it to save time spent on signatures. I never realized how much paperwork is involved in establishing one's independence.

While my life was beginning, another life had ended. On the way home from my initial visit to the humane shelter, I stop to watch a crane-like vehicle pick up trash in a vacant lot. I become fascinated by the workings of the giant mouth on the piece of machinery, imagining the angry jaws of a prehistoric giant, munching on a long overdue snack. The neck goes down, the jaws open, and then clamp shut on the debris on the ground. Slowly, the monster lifts his head high, turns it to one side, and spits out his mouthful, as if he knows it is rubbish. He performs this action again and again as if each, next bite might taste a little better. He is repeatedly disappointed. I look on for 30 minutes or so. Each time, I hope that the beast might decide to enjoy his meal. After watching this cycle 16 times, my interest wanes. I walk back toward my car.

"Wait! Stop!" I hear a man yell. I stop, turn around, and wait. A heavy man with a graying ponytail is waving his arms. He is not talking to me, but to the big, orange giant. "Stop the trackhoe! Stop the trackhoe, now!" he screams pointing at the mouth. "Look in the clamshell!" I look, too. "What in the hell is that?" That's when I see the two legs jutting out between the clamped teeth of the dinosaur. The dangling feet are still wearing tennis shoes. The giant dinosaur halts, and I recognize the smirk of satisfaction on his steel face.

The body is later autopsied and identified. Police determine that the victim died from a knife wound in the chest as a result of a drug deal dispute. So to correct my original statement, I didn't actually witness a murder, but the evidence of one.

A few crystal grains remain on the rim of my glass, so I don't even bother resalting it this time. I just dump a palmful of Morton's into the glassful of tequila and margarita mix. I take my fresh drink into the den and plop down on the floor. The apartment is empty except for cardboard boxes, a desk, a director's chair, and a few other small pieces of furniture. I've only unpacked a few books and some paper in the week I have been here. Scribbling and scratching on a legal pad, I reduce my thoughts to seven words: *Thanks. All impossible without you. Love, Lindsay.* My telephone is on a piano stool atop a stack of books; therefore, I don't have to scoot far to reach either it or the telephone book.

I dial Western Union. One of those genuinely friendly telephone voices greets me and, after first asking about the weather, offers assistance. I enjoy speaking with these rare telephone personalities who can converse without hurry or script while providing their services. Also, except for the puppy that I picked up on my second trip to the shelter, I haven't interacted with another living soul all day. In a developing conversation, I mention that I have just moved to Montgomery.

"Montgomery, Alabama? I'm in Reno, but I've been to Montgomery before," says the voice on the other end of the line.

"I didn't realize. I thought I dialed a local number." I am amazed that I have to talk to someone in Nevada to send a telegram to Georgia.

"Oh, no. I'm not in Montgomery. I haven't been back in nearly 25 years. Montgomery . . . I was there during the civil rights movement, actually."

"Really? Things have definitely changed since you were here. How do you remember Montgomery? I start teaching here at the end of the month." I am truly interested in how different I imagine Montgomery must have been in those times of intolerance and hatred.

"I participated in many protests. Back then, I was much hated; not only in Montgomery, but also in Tallahassee. That's where I was hit in the head with a brick. I still have the scar."

"You must be one tough cookie," I say, hoping I don't sound facetious.

"Well, maybe so. At the time, I had red hair, blue eyes, and weighed about 85 pounds. I didn't look too tough."

As she describes herself, goosebumps form on my freckled forearms. She seems to be describing me. I have forever considered myself a redhead, ever since I was in the second grade and decided to be Pippi Longstocking for Halloween. Mother helped me plait my hair into two seven-inch braids. Afterwards, she clipped two pieces from a metal coathanger and stuck the wire into each braid. The braids stood straight out in 90-degree angles from each temple.

Everyone in the world, except for my hair stylist, calls me a redhead. He says my hair is really more of a dishwater blond with brassy highlights. My eyes are blue, and I do weigh about 85 pounds, give or take, depending on the last time I've eaten a Turtle from Darrell's or onion rings from the Red Bird Inn.

I am definitely not tough, though. I'm on the puny side, long and wiry. I was teased in school because I had the build of a basketball player, only on a smaller scale. I still have no calves, and my ankles are only as big around as most people's wrists. Witty classmates used to lift the leg of my pants and ask to see my Timex.

". . . and I believe that conscience is wasted if we don't take a stand. I can sense you have a strength that you are not fully aware of," the voice continues. My throat becomes dry. Take a stand against what? When had this conversation taken such a philosophical turn? I just want to send a telegram.

"Keep a stiff upper lip, you'll need it. I'm so glad that there are people still trying to keep our tradition alive," the voice advises. Doesn't this flake know that segregation ended long ago? Doesn't she know that blacks and whites live and work together happily, even here in Montgomery?

My palms sweat and my upper lip tingles. Who was this fruitcake to tell me to take a stand? I end the conversation as quickly as possible, and hang up the phone.

"Not now, Leshy! Go away," I say quickly, but quietly. I take a swig of my margarita and get up to fix another.

I'm not usually in the habit of talking to myself, out loud, at least. Long ago, I dubbed any unexplainable discomfort or fear Leshy. This habit started when I was a sophomore in high school at Bankhead School in my hometown of North Georgia. I became dizzy one morning while sitting in my mythology class. On that particular day, Dr. Vande Brake was trying to cover Slavonic mythology in one class period because he wanted to have at least a week for Finno-Ugric and Persian myths.

My heart was already racing as he mentioned Leshy, the spirit of the forest, a dwarfish creature who wore a red sash and always had his left shoe on his right foot.

My palms started getting moist. I couldn't write as fast as he was talking. I did catch that Leshy led astray travelers through the forest. He would make them blunder in every direction, then bring them back to the same spot again.

I became more curious about the little prankster. He seemed quite good-natured. He did offer the lost travelers a chance to be released from his spell. To be free, a wanderer must sit down under a tree trunk, remove his clothes, and put them on backwards, including putting his left shoe on his right foot.

Dr. Vande Brake explained that Leshy teetered between his good-naturedness and complete anguish. Sometimes people in nearby towns could hear his shouting, sobbing, wild calls, and hysterical laughter coming from the forest.

I was instantly endeared. I got so interested in the little silvan creature that I forgot about my nervousness. I decided to adopt the little imp. I would keep him busy, and he would keep me lighthearted.

Only recently, Leshy had become a more frequent visitor, becoming quite a nuisance.

"Leshy, I'm getting really sick of you," I chuckle because I know just how to get him off my back. I take a huge swallow of tequila straight from the bottle until I feel warm. Then I say, "See" and go down to the pool with a new drink in my hand.

The most god-awful noises were coming from under the bed. Clicking, gnawing, licking, and then smacking. Momentarily, I am overcome with a fierce desire to scream, or even to kick the dog. Of course, I don't do either. I consider that I am experiencing the same cringing irritation that my students feel when I purposefully "accidentally" scrape my nails across the chalkboard as I erase. It usually gets their attention when thing are going slow. I've learned many such tricks in my year of teaching.

I turn my attentions back to Warren. He wipes his face on the pillowcase. Then he sits up and reluctantly starts to get out of bed, testing the bare, hardwood floor with the toes of one foot.

"Yow!" He quickly jerks his left leg back into bed and under the covers. I admire his shiny arm as he reaches over to the nightstand and picks up his white, ribbed undershirt.

He searches under the wool blankets for more clothes. He manages to find his socks, and by making a tent with the sheets and his legs, put them on.

Warren tries again. It is 10 p.m. and bone-chilling cold, but he is determined to complete his mission.

The tall, muscular man steps on the floor, this time with both feet at once. I giggle, almost releasing the swallow of flat beer in my cheeks. Half clad, he walks over to the bureau, lights a Salem, and snatches up a previously useless brass trinket to serve as an ashtray. Then he takes a running jump back onto the bed. I worry about the dog, who is still under the bed gnashing away at its dry skin. Fortunately, the creak of the boxsprings silences it.

For the first time tonight, everything is still. I notice in the background the music from Warren's record player. Phil Perry is hitting those high notes about amazing love. For the first time tonight, I realize that I'm exhausted. I have not forgotten that I will have to get up early in the morning.

Warren wants to chat. He is one that needs little sleep. He can teach all day, work the register in the Parisian's men's department at night, sometimes finding extra time to model for their flyers. He never seems to tire. Unlike me, he is consistently warm, dynamic, and completely hilarious.

"Baby, what are you thinking about? Warren asks while rubbing my shoulders.

"Work," I lie.

"Are the kids giving you trouble, again?" he asks, concerned. "You've got to show them who's boss. You're too nice. They'll run all over you."

"Warren, it's too late. I can't rule by force. I try to treat people with respect, whether they're grown or not. I never, in all my life, imagined that the main duty of teaching would be crowd control. I'm a pushover, and they know it." I kiss the side of his neck.

"Yeah, I know. You've just got to be mean."

"You mean like this, 'Sit down and shut up! I'm not taking any more of this shit!'"

"You're straight, you're straight," he says through his laughter. "Pretty good for a white girl," Warren can barely get the words out. His laughter comes all the way from his belly and echoes up his chest. It comes out as a deep, Barry White growl.

"What do you want for breakfast in the morning? Bacon? Eggs? Bacon and eggs? Toast? Biscuits? Grits? Champagne and caviar?" Warren asks, seriously.

"You know I've got to leave before breakfast. You're too good to me. What am I going to do with you?" I ask thinking *What would I do without you?*

As if reading my mind, Warren replies, "Baby, you know you got me 24-7." I make a mental note to ask my students what "24-7" means.

I wake up with my head on Warren's chest. His large hand is cupping my head. I can hear his heart thumping, steady, but very loud and forceful. My own heart gives a flutter. I look at the clock: 4 a.m. Getting up quietly, I depend on the red glow of the alarm clock to shine the way to the bathroom. Only after the door is closed do I switch on the light. I pick up my pile of clothes heaped on the floor and put them on: panties, bra, black tights, black and white checked stretch pants, black leather pull-on shoes, and an oversized grape sweater.

It takes only a few minutes for me to locate my purse and get out the front door. The warmth of Warren's house does not prepare me for the biting, winter winds outside. At once, I wish that I had brought my coat. I get into my car and lock the doors. The windshield wipers and fluid remove most of the frost from the windshield.

My next concern is getting into my apartment without waking the neighbors, taking a shower, and getting to work on time. My head pounds, and my stomach clenches. For a moment I'm lost until I come to Fairview, the road that leads back to the east side of town. "Thanks, Leshy." I say to no one. At the end of Fairview, I stop directly in front of the country club. Both arms shudder as I choke my steering wheel. On green, instead of making a right in the direction of my apartment, I take a left. I make a few more turns on the narrow streets until I'm on the Wetumpka Highway, heading out of town. It is still dark, and there's not much traffic. I loosen my grip on the steering wheel, turn the heater down, and let out a deep sigh.

The new burlap smells like fresh hay as I stretch it across the bulletin board.

The laminated cardboard footprint is slick between my thumb and forefinger. "Steps Toward a Successful Future." The thumbtack draws blood. I look for a paper towel. Something sanitary.

I notice the cheap paneling as I glance toward the wood desk. Mildew. Dampness. The spoiled smell must be the carpet in this dilapidated doublewide, called a "portable" in educationspeak.

I reach Wetumpka. I go through the Hardee's drive-through to get a sausage biscuit. Eating in the car, I get on Highway 9 and go north. The biscuit is tough from being microwaved too long. It burns the roof of my mouth, so I take a giant sip of Dr. Pepper.

85 degrees. My hairline and upper lip are sweating. Not from the heat, though. I am sitting on the bleachers with 1200 adolescents half-watching an unorganized pep rally. A voice comes over the intercom, "3:05. You may be dismissed. Please walk back to the building in an orderly fashion." Hundreds of nameless faces rush by me. I recognize a few. Tall, lanky, and especially dark is Wendall. I look at his torn red T-shirt and worry that he is going to trip on his soiled, saggy jeans that are riding way below the waist.

"Yo! Black Boo! Wait on me!" a voice calls out. To the side of me—Jermont, the heavy one who warned me that the principal promised him a passing grade in my class, regardless, because this is his third year in the ninth grade. Quickly, he's far ahead.

Pushing, shoving, chaos. Like the Rolling Stones concert in Birmingham.

A smiling face. A beautiful gap-toothed grin. Facing me. Steady, against the flow of the crowd. He reaches his hand out to me in high-five fashion. I grab it and don't let go.

"How was your first day at Parks Junior High?" the man with the warm laugh asks.

Just now, I pass through Santuck, then Central. I head for Equality.

Overheard at the Hillstreet Café. "Can you believe she lets her son invite a black boy over? What happens if he has to go to the bathroom? It's not the kind of situation I'd allow in my house," says a lady in a short, black skirt and a tailored turquoise jacket with matching silk blouse.

"I wouldn't let one in my house. They're taking over, I tell you. East Montgomery is not even safe. I've heard some have even moved into Cedar Lakes. Why can't we ship all of them off to Montana, or some obscure place like that. Let them rob and kill each other?" responds her companion.

"What's this world coming to?" The woman pulls out her compact and examines her eyes. Then she uses a cocktail napkin to blot her nose. "David, dear, you need to take me home. We've only got a few hours before your wife expects you home."

The sun has risen by the time I reach Goodwater. I am close to my destination.

"Miss Hayes, I think I know what hyperbole is. It's like when you say, 'Yo' mamma's so skinny, she has to tie knots in her legs to have knees,'" says Jermont

excitedly.

I don't notice when I leave Ashville and enter the Lineville City limits.

I can't remember where I parked. My cart is full of groceries, and I don't feel like pushing it all over the whole parking lot. I see it. Just where I left it. I get closer. I notice the big white letters on the windshield NIGGERLOVER.

I'm on Highway 49 now. I've just completed the winding, uphill course to Cheaha State Park. Cheaha State Park has the highest peak in the state of Alabama, 2405 feet high. My family camped there often when I was a child. I pass by the restaurant and lodge at the top of the mountain, and start my way back down the other side. When I complete the hairpin curve, I know I'm near. Before I reach the lake and the campground, I take a left on an unpaved road into the woods.

I park in the primitive campground. The place is empty. I get out and walk by old campsites. The wood is damp and smells like ash and urine. I walk a little ways until I'm out of sight of my car. I sit down to rest against a tree, remembering the whoops and hollers that we heard from this area when I was a child camping in the less barbaric camping section. I can feel the dampness from the morning ground soaking through my pants. I start to cry. I can't stop. Through my sobs, I let out a scream. Not the playful yells of the primitive campers of yore, but a tormented scream. Finally, I laugh hysterically until my voice is hoarse.

Exhausted, I lean back against my tree. I close my eyes, pull my sweater over my head, as I kick off my shoes.

Janet Mauney

excerpted from Tattoo

My mother met Marvin Arthur Stiles on the Tilt-A-Whirl at the King County Fair in July. Sioux's dad had been gone for five years, and my dad hadn't been around since my conception. Sometimes a biker or a sailor would ask Mom for a date. Nothing serious. They came around for tattoos and fell in love with her, just the way men fall in love with nurses or therapists. The bottom line was that she didn't like to mix business with pleasure, and she thought some of these men had so many tattoos, they looked like convicts, and some of them probably had been. When I pointed out that she was the artist behind some of these tattoos, my Mom said, "It's a living." These were harsh words coming from someone with a soft heart. Every time Sioux and I wanted her to give us a tattoo, even a tiny small one, she would say no. It was just the way she made her living. Lots of people had to do things they didn't like to make a living. Besides, she didn't have time for boyfriends. She was busy trying to discover her heritage and make a living for her family.

During the first week in July, Mom stopped working early in the afternoon. "Okay, girls," she said. "It's time to start enjoying your summer vacation." Sioux and I had been sitting around watching Hoss and Little Joe on re-runs of *Bonanza* on the Family Channel. We put on clean shorts, climbed into her car and headed over to Emunclaw. Mom's shirt was the kind of red that shows off her dark hair.

We scuffled through the sawdust floor of the animal pens to look at baby pigs, lambs, calves, ducklings and chicks. Mom bought some jars of homemade jelly. We ate hotdogs, cotton candy and drank big oranges, the junky kind of food she never let us have at home. The day was warm and sunny after an early morning rain. We threw darts at balloons and aimed guns at bottles that wouldn't tip over even when we hit them, but we didn't win anything. The carnival workers had tattoos, and Mom inspected some of the better ones, especially the horses, and asked who did them. She knew the famous tattoo artists on the west coast and had even studied with Vyvyn Lasonga. We rode the ferris wheel and could see the land and the orchards spread out below us like patches in a quilt. Mom stood her ground about not getting on the roller coaster, but we finally talked her into the Tilt-A-Whirl after she watched it run four times.

Sioux, Mom and I had climbed into a pod, strapped ourselves down like little astronauts, and sat waiting for the ride to start. The lights of the ferris wheel were spinning around next to us. Thin, tinny music produced off-key sounds that mixed with the cries of children on the merry-go-round. There were two more empty seats in our pod. Marvin jumped on at the last moment, sat down beside Sioux, hooked his strap and grinned at all of us. As soon as I noticed his cowboy boots, I knew we were in trouble. Mom has this thing about guys in cowboy boots. Right now, she thinks her father must have been a cowboy with a Mexican wife. Last year at this time, she thought her father had been a cowboy with a Pawnee wife. How they ended up in Bessemer, Alabama, is a mystery. I can't ask too many questions about that. It upsets her because she's thinking so hard, trying to figure out the scenario of her own birth.

The Tilt-A-Whirl threw us up in the air and spun us around, so Marvin was leaning on us. He smelled like leather and some kind of men's cologne. Then it dropped down and threw us the other way, so we were leaning on Marvin. Toward the end of the ride, Sioux lost her lunch on Marvin's lap. Mom was terribly upset. She told me to take care of Sioux, who was actually fine once her feet were planted on solid ground, while Mom got a cup of water and took the kerchief from around her neck to clean Marvin's trousers. He just grinned through the whole ordeal, like he was watching the comics on TV. Even I noticed that Mom was looking pretty—her cheeks were pink with embarrassment and she had on make-up. When she wears make-up, she looks better than other people. Strands of hair had come loose from her barrett and were curling in the afternoon heat. He offered to take us to a quiet restaurant where we could calm down, and Sioux could have a Coke to settle her stomach. Sioux and I figured Mom wouldn't let us ride any more today, so we stubbed back through the sawdust and out of the carnival with its greasy sweet smells.

Our old aqua Civic coughed a little, then followed Marvin's black Dodge Ram to a Burger King. Sioux put down a cheeseburger and some french fries with her coke. The color came back into her face, and she chattered away at Marvin, asking him questions that would've seemed rude if she wasn't such a child.

"Where'd you get the boots?" she chirped.

"In Texas, God's country," he answered.

"Wow! You're from Texas." She looked at us. "He's from Texas."

I had a chocolate milkshake and Mom drank a cup of coffee. Marvin had the works—a Whopper cheeseburger with onions and tomatoes, large fries and a large Coke. He finished off with an apple pie. He was a cowboy who came to Seattle to find work.

"Do cowboys make a lot of money?" asked Sioux, using her hands now to tame her berry-red Jello hair.

"What kind of work?" My mother looked at him over the rim of her coffee cup. All her eyelashes had grown back, but seemed to flutter nervously as she talked.

He didn't know a lot about anything but cattle, but thought he might like to work for Boeing and learn about the airplane industry. Or he might apply over at Fred Meyers and learn about retailing, but he wasn't sure he could stay inside all the time.

"How about landscaping," asked Mom. "There's a lot of beautiful gardening going on in Seattle."

Marvin turned his nose up at that. "That's too much like farming. I can't make that leap. Farmers and cattlemen don't get along."

"Have you given up cattle ranching?"

"Beef is getting a bad rap. The bottom dropped out of the meat market, so I don't know. But I can tell you one thing for sure. I'm so glad to meet a friendly bunch of people like ya'll. People from the South. I don't know anybody in Seattle. It's been lonely."

Mom was hooked. With his rumpled hair and sunburned face, Marvin had just turned her heart over, and she liked to help people who were having trouble. I didn't like his eyes. He squinted, even when he wasn't smiling, and I just couldn't get a good look at them to decide if he was a hard man or a kind man. She invited him to our house.

When we got in the car, Sioux and I started talking at the same time. Dr. Scott had told her she was too trusting, and she allowed people to take advantage of her. "Oh, come on girls. He's decent. He bought ya'll a meal, didn't he?"

"At Burger King! Get real, Mom," I said.

"He's good looking. That's why you like him," said Sioux.

"He's unemployed," I said. "Mom, Dr. Scott said the minimum criteria for a boy friend would be that he have a job."

"Jimmy T. had a job when I met him," said Mom. "He didn't quit working until after we married." It wasn't quite dark outside. Lightning flashed around us even though there was no rain. My mother was oblivious.

Marvin followed our car and settled down in our living room, telling us one cowboy story after another. His stories sounded kind of far fetched, like the one where he had to battle a bunch of sheepherders to get his cows from Wyoming to Texas. It sounded like a *Bonanza* episode, and I was sure cattle were transported on the railroads these days. This guy was hokey, and he didn't have any calluses on his hands. He couldn't be a real cowboy. It made my chest hurt to think my mother was falling for a stranger in cowboy boots who wore a wide grin that could be phony. After about a half hour, Mom and Marvin moved to the kitchen where she drank coffee, and he drank cold beer from our refrigerator, while she showed him her new drawings for tattoos. Amid flashes of lightning, he praised her Alabama birds and said he wanted to get a tattoo as soon as he got a job. Mom didn't offer him credit, so I knew she hadn't completely lost her head.

Sioux and I drifted upstairs. She took a shower and washed the Jell-O out of her hair, taking time to put in a cream rinse and run a comb through it. I think she sort of liked Marvin, too. Wearing her nightgown and putting on earphones, she began listening to her tapes of Guns 'N' Roses while staring out the window into the darkness. Night noises of crickets and traffic mixed little jolts of lightning and Marvin's booming laugh punctuated the low hum of their conversation. The leafy smell of wet ivy and summer flowers drifted through our room. I got a ladder from the basement and worked on the ceiling stars, trying to put the big dipper where it ought to be.

A couple of times I climbed down and looked out the window to check and see if Marvin's truck was still parked outside. Once, Sioux took off her earplugs and called to me. "Come here, Phoenix, there's Mr. Brockle." He was walking back and forth from his house to the street, carrying boxes full of stuff too dark to see. "What do you suppose that is?"

"I don't know, but I can guess," I answered.

"Marvin's still here," she whispered.

"Yeah. I can't go to sleep until he leaves."

"Why?"

"There's no telling what he's up to. Mom doesn't know him from a stray alley cat. She has no business bringing him into our house until she knows him better. Sometimes I think she's got a chip missing when it comes to men."

"Do you think he'll move in with us?"

"No way. She's not that dumb."

Marvin came out the front door and ambled slowly to his truck. Before he got in he looked back at the house. "Duck!" said Sioux.

"Why?"

"He might think we're spying on him."

"Who cares? It's our house. We can look out the window if we want to."

Marvin raised his hand and waved. "Goodnight, girls," he called with a laugh. I felt a little stab of anxiety right in the center of my throat. His hair stood up like a rooster's comb. Mom was a strong lady, but I knew she was lonely or she never would have asked him over. I thought about hiring a detective to get the real scoop on him, but I only had fifteen dollars put aside—not enough for an official investigation. His truck was out of sight before Mr. Brockle came out with another load of junk.

Patricia Mayer

excerpted from Terminal Bend

March, 1996
Bink and T-Coyote

*I*f you passed through Terminal Bend, Alabama, you wouldn't see what I see because I'm looking through the eyes of living seventy-two years in the same place. All you'd see is the town with the most murders in the state, but I remember when "drive-by" was what we did when we went to see the live Nativity scene in front of the Methodist Church. I've come to understand the strata of change. I know that there are layers of history below the line of vision.

Terminal Bend got its name because it's the place where trains from Pensacola to the east and New Orleans to the west turn north toward the cold cities we've only heard about. South Alabama is a warm place. For our children, snow exists only in the scenes on Christmas cards. They are unaccustomed to the erratic nature of change. They have been lulled by a compliant climate.

In the spring of the year, when azaleas bloom, I always remember two people. One is my brother, Bink. The other is T-Coyote. Now, where Bink is concerned, I would have to quote my older brother, Earl, when he said to me, "Dorothy, far as I can tell, I got two sisters—you and Bink."

When Bink overheard this, he started bawling. His ears turned the color of azaleas and that's why I always think of Bink in the spring. I remember the tragedy of T-Coyote for reasons that run a lot deeper.

To tell you about T-Coyote, I have to go down a few layers to the end of the first World War, which was the war to end all wars, only it wasn't, and we had to start numbering them. Terminal Blend was little more than a lone railway station and what would become the surrounding town was still Noel Sly's cow pastures.

People were restless, the way they always are after a war, and a lot of them moved south. Noel could feel the aftermath of the war's winds of change blowing across his pastures and he sold out to land-hungry developers with rolled-up blueprints under their arms. Soon, the grinding roar of John Deeres filled the air. The electric company jerked tall pines out of the ground, roots and all, then plunged creosote poles into the ulcerated earth and festooned them with humming power lines. The land was mauled and carved, humble little houses popped up, and businesses moved in to siphon off the paychecks of the new families. A town was born and the Southern way of life was perpetuated for the next generation. My brothers and I were part of that generation. And so was T-Coyote.

The land developers deeded fifty prime acres to the Mayor. His Honor had been more than helpful in advancing the cause of several questionable permits. The Mayor was a passionate fan of baseball and an avid gambler and he planned to put a stadium on this land to show off his new bush-league team, the Terminal Bend Slammers, not to mention booking profitable wagers on the games. He was looking for a backer to bankroll the stadium construction and that's where Vernon Potts, a crafty little weasel from Atlanta, comes in.

Now, Bink and I used to go to the Roxy Theater all the time and once we saw a picture show about carpetbaggers, and it seems to me that Vernon Potts was a carpetbagger, just like those Yankee scoundrels, even if he was from Georgia. Vernon blew in and greased up the Mayor with an irresistible proposition. Vernon offered to foot the entire bill for the stadium in return for twenty of the fifty acres which the Mayor got free in the first place, just for looking the other way which ain't hard to do when you got two faces. Just for icing on the cake, Vernon said he would start a new business on his twenty to bring jobs into the town (and tax dollars into the Mayor's pockets). Vernon even promised to build his own house on the back of his twenty for the purpose of keeping a close eye on things, which, as Vernon and the Mayor both knew, is a vital part of double-dealing.

Have you ever stood a quarter on edge and thumped it with your finger so it spun around real fast? I'll bet the Mayor's shiny little eyes spun just like a quarter when he heard Vernon's proposition and it's no wonder he couldn't see a downside. The greed in that office must have been so thick you could fall into it and not hit the floor, because nobody bothered to check out what kind of business Vernon planned to run when he got the go-ahead. Thus was born the great source of misery known as the Pulley Works, or as Brother Earl called it, the Pull Your Works.

Vernon was as good as his word, which is no compliment. He threw together a rickety wooden stadium that started rotting almost immediately, and a gloomy factory that provided the jobs he'd promised, although the grime covered, sweaty men who made the pulleys would tell you that he did them no great favor. Vernon's factory looked for all the world like an aircraft hanger from Hell, clanging and belching steam and sparks and sooty filth into the air.

Vernon slapped up a tiny, crude house behind the factory, encasing it and five acres within a high concrete block wall. It was a symbolic weasel hole of sorts, isolated from the perversion of the factory, or so he thought. From this vantage he ran his factory with a hand that was hotter and harder than the iron in the pulleys. Vernon was feared by his exhausted, underpaid workers who could barely dredge up the energy to hate him and he was condemned by the townspeople who were forced to breathe his noxious fumes. The soot from his low grade coal coated everything with the blackness of Vernon's greed. When he died of lung cancer ten years later, a few folks were honest enough to narrow their eyes and smile with one corner of their mouths. The whole town didn't give a hoot if Vernon's carcass was tossed into the furnace and went up the smoke stack with the rest of the soot and that would be Vernon all over.

He willed the factory to a disinterested sister in Georgia. She hired a manager, and fortunately, the man was a decent sort. He gained respect from the workers and thanks from the town because he raised wages and burned a higher grade coal. The fumes were gone and the filth was incorporated by nature and disappeared just like Vernon. The sister put the house and five acres up for sale and that finally brings me around to how Terminal Bend acquired T-Coyote and vice-versa.

His name was actually Tekayote. He was a Japanese-American who came to live in Terminal Bend by chance. He once told me that his grandmother had been a pearl diver in the Sea of Japan, and it was from her that he inherited his unusual height.

His parents immigrated to America by way of Hawaii, where they paused for a while to cut sugar cane. When they arrived in California they found work in the vegetable fields where they labored sixteen hours a day under the sun until they wore themselves out and died. Their only hope was for their son, Tekayote, who had been born between the rows of a California lettuce field. His mother was docked a day's pay for slacking off.

Their legacy to their son was twofold: a love of green, growing things and a surprisingly large sum they had saved. Tekayote was a humble man who thought that the California sun and soil were dedicated to forces more powerful than himself and he never established his sense of place, so finding himself alone at the age of twenty-nine, he climbed into a boxcar of an eastbound train. He had the art of farming grafted to his soul, hope in his heart, and his parents' life savings in his pocket.

After eight days, his train pulled across the open flatness of South Alabama. He leaned his back against the frame of the boxcar door and studied the quality of the Southern sunlight. He lifted his nose like an animal to draw in the warm, moist air that carried the pungent green scent of life. He could smell it, even over the hot grease of the train's wheels. Tekayote's mind spun with the possibilities of a place such as this.

The year was 1932, and my father was foreman at the Terminal Bend freight yard. He was surprised to see the tall, thin man climbing down from the box car. Hoboes were common, but this, Daddy laughed later, was a different breed of cat.

Daddy approached him cautiously because the only other Orientals he had ever seen were the two Chinese families who lived on Dexter Street. Daddy asked, "Can I help you, Mister?" He wasn't even sure that the guy spoke English.

"Yes," Tekayote answered politely with perfect clipped California twang. "Can you tell me where I might purchase a plot of land?"

Daddy did a fast mental inventory. Then he remembered the Potts place. It was a wreck, with a nasty feel about it—Vernon's legacy to the world. The price had been cut and cut. My father gave Tekayote directions and wished him well. Several days later, Tekayote was the new owner and he turned it into an Eden for us all.

He was so trusting that even the beer belching boys from the Pulley Works took to him. Their relaxed Southern drawl wove around his name and turned it into "T-Coyote." It was all we ever called him. Years later, when they took him away and we tried to find him, no one could remember his rightful name.

T-Coyote set about nursing the soil of his new home back to health, then he opened a flower business that took off right smart. His yard was a riot of color and a cagey demonstration of his skill. He eventually became the horticultural wizard of Terminal Bend. Things cooked along for T-Coyote and all of us for a few years until the world shifted sideways into World War Two.

T-Coyote managed to turn even war to his advantage. When all the fertilizer was used up making explosives and there was none to be found for our Victory Gardens, he drove away one night with his wheel barrow and shovel rattling around in the bed of his old truck and came home the next morning with the truck sagging under the weight of a ton of cow manure. People came running with buckets and sacks. It was a sight to see our neighbors jostling shoulder to shoulder to get free cow patties. "T-Coyote's gen-u-ine hockey pucks," Brother Earl called them, although I don't know how he knew about hockey—the game, I mean.

After Pearl Harbor, when the government began uprooting Japanese people and moving them to relocation camps, none of us gave it any thought. The only Japanese person we knew was T-Coyote, and he had been one of us for ten years. He even planted the new azaleas in front of City Hall. He lectured to the 4-H kids and he spoke at the ladies' garden club. He could balance a cup of tea on his knee with the best of them while he chatted with the Mayor's wife about roses. If T-Coyote himself had run for Mayor he probably would have been elected.

For the first few months of 1942 the government overlooked T-Coyote, then one day in late September he disappeared. They had taken him away. A CLOSED sign hung on the gate of his padlocked business and slowly the weeds took over, then the winter set in and everything died of cold and neglect.

Principal Parker from the high school formed a committee to appeal on

T-Coyote's behalf. They petitioned on the grounds that he was a *nisei,* or American-born Japanese. An indifferent official said it didn't matter. When Mr. Parker pressed to find out where T-Coyote had been sent, the man said that things were "temporarily out of order" as though T-Coyote was some sort of machinery. The bottom line was that they didn't know where he was. The red tape was endless and the heavier priorities of war took their toll on the attention given to T-Coyote's case. Nobody in the government seemed concerned about the fate of one insignificant Jap gardener. He had vanished and Mr. Parker decided that clever T-Coyote had managed to slip through their hands and was lying low until the trouble blew over.

That might have been the last we heard for a while if it hadn't been for Buddha Mose, the grandson of the town's black moonshiner, Jonah Mose. Buddha and Bink and I played together years back, so when Buddha was home on leave, we all walked down to get a strawberry cone like we did when we were kids. I went inside to buy the cones because blacks weren't allowed in Duvall's Drug Store in 1942. By the way, that's another thing that changed because now blacks own it, and ain't that what you'd call a reversal of fortune for Old Mr. Duvall? Anyway, I came out juggling three cones and we took off down the street, walking and licking, and that's when Buddha said it and knocked the socks right off Bink and me.

He pushed his glasses back up on his nose and said, "My eyes is good enough for stateside, but not for combat. Firs' time in my life I been happy to wear glasses. They got me workin' at one of them camps where they send Jap'nese folks 'cause they afraid they gonna be spies. It's mis'rable duty. That's why the colored troops have to do it. I hate to say it, but all Jap'nese folks look alike to me, but one day I saw a face I knew. You 'member T-Coyote? That Jap'nese guy sold plants out b'hind the Pulley Works?"

When we heard this, Bink and I froze in place and stared at him. Buddha just kept walking and talking, and he didn't even know we had stopped. He was right about one thing—he was half blind.

He continued, "I 'membered him 'cause he put in some 'zaleas round City Hall and paid me to help. I rec'nized him 'cause he was a head taller than th' rest. He didn't stay long. He got sick so they shipped him out. Said he had some kinda heart trouble but I think he jes' had a broke heart, is all. He couldn't understand what he done to make folks tear him away from his home and rob him of everthin' he worked for and he jes' give up. Anyway, I thought it was sorta special, both of us from Terminal Bend in the same place at the same time, on opposite sides of the barbed wire fence, and neither wantin' to be there. Life's strange, ain't it?"

Buddha had to start back for the camp that afternoon, so we hustled him down to see Mr. Parker and made him repeat the story. After that, Bink and I put him on a bus back to the relocation camp in Arkansas, where there was enough barbed wire to break a gentle heart.

At Mr. Parker's prodding, the official confirmed that T-Coyote had been in Arkansas, but didn't know where he had gone after that. Finally, after months of dogged persistence, Mr. Parker was bluntly notified that T-Coyote had died in a camp in Utah at the age of forty. Cause of death: *classified*. Known survivors: *none*.

The government sold his property to the Pull Your Works for expansion and his bank account was confiscated by the state. He had literally been erased. That was the end of T-Coyote, who died of a disease called *classified* and left no survivors except the entire town of Terminal Bend to mourn for him.

After we got the news, our gardens continued to flourish and the azaleas around city hall bloomed bright pink but nothing was the same. Every spring, even after all these years, I still remember T-Coyote. I like to think that, for a time, a few stubborn flowers pushed through the trampled soil of the Pulley Works expansion on T-Coyote's lost home and opened their bright, defiant faces to the sun.

That brings me to the other person I always remember in the spring and that's my brother Bink, and I was joking when I said it was because his ears turned pink when he cried.

Bink was a fine companion and loyal friend. Brother Earl was right—Bink was as good as having a sister, even better, because I didn't have to share my clothes with him—not too often, anyway—just on special occasions, and usually just undies.

When we were kids, and unaware of the nature of change, we moved into a new part of town that was dirt poor from the start (economically challenged as they say today), and this always embarrassed Bink. We were crammed in pretty close and it was part of life to hear the neighbor's toilet flush or doors slam. We could stand in our yard after school and catch a whiff of their collards boiling and sausage frying. Those greasy, pungent smells floated on the hot afternoon breeze and coated the inside of our noses; tempting and revolting and laden with exotic possibilities, like our neighbor's wife's cleavage. Let me assure you that Brother Earl was on the case where that cleavage was concerned. He called it The Great Divide and he always found reasons to putter around outside while she hung out her laundry. Bink said she was disgusting, but he did take an interest in her undies hanging on the line.

The War took them both, Brother Earl and Bink. Brother Earl came back in one piece, but only part of Bink came back. The other parts were left on a field in Italy. As Brother Earl put it, they shot off one of most everything Bink had two of. Everybody knows that this wasn't completely accurate, because it was really a land mine and not bullets that separated Bink from his parts, but the result was the same, and Brother Earl thought it made a pretty good joke, so we let it be.

In my layers of memory, I see Bink the way he was when we were kids. I recall how he played dolls with me under the oak tree where it was cool, while clouds of mosquitoes spun and danced around us in the tree shade.

TERMINAL BEND

Sometimes fat little Duke Piranno would waddle over to play with us, and when I was eighteen I married Duke, even though Brother Earl called him Ton-O-Fun and Pukey Dukey. Time evened it all up for Duke, though, because he watched them plant Brother Earl in the Magnolia Street Cemetery. Duke wore a red bow tie to the funeral, and ain't that the ultimate one-up? But I don't need to go off on the subject of Duke, because I remembered Duke in the fall, and this is spring and the memories belong to Bink.

Of all the fun that Bink and I shared, our A-Number-One treat was going to the Roxy. Some towns have their big movie palaces with plaster Cupids and chandeliers glowing yellow through a greasy coating, but the Roxy was Terminal Bend's, plain and square, with a marquee where the names of the stars were misspelled. It was a mystical place.

The seats were covered with scratchy wool and flanked by wooden armrests rubbed smooth by countless sleeves. The undersides of the seats were pimpled with petrified wads of gum. Down the aisle ran a long slice of stained carpet worn so slick it was dangerous. On the side walls were rusted light fixtures tilted like drunken sentries holding burned-out bulbs fluffy with dust. Mildew garnished the screen's faded blue curtain. The curtain creaked open so slowly that we always saw the first few minutes of the movie through a dreamy veil of blue.

Bink and I could hardly wait for Saturday afternoon, because that was when the feature changed. We loved to sit in the cool oily-smelling dark, sniffling and glued to the screen while the aroma of roasting peanuts snaked in from the lobby and coiled around our heads. I always had to nudge Bink two or three times to get his attention when I passed him my damp hanky. We soaked up the romance that flickered at us from the screen and lit up our faces with magic. Upon that screen, Clark Gable said "damn" and scandalized the entire country. I always wondered what the country would think if Brother Earl ever got a chance to say his favorite word on film. Bink never admitted it, but I know he fell in love with Fred Astaire and I fell in love with gorgeous Laurence Olivier.

Lulled by a movie viewed for the umpteenth time, the projectionist, old Mr. Wilcox, napped while the reels turned. If we were lucky, Mr. Wilcox would rouse up halfway through the movie in time to switch on the second projector. Likely as not, he would sleep through, and the finished reel would run off the feeder spool, causing the projector to throw a blinding light on the screen. The audience would yell, "CHANGE REELS!!" in the direction of the booth. If this didn't wake him, Bink would call out, "I'LL GO!", bolt out of his seat, across the lobby, and up the narrow stairs to the booth where he would find Mr. Wilcox snoring while the reel spun, flapping its loose end like a flag in a windstorm.

We'd leave the dark theater, blinking in the sunlight and drunk on our own imaginations. Looking back, I realize my ideas of romance sprouted in that theater the way toadstools sprout in the dark and that's why I married

Duke—it was time and he was the only one who asked and there was plenty of him to love. It turned out okay, though. Duke was a ton of fun. Brother Earl was right about that, too.

After Bink came home from the war, he got a medal in the mail and we pinned it on him every Veteran's Day. I think that gave him some pleasure, but it was hard to tell. We got Bink a wheelchair, but since he only had one arm, all he could do was go around in a circle until we put a motor on the back of it. After that, he puttered down the street in the Veteran's Day parade with his medal bouncing on his chest. I even took him to the Roxy once, but he didn't enjoy the movie very much—and he used to just love Fred Astaire—so we never went back. After a time, they boarded up the Roxy and later tore it down and put up a big Winn-Dixie with a deli and a bakery that makes the best brownies I ever ate. At first I felt bad about the Roxy, but I finally decided it was just another layer laid in place.

When Bink died of what Brother Earl called "Bink's Amputation Complication" we laid him out in his uniform and I pinned his medal on him, but it just didn't seem to be enough, and then I got a brainstorm. I asked Mr. Merkel down at the Oakdale Funeral Home about it and he said to go ahead because people do strange things in times of grief.

So, just before they closed the lid on Bink, I slipped a pretty pair of brand new lace undies into his coffin for old time's sake and if you think this sounds too bizarre to believe, just ask Mr. Merkel because he was the only one who saw me do it.

And then we laid Bink to rest.

Well, that's it; that's my springtime memories, all about Bink and T-Coyote and the Pulley Works and the Roxy, but they're really about change when you look under the layers. If you're ever passing through Terminal Bend in the summer, and you want to hear the story of the time Duke punched out Brother Earl, and about Buddha Mose and his Concrete Jesus, and the time Jonah Mose's moonshine-making-still started a riot and got the preacher arrested, come see me and we'll talk.

Julia Oliver

A Touch of the Spirit

"It's a beautiful day, Miss Sadie."

"That it is." She stiffened her cheek for his kiss. Porter was her first cousin, only two years her junior. "Miss Sadie" indeed! At least he got the salutation right. She was too old to be a "Ms." and had never been a "Mrs."

Porter eased himself into the other porch rocker, ruminating over what to say next. He liked to keep conversation going full tilt. "Alma and I want you to come to church with us tomorrow. The new preacher's a real fireball."

"You know Sunday's my day for solitude." Soon after her mother died from grieving over the loss of Sadie's father (who committed suicide by pickling his liver with alcohol), Sadie gave up regular church attendance as though it were a bad habit. To reassure him—Porter worried about her salvation—she added, "I don't feel the need to get all gussied up and go into town to church. I get a touch of the spirit whenever Joseph is on the premises. He announces his arrival with some hymn or other."

Porter nodded in approval. "Those old spirituals are powerful religion. I remember summer nights out here, when Joseph's daddy sang 'Amazing Grace' while you and I caught lightning bugs . . ."

"Joseph's daddy dropped dead chopping wood when I was three years old. You would have been in diapers." Porter had only visited the house she had lived in all her life.

"Must have been one of the other Nigras then," he said amiably.

In the progressive Alabama town a few miles away, Porter was president of a bank where just as many black people handled the money as white, and where he wouldn't dream of uttering that obsolete term "Nigras." Sadie was about to point that out when he leaned over to examine the porch railing and changed the subject. "We got a good paint job this time. I wish you had let me have the front rooms done, too."

"You'll have to wait till I'm dead to get at the inside." Years before, Porter had quietly assumed responsibility for the maintenance of her house, which he called, as though it were a title, "the homeplace." His latest idea was to install a burglar alarm, but Sadie told him to forget that, she would never turn the thing on; she kept a gun handy and wouldn't hesitate to use it.

He had taken the hint that she didn't like him to visit too often; hospitality did not come naturally to her. Since he'd called ahead this time, she had ready a pitcher of tea, brewed to the color of a dark jewel. She was almost as fond of Porter as he was of her—neither had siblings or other first cousins—but she got impatient when he reminisced about how her house used to be the center of a prosperous farm. The gracious living part was over before her time. Most of the land had been sold off piecemeal. She and her parents had lived with Grandmama because Sadie's daddy was a drunkard who couldn't earn a living. Grandmama left Porter's mother, the daughter who had married well, a silver tea set and the bone china; Sadie's mother got the house and the rest of its contents. Never once had Porter intimated that he felt his side had been slighted. If the shoe had been on the other foot, Sadie would have raised some hell.

She had to hand it to him: Porter was more than a lip-service Christian. He even tithed, which wasn't required of Methodists. But unlike her, he cared a lot about worldly goods. Now he glanced, with anticipation, through the screened door into the shadowy interior. Sadie kept the windowshades down so she wouldn't have to run the central air conditioning he'd installed a few summers back. Except to occasionally flick a feather duster over the surfaces, she ignored the dark, heavy furniture that stood against the walls like trees in the oldest part of a forest. Porter would stroll through the twin parlors nodding cordially at the spool-turned sideboard, the oversized planter's desk, and the console with the petticoat mirror as though they were acquaintances.

Alma had furnished their house with antiques finer than anything Sadie had, but Porter revered things that had been in the family. As her closest relative, he would probably get it anyway, but Sadie had done the right thing and made a will bequeathing him her meager estate. He would keep the homeplace for his private retreat, even though his grown sons (who had deserted Alabama for Atlanta) had mentioned turning it into a hunting lodge. Sadie didn't care what they did with it. She'd never know, anyway.

It was a ritual on these visits that she allowed Porter to select from the clutter of small stuff. Once he chose a shaving mug with a moustache rim; most recently, he took a set of pressed glass fruit dishes. She said sassily, as she preceded him through the doorway, "What do you aim to talk me out of this time?"

"Nothing for myself. I'm asking on behalf of the museum they've started in the old depot. I want you to donate something of substance that belonged to our great-grandfather, in his memory." He paused to stroke the plump arm of a Victorian lady's chair. "Your name would be engraved on the donor's plaque, of course."

She glanced significantly at the gilt-framed image that hung over the mantel. Alexander Powell's icy blue eyes and gaunt cheekbones reminded Sadie of her own face. Porter was almost handsome. He wouldn't want people to know what an ugly old goat this great-grandfather had been.

He waved the suggestion away before she made it. "Not the patriarch's portrait. What I have in mind wouldn't be missed."

"That could be anything. Most of what's here is useless, except the Fridge on the back porch. Joseph puts fish in it for me."

Porter peered through a window at the small frame house a stone's throw from hers. "How many are living there now?"

"Just him since his wife died. His sons are in the Army. Daughter's in Birmingham."

"Hasn't been long since that whole family was available to work around the place."

Sadie said, "I'm glad those days are past. I don't want anyone to depend on me for employment. Joseph draws Social Security. I let him fish in the pond and use the tractor to break his ground, so he doesn't charge me much to help out around here occasionally."

"You probably know that Joseph's ancestors took the Powell name after they were freed."

"They had a right to it. Joseph's granddaddy was our grandmama's half-brother." The idea of her nearest neighbor as a blood relative had not occurred to her before, but it certainly made sense.

"You have a wicked imagination." As though to prove he didn't, Porter turned his back on the life-sized painting of two women, in flowing garments, pressing their bosoms together.

She said, slyly, "The museum is welcome to Ruth and Naomi."

"Well . . . No. Wouldn't want to leave such a large gap on this wall."

"I doubt anybody besides us knows there ever were any white Powells around here."

"It has been a long time. The last male with the surname in our line was Alexander, Grandmama being his only child."

"Only pure-white child," Sadie amended. "Our great-grandaddy got a slave woman pregnant, then gave them that dab of land to ease his conscience."

Porter frowned. "Did you make that up?"

"I figured it out. One of Joseph's eyes is blue." Actually, it was the color of skim milk. A cataract, or maybe a mule had kicked him. Joseph never discussed his misfortunes with her.

Porter sighed indulgently. "Well, we're all kin in the eyes of the Lord." He turned to admire the droopy peacock quills that languished in a fan-shaped, hobnail vase. "Do you rearrange these often?"

"They haven't been touched since Grandmama put them there, unless she manages to shift them around herself from wherever she is now."

Porter's heaven wouldn't accommodate earth-roaming ghosts. He frowned. "Your conjecturing is getting out of hand. I have found it's best to stick to the facts."

Sadie ignored the reprimand. "Porter, do you have cancer?"

"Not that I'm aware of. Why do you ask?"

"No reason except you're old enough to have something bad wrong with you."

"So are you, but as always, you're the picture of health. I hope you're not ill?"

"I'm fine," she admitted.

"Have you thought what you will do with all that energy after you retire next year?"

Sadie had been a traveling nurse in the county school system for over four decades. She had once hoped to be a veterinarian; two years of nurse's training was as close as she got to that goal. "Sure have. I plan to raise Labs. Tarbaby could use the company."

Porter glanced at the toothless, ancient black dog that stayed as close to Sadie as her shadow. "Isn't it about time to put that creature out of his misery? How old is he?"

"He's a teenager," Sadie said. "And he's not miserable."

"Well, breeding dogs should keep you busy, all right."

The table-top piano took up most of one wall. Sadie had almost forgotten her disappointment at not having had music lessons. She raised the curved lid and flattened one hand over keys that were cracked and stained like old teeth. The sound was as harsh as a tree full of blue jays. She shouted above the reverberation, "How about the Chickering?"

"The museum already has a piano." Porter peered at the instrument through his bifocals. "You know, I don't recall ever having seen the keyboard before. I must have assumed the lid was sealed shut."

"Like a coffin?"

He rubbed his hands together. "Now you're close to what I have in mind."

Sadie sighed. "Just tell me."

"You'll recall this story: Alexander Powell had a casket built to accommodate his long frame and await his need. But he died in a steamboat explosion, and there were no remains to bury."

"You mean the casket we shut Joseph up inside."

"We were children; we didn't know any better." Porter's face flushed with guilt and remorse.

"We were lucky he didn't suffocate." Joseph had been tall for his age, the color of weak coffee, in starched overalls that stood out from his scrawny body. "Far as I know, that old box is still in the basement. I haven't been down there in years."

The basement smelled like English cathedrals she had visited on her only trip abroad. In the murky light of a chain-hung bulb, the polished wood gleamed through layers of dust. The interior, she recalled, was lined with feather-padded linen. She had made Joseph brush himself off before he climbed into that pristine whiteness.

"Just as I remembered—it's a genuine, pinch-toe coffin." With his handkerchief, Porter skimmed off some of the dust. "Look at that remarkable craftsmanship. Slave-made, no doubt, from pecan trees that grew on the place."

"What a waste," Sadie said. She could have used it for one of her parents and saved herself some money.

Joseph had climbed in, eased himself into a prone position, closed his eyes, and crossed his hands over his chest, exactly as she instructed. She couldn't recall whose idea it was to fasten the latches, only that it took both her and Porter, working frantically, to get them open again. After that, Joseph gave her a wide berth that lasted until they were grown.

Sadie said, with a shrug, "The museum's welcome to it," having just decided that she would not be buried in this or any other container. She would leave instructions with the lawyer who'd made her will: her remains were to be cremated—they'd have to haul her to Birmingham to get the job done—and the ashes scattered on the fishpond.

Porter gripped her elbow and steered her up the stairs. "I'll come out first of next week with a van and some men to load it."

"Joseph could haul it in his truck."

"I'd rather not involve him."

"You can put your name alongside mine on the donor plaque," she called out, as Porter was getting into his car. She'd forgotten to offer him the tea. Later, as the sun disintegrated behind the empty field, her solitude was interrupted again, by Joseph's sonorous rendition of "What a Friend We Have in Jesus."

The singing ceased as soon as it got her to the back porch. "Brought you some nice bream," he said.

"Don't they look delicious!" She couldn't stop herself from asking: "Remember that time we played dead with the coffin in the basement?"

"Sure do." His expression, as always, was impassive.

"My cousin and I shouldn't have shut you up in there, and I shouldn't have waited all these years to tell you how sorry I am that we ever thought of such a thing." To her dismay, she sounded flippant.

"Just a little game is all that was." His voice was rich with forgiveness.

She cleared her throat. "I have trouble sometimes with my memory now. Would you tell me—What color was your eye before it clouded over?" She waited for his answer as though it would explain things the churches couldn't.

"Same as yours. Kind of blue."

She said, in a rush to get the words out, "I want you to have something from my house. What would you like?" The alien force of generosity made her heart pound.

As though to give her an opportunity to withdraw the offer, Joseph waited a few seconds. Then he said, as smoothly as if he'd rehearsed it: "While I was getting the window screens out of the basement for you not long ago, I thought to myself, now I'd be proud to make my final journey in that old coffin."

"It's yours." She crossed her arms, bracing herself against his gratitude.

She would tell Porter he'd have to pick something else for the museum. "Bring some boys with you to get it. The thing probably weighs a ton."

She noticed, with a sharp shiver of regret, that he had dried out with age, like unvarnished wood. With unaccustomed prescience, she knew she would outlive Joseph, and Porter, too. The boding smote her like a cold, out-of-season wind.

Joseph was placing the best of the day's catch on a shelf in the icebox. She said, "Stay for supper. I'll fry the bream and cook the greens you brought yesterday." The invitation surprised her as much as it must have him.

"Thank you all the same, I best be going on. I got things to tend to at home." He turned and started down the steps. In the last of the day's sunlight, the man glowed like the string of fish he carried over one shoulder.

Sadie was reminded of saint-statues in the English cathedrals.

She called Porter and told him she'd decided to give the coffin to Joseph so it would be put to practical use. He masked his disappointment gallantly. Then she heard herself say, "If the offer's still open, I'd like to go to church with you and Alma tomorrow."

She didn't want him to think she was making some earth-shaking commitment, but she hoped he realized she had spoken the truth. Whatever truth was.

Ann Vaughan Richards

excerpted from Miss Woman

Miss Woman sang the blues. Deep, low down, gut wrenching blues. Mad Dog Blues, Memphis Blues, Don't Care Blues, You Can Have Him I Don't Want Him Didn't Love Him Any How Blues. And the words and notes floated out over the courthouse square in the sweltering month of June. They bounced off the plate glass store windows and rolled down the alleys. Wailing, moaning, misery loving blues.

And the flowing well kept on flowing, absorbing the notes and spewing them back, gurgling and foaming, into the algae encrusted pool. Whining, crying, man done me wrong blues. The hot asphalt sucked up the melodies and steamed them skyward into the sweating fly swatting air. And the air did its best to beat the lyrics back down with its heavy sweet breath until they hung in limbo, trapped between the weary cracked roof tiles and the gum clogged drains. And there they hung, swinging back and forth, seesawing to the left and veering to the right. Throbbing, thumping, ain't it a crying shame blues. Groaning low, spiraling high, Miss Woman sang the blues.

Miss Woman suddenly appeared—full blown and grown—sitting sassy and big as life at an upright piano on the top floor and right above the Victoria Thrift Store. Right in our midst she materialized, a strange and alien presence, a lush and fanciful image. Plucked out of the heavy honeysuckle air, she was there. One day, we were a normal small town. We made axe handles, we worked in the sewing factory, we bought pork chops, we brushed our teeth and ran our stores. We conducted our lives with normal, everyday, small town decency. We were doing fine, thank you. Not great, but fine, just fine. The next day, she was there, sitting in front of the open window of the top floor and right above the Victoria Thrift Store, playing her heart out and singing the blues in a rich chocolate voice. And then, we were not so fine. Because on the first day of June, it was hot and she was there.

And shortly thereafter, somebody took a shotgun and blew off Glenna Bedsole's head. Some say it wouldn't have happened if Miss Woman hadn't come to town, if she hadn't sung the blues. "Maybe," I answer, but I know now that the wheels began to turn a long time before Miss Woman came to town. Miss Woman sang the blues. That's all she did. She sang wonderful warm blues. Somebody else took a shotgun and blew away Glenna Bedsole's head. And somebody else blew away a part of my soul. Miss Woman just sang the blues.

Chapter 1

It started the day Miss Woman came to town. I didn't know it then. I know it now. Now that it's too late. I wish I could go back to that day. Maybe I could have done something or said something that would have changed the course of events. Maybe I could have stopped the hate and the hysteria. And maybe if I hadn't been so busy trying to come to terms with my life I could have saved the life of someone I cherished. Or maybe it was already too late.

I remember that day vividly. I guess we all do. It started out as a typical rainy June day, a few giant splats plopping down on the sidewalk, followed by sheets of rain. One sheet passing through, drenching everything in sight, and hitting the ground too fast to be soaked up so that the water swirled in dirty rivulets down the street, pushing Baby Ruth candy wrappers, cigarette butts, Pepsi Cola caps and bubble gum wrappers in a zigzag line until they were deposited without ceremony in the ditches. Then that first sheet of rain passed over, heading to Enterprise or Dothan or Montgomery, and we relaxed just in time to feel the impact of the next onslaught, the new sheet—white and determined, thick and heavy. And we helplessly watched as it marched forth, an army of drops in formation and advancing.

We watched it progress, coming up from behind the Victoria Drug Store and the Victoria Hardware Store until it grabbed the roofs and engulfed the stores on the far side of the square. We watched it surround the old brick courthouse like a cocoon. And then, of course, it was upon us, slamming against the display window and trying to beat its way inside my book store.

Right after that first rain, when the sky cleared, the window above the Victoria Thrift Store was thrown up and there she was, unnoticed at first. Unnoticed until a chord banged and the blues came forth. Soul searing, heart tearing blues, riding on the languid air of an overripe June day.

Across the square in front of the Victoria Dry Cleaners, Callie Thomas bent to scratch a mosquito bite on her scrawny anemic leg and froze in place as the first words made their way past the courthouse and into the Pussley filled sidewalk cracks. And Callie sat down on the spot and listened. Right in the middle of the hot wet sidewalk, mute Callie Thomas sat and cocked her ear toward the sound.

The words and the chords came right through the plate glass window of my store. Mary Jo and I looked at each other and, in unspoken agreement, we walked to the door. The blues got louder as we got closer.

"Somebody," said Mary Jo, "is singing the blues."

When we opened the door, the heat slapped us in our faces. I reached up, wiped my brow and dried my hands on my jeans. Mary Jo unbuttoned two buttons on her blouse and fanned her face with the literary reviews. We looked upward to the source of the blues. We were not alone.

Corinne and Frank Morrow, who ran the jewelry store next door, were standing side by side, their hands cupped over their eyes as they peered upward. Their faces were lined and haggard as the misery of Christmas before last etched their countenances and stooped their bodies. On the other side of the square Miss Minnie Henderson, self-appointed consoler of the ailing and the bereaved, having completed her daily chat with the pharmacist, pushed open the drugstore door. Her drab, virginal body and her dreary face displayed outrage as the blues fell upon her.

Thus it was, all around the square—platinum haired Betty Sue Jenkins, in front of the beauty shop, squinting through melting eye shadow; Jessie Ed Harper, my uncle and the mayor, outside the Victoria Feed and Seed Store shielding his bloodshot eyes from the glare of the sun; Judge Rhinnart and the city clerk standing on the courthouse steps; and Sheriff Grice Hadley and Deputy Tommy leaning on the streetlight in front of the Victoria Police Station. They were all looking heavenward to the sound of the blues.

In a voice loud enough to be heard over the strains of the Risin' High Water Blues—a voice that could be heard all the way down the block to my store, Nettie Tucker screamed "Betty Sue! You come right back in here and comb me out, you hear?"

In front of the Victoria Dry Cleaners, Glenna Bedsole's face registered her disgust. Noticing Callie Thomas, who was sitting rapt and spraddle legged, smack in the middle of the hot wet sidewalk, she furiously waved her hands to shoo the child away.

And the next thing I remember is seeing Grice and Tommy running through the stiffling heat to a silent heap in the middle of the street.

"Mary Jo!" I cried, "Something's happened in front of the dry cleaners!"

Forgetting the heat and the stickiness, we loped up the street and across the square to the bundle that was Callie Thomas.

As Grice attempted to help Callie up, she fiercely shook free and stood up on her own two feet. I tried to touch her, but she pushed me away with all her adrenlin-charged might. She glared at us, turned and stared at the Victoria Dry Cleaners, limped to the courthouse square, sat down on the lawn, and cocked her ear toward the blues. Her face was hard and expressionless. And determined.

"What happened, Grice?" asked Mary Jo, as Miss Woman launched into the Mean Woman Blues.

"I don't know. I looked up and saw her hit Mr. Stroud's car."

We didn't know what happened, but Glenna Bedsole knew and Callie Thomas knew. And, sitting in the alley beside the Victoria Dry Cleaners, O.K. Maylo knew. He had seen it all. He had seen Glenna Bedsole heap curses upon Callie's head, and he had seen her enter her store and come back out with a handful of wire coat hangers, he had seen her throw the coat hangers on Callie's unsuspecting body, and he had seen Callie start in fright and run into Mr. Stroud's car. O.K. Maylo knew, all right.

"Does she look hurt to you?" asked Mary Jo.

"Not from here." I replied. "We need to get closer to her, but she won't let us."

"I don't know what's to become of that child," said Mary Jo. "She's like a feral child."

"She never had a chance from the day she was born to Ludie Thomas," I said. "That Thomas Clan is as low on the human scale as they come."

"She dropped out of school this year," said Grice. "Twelve years old and a dropout!"

"The teachers couldn't do anything with her so the school system gave up," said Mary Jo. "Ludie wouldn't cooperate or even bother to get her to school. Finally, Callie stopped going altogether."

"Ludie doesn't care what she does as long as Callie leaves her alone so she can stay drunk!" said a disgusted Grice.

I leaned against a parked car and watched Callie. Mary Jo leaned with me and we fanned our faces with our hands as we tried to create enough breeze to drive away the flies.

"I'm going to get that child a cold drink," I said.

I fished in my pocket for some change and loped up the courthouse steps. I fed nickels and dimes into the Coke machine and walked back into the sun with the cold can held to my chest. I got as close to Callie as I dared, stretched out my arm, and said, "Here, Callie. Here's a Coke for you." My offer went unanswered.

I edged nearer and set the can in front of her left knee and walked back to the parked car where Mary Jo was waiting with worried eyes. Callie continued to sit and listen to the blues. For five or more minutes, Callie sat unmoving. Then slowly her left hand reached out, grasped the can, and brought it to her mouth. Gulping thirstily and greedily, she downed the Coke, threw the can aside, and resumed her attention to the blues.

Once again, I approached Callie, who steadfastly refused to meet my eyes. "Callie," I said as softly as I could over the blues, "Let me know if I can help you." Not expecting an answer, and not getting one, I turned away.

"That child," said Corinne Morrow, with her sad eyes emitting so much pain I couldn't return her gaze, "What's wrong with that child?"

"She ran into Mr. Stroud's car."

"Is she okay?" asked Corinne.

"She's not hurt," I evasively replied over the sound of the blues. Callie Thomas was not okay, but the accident had nothing to do with that.

"Hello, my darlings!"

We all looked up to the window above the Victoria Thrift Store. As abruptly as they had begun, the blues had stopped. And into that silence came a deep melodic voice, calling down to us, demanding our undivided attention. Red satin encased mountains of breasts rested on the window ledge, and a mocha beaming face with gigantic golden earrings looped from each ear looked down upon her grim subjects. Bejeweled fingers and a bangled arm waved down.

"Hello, my dear ones!" shouted the face, "Miss Woman done play for you the blues!"

We stared back, gaped mouthed and speechless.

"No need for the thank yous very much. It done be my pleasures!" And with that, the window slammed down and the blues ended.

And Victoria went on about its business as usual, unaware that the fragile straw of sanity which held one of us together had decisively snapped.

Judith Richards

excerpted from Summer Lightning

Terry walked out the Chosen road, detouring through a cane field where black men with machetes were harvesting thick, juicy stalks. "Peel me a stalk?" he inquired of a gleaming ebony worker.
"Sure nuff."

The man flashed startling white teeth. His accent told Terry this was an islander from the Bahamas, come to cut cane and make a few dollars American before returning to his own home. The cane dripped around Terry's hand. He had no way to cut off plugs, so he chewed from top to bottom, reducing each bite to a tough fiber sucked dry of fluid.

He ate as he walked, still carrying his books, chewing cane and wondering if he'd see Mr. McCree today. Snake man, they called him. McCree called Terrell Terry or Little Hawk and never asked discomforting questions.

Terry heard a car coming and got off the road. His second week of school had taught him about Miss Ramsey, the truant officer. She came this way every morning, gathering the unwary to haul them back to Mr. Hammond's office.

There were stories that Miss Ramsey had caused a tenth-grader to be shipped to Marianna, to the boys' reformatory, because he skipped school. And stole things.

The car passed. It was not Miss Ramsey. It was the greens keeper at the golf course, on his way to work. Dust swirled from the roadbed, settled on saw grass and temporarily colored the air russet.

Terry crawled down a bank to reach canal water, ever mindful of snakes. He pushed aside blue-blossomed hyacinths, a favorite resting place for the cottonmouth moccasin, and washed sticky cane juice from his hands.

He nearly slipped. Only a quick grab for the belt around his books saved them from total loss. He retrieved the dripping bundle and moaned. A red dye from the cover of his reader bled onto his fingers. He knew his problems had just been compounded.

He continued toward Chosen, alert to the sound of an occasional approaching automobile; dust, sweat and red dye from his book turned his hands and all he touched a dingy brown. He followed a familiar path from the road down a canal bank, to a crossing board, through a thicket of Australian pines and into a small clearing. Here lived Eunice Washington, a stout black woman, and her sole grandchild, LuBelle.

"Hey, Eunice."

"Lord God, boy, you near scared me to death! Don't come creeping up on Eunice like that."

"You seen Mr. McCree?"

"Not yet. He'll be along directly."

"Can I wait?"

"Help yourself." Eunice poked a bleached broomstick into a boiling cauldron of lye soap, rainwater and "took in" clothes, which she washed and ironed for pay.

"LuBelle here?"

"Ain't she always?"

"Inside ?"

"Most likely."

The house was built on stilts, over earth packed hard by years of foot traffic. There were no windows, only holes cut in the siding with hinged shutters, which opened from the bottom. No screens kept out insects, and the inhabitants shared the cool, dark, three-room building with whatever chose to enter. The house was always an odd mixture of odors. Boiling beans simmered on a wood stove, where Eunice also heated her irons, and the damp, musty aroma of fresh dirt rose through cracks between floorboards. LuBelle was sitting in the middle of a bed, naked. A year younger than Terry, she never wore clothes. It had not occurred to him to give this a second thought. He had never seen her otherwise.

"You want some taffy?"

"No," Terry said.

"Mawmaw made it last night."

"Listen, LuBelle, you got any worms?"

"No."

"Reckon we could go dig some? I'm going to ask Mr. McCree to take me fishing."

"He ain't going. Today's his day to trade with Mawmaw. Mr. Cree don't do nothing on trading day, except trade."

"Today?"

LuBelle pointed at two quart jars on a bare table. The contents looked like kerosene. But they weren't.

"Ho, Eunice."

"There he is," LuBelle grinned.

"Look what I got you, Eunice!"

"Lord God, Mr. Cree," Eunice always dropped the Mc from his name, "what you doing bringing that here?"

LuBelle and Terry ran to the front porch. Mr. McCree was standing in the yard, laughing, Eunice holding him at bay with her broomstick. The old man gripped the heads of two huge rattlesnakes, one in each hand, tails whirring a dry staccato warning.

* * *

LuBelle scratched her belly, the pupils of her brown eyes surrounded by white as she observed the ritual of slaughter. Terry watched Mr. McCree lop the heads from both rattlesnakes, letting the writhing bodies fall to bleed in a washtub.

"Don't touch the heads," McCree warned. "They still bite."

"I ain't touching nothing," LuBelle said.

"You two young'uns stay way from them snakes," Eunice called, stirring her wash and kicking hot embers back under the blackened cauldron.

"With your mawmaw's beans, fried rattlesteaks," McCree said, his voice deep, graveled, "we got us a feast ahead."

"Mawmaw don't eat no snakes," LuBelle advised.

"Reckon not," McCree said. "But I got fish for her."

"I be of a mind to eat some fish myself," LuBelle mused.

"Plenty for all," McCree agreed. He skinned the headless carcasses, which still twisted in his hands.

"That hurt them?" Terry asked.

McCree leaned over close to a rattler's head on the ground. "That hurt you?" he asked the head.

"Spect his head hurts," LuBelle said, "if anything at all."

"Without a head, he's dead," McCree explained. "Dead things don't feel nothing, except pain in the soul."

"Snakes got souls?" Terry inquired.

"Like as not." McCree sliced pure white reptile flesh into wafers suitable for frying. "Seminoles think so. They think trees and grass and all manner of things have souls. I never talked to a dead man, so I couldn't rightly prove it right or wrong."

"Only folks got souls," Eunice stated.

"My dog died and went to heaven," Terry said. His wirehaired terrier had been struck by a car.

"Whose heaven?" McCree grunted. "Yours or his?"

"What do you mean?"

"Your heaven might be full of chains and locks and pens to keep a dog from running in God's backyard. His heaven might be full of rabbits and star-nosed moles and crunchy bugs to chomp on. If you was a dog, which would you want? A tether, or freedom?"

"I never tied up my dog."

"Got killed, too," LuBelle said.

"That isn't my fault!"

"Nobody's fault," McCree responded. He lifted a quart jar with a bloodied hand, unscrewed the mason lid and took two huge swallows. He wiped his unshaven chin with the back of a gritty sleeve.

"Mind what you teach them children," Eunice chided. "I don't want no bad dreams or long questions after you leaves."

"Boil your clothes, woman."

LuBelle laughed and McCree winked at the black girl. "Fetch some salt, child."

"Can I have the rattlers?" Terry asked.

McCree handed them to him. Terry stuck the appendages in his pocket with the two cigarettes. Feeling these, he asked, "Want a cigarette?"

"Nope. Want a plug of Bull of the Woods?"

"Nope," Terry said.

McCree took a round box of iodized salt from LuBelle and liberally applied it to the diced rattlesnake meat. This done, he went to his battered pickup truck, followed by the two children.

"Where's your dog?" Terry asked.

"Round about. Dog!" McCree withdrew a burlap sack from the bed of his truck and reached inside. He pulled out two catfish, considered these, pulled out two more. "Dog!" he hollered again.

Dog was the animal's name. A mongrel with one blue eye and one green, the old man's companion and "chief snake sniffer," the pup had taken refuge in a hollow under an elephant ear plant.

"There's Dog," McCree said.

"Go stir them beans, LuBelle!"

"Yes ma'am."

"Stir to the bottom now, so's they don't stick," Eunice commanded.

"Mr. McCree, reckon we can go fishing sometime soon?" Terry questioned.

"When did you have a mind to?"

"Today."

"Not today, Little Hawk."

"You said you'd teach me how to catch fish with no bait."

"I did that, and will, too."

"When, you suppose?"

"Oh, tomorrow maybe."

"You think I can do it?"

"Anybody can."

"Them beans bubbling?" Eunice called, lifting clothes on the end of the broom handle, transferring them to a bucket.

"A little," LuBelle replied.

"Eunice knows about beans," McCree said, cleaning catfish.

When the washing was done, they cooked the snake meat and catfish in large frying pans over the remaining embers, the odor of lighterknots burning, sap crackling, the aroma of food making their bellies churn. McCree cut a green bamboo stalk, split a section into slivers, and they used these to spear meat directly from the pan onto plates heaped with soft butterbeans and green onions.

"Old *Crotalus adamanteus* served us well this day," McCree observed. He called most things by their "true" names. It seemed only proper, he said, to call things what they really were. Names meant something, McCree told Terry. *Crotalus*, big rattler, *adamanteus*, unyielding.

"Don't smack your lips," Eunice said to Terry. "If a bite's too big to shut on, make a smaller bite of it."

"Yes ma'am."

"Don't say ma'am to me, either."

"Yes ma'am."

McCree passed his jar to Eunice and she helped herself to several small swallows, winced, handed it back.

"Can I have a taste?" Terry asked.

McCree gave it to him and Terry took a sip of the liquid, felt it sear to his innards, a lingering kerosene scent in his mouth.

"I don't like it," Terry said.

"Didn't think you would."

"I have some?" LuBelle asked.

McCree handed it to her with one hand, spearing more snake meat with the other. LuBelle put her tongue in the tilted jar, withdrew it, face contorted. "Tastes like coal oil smells."

"It does," McCree agreed.

"How come you drink it then?" Terry asked, speaking to McCree and Eunice.

"Punishing myself for long-ago sins," McCree said. Eunice laughed.

"What kind of sins?" LuBelle questioned.

"Minor infractions, mostly against the flesh," McCree stated. Eunice laughed again.

"Now and again, taking the Lord's name in vain," McCree added.

The sun was settling behind the tops of Australian pines, making tatted patterns through the topmost branches. Crickets had begun the first evening serenade. They sat around the fire, lying back against a tree, bucket or stump, watching the embers pulling ashen blankets over the reddish glow below.

"I had aplenty," Eunice said, refusing McCree's second jar. McCree took noisy, sucking sips, exhaled a sigh of satisfaction and began cutting a plug from a tobacco patty he carried in his top pocket. He offered this around, the children soberly refusing, then put it away.

"I saw a wonderful thing today," McCree said, settling back. "I saw a snake eat a buzzard's egg."

"You did?" Terry slipped nearer. McCree took LuBelle under one arm, Terry under the other, sharing his leaning spot.

"Commenced to eating that egg with a head no wider than my thumb. The egg was big as this—" He showed three fingers wide, "I seen that before, but it always confounds me. Egg so smooth and that snake just unhinges his jaw, his bottom jaw stretches apart and he ain't got no place to hang a fang; still he does it and down it goes. A big bulge like a tater in a long sock. He'd have eaten more, but Mrs. Buzzard came back right about then, mad with the snake, and me for letting the snake do that."

"Why didn't you stop him?" LuBelle asked.

"Ain't my right to do it," McCree said. "Snakes got to eat just like the rest of us folks. He was hungry, he found the egg and it was his to eat. People who go around trying to choose up sides with nature do no living thing a favor. But I don't suppose Mrs. Buzzard would agree."

LuBelle had her head against McCree's chest, eyes catching the last of the firelight, reflecting it at Terry, who assumed the same position and stared at her across McCree's body. The old man smelled like cured tobacco, his breath a miasma of the weed he chewed. His words came to Terry's ears two ways, from overhead in words, from within a comforting hum behind a rib cage.

"Some of these days a gator or cougar is going to feed on my bones," McCree said.

"Hush such," Eunice said, but not firmly.

"As it should be. I been eating their kind nigh onto eighty-three years, more or less."

LuBelle's eyes fluttered, closed. Fluttered, closed.

"Go to bed, child," Eunice admonished.

"Let her be," McCree squeezed LuBelle slightly.

Bullfrogs burping, tree frogs in key on a higher note, crickets fiddling, cicadas chirping, wind whispering, bellies filled, pine smoke holding off mosquitoes, the final light of day gone, Terry sighed deeply, eyes closing.

"Where you reckon that boy's mama be?" Eunice asked softly.

"Says he ain't got none."

"No mama?"

"Says that."

"Dressed the way he do? He got a mama."

McCree lifted Terry aside, putting him on a mat of fallen pine needles. He carried LuBelle to the house and placed her in bed, covering her over with a thin sheet to ward off pests.

"Got a daddy then," Eunice said, when McCree returned.

"Says not."

"You believing that?"

McCree gazed down at Terry, sleeping. "I tell you about believing, Eunice. I believe what he believes, even when I believe it ain't true. What he believes is what is."

McCree shook Terry gently. "Little Hawk?" He shook again. "Little Hawk, the owls are coming out to play."

MICHELLE RICHMOND

The Last Bad Thing

I saw him at Sabrina's on Seventh Street. I left without speaking to him, and for the next two days hated myself for allowing him to pass so quietly through my life. When I returned two nights later, he was there, wearing the same vest, holding the same stance. I gave him my address. He wrote his name with a nub of a pencil on someone else's business card. By the time I left New York and headed home to Mobile, the "I" in Ivan had already begun to rub off.

Since then, he has been writing me. In his first letter, Ivan explained that he teaches math at Rye Country Day School, but his National Guard unit has been called up and the address on the business card will no longer be valid. The address I have now begins with the letters SPC, followed by Ivan's social security number, followed by more words and numbers I can't pronounce, and all I can deduce is that he is stationed somewhere in Saudi Arabia.

I am only the second person he has ever met from Alabama. In my letters, I try to explain what it is like.

The beaches to the south justify this state's existence. They make up for our governor, for Mobile politics. The dogwoods and azaleas make a pretty good case for us too. I have been to the California coast and it can't compare to ours. There is such a sense of spaciousness here, of temporal ease. Most other places I have been left me feeling closed in. But there is something to be said for tight spaces. Otherwise, I wouldn't be moving to New York.

Here is what I know. It is Ramadan. Many times a day the people come out of their homes—the men and boys white-robed, the women cloaked in black—and bow toward Mecca. From their apartments the American soldiers can hear them chanting and wailing. Everything white, and the sound of all those voices, and inside their rooms the Americans read love letters and play Nintendo.

I will tell you what moves me: a slow swing on the saxophone, chocolate, a man alone in a restaurant reading a book, womanhood. The boy in my neighborhood who watched me this afternoon as I walked by.

He was twelve or thirteen and had just set a sprinkler out on his lawn. He stood by his door, watching. The shower caught me as I passed. I admired him for not looking away when I saw him, for being on that edge where he is deciding how he will live his life. I smiled at him and thought of the boys I knew when I was his age. Of Jamie, who gave me my first kiss.

I was fourteen. I was spending the night with my friend Andrea, whose parents were away. I didn't tell my own parents that Jamie would be there—Jamie who was eighteen and had introduced himself to me and Andrea at a youth evangelism conference in Lookout Mountain, Tennessee. He claimed to be Canadian, said he spoke impeccable French. "I may not look muscular, but I have wiry strength," he said, and he broke a broomstick over his knee to prove it. We watched the 1984 Olympics on TV, nestled on the couch like lovers who had been together for years. That was the year May Lou Retton ran off with two gold medals. If you were an American girl and your parents had said dream big, you wanted to be Mary Lou. She represented the best of what a girl could be.

The next morning Jamie kissed me by the window as my father's dark blue Chevrolet pulled into Andrea's driveway. I am certain that my father saw us. On the way home from Andrea's, my mind was on the thing that was between us now, my father and me, and I didn't know what I would say to him about the boy in the window. But when he said, "You have to listen," he didn't talk to me about Jamie. He said, "Mr. Carlisle is dead."

Mr. Carlisle was a friend of the family, a man who had been coming to my birthday parties for as long as I could remember. When my mother was in the hospital after a car accident years earlier, the accident that left her nose slightly off kilter, it was Mr. Carlisle who picked my sister and me up from school and took us to Dairy Queen. His house was full of animals he had shot and stuffed, the walls decorated with antlers and skins. A drunk driver had hit him head-on while he was driving home late from work, while I was watching the Olympics, holding hands with a guy I hardly knew. Mr. Carlisle's jeep landed upside down in a ditch. The picture that came to me, that day and for years after, was a picture of four tires turned up to the sky, so still beneath the moon, and underneath the tires, somewhere down below, the body of the man we had known. For years I felt responsible for Mr. Carlisle's death. It is not unusual for Baptist children to feel this way. Whenever something terrible happens to someone you love, you automatically think of the last bad thing you did and wonder if it is somehow connected to the tragedy. And you wonder when a friend or a cousin will do something equally bad, something unspeakable, and exactly when it will come back to you in the form of disease or disaster.

Pardon me for talking about the weather, but it's relevant. Here it is tempting 80. Yesterday I wore a tank top and shorts well into the evening, when it began to cool. The driveway has already begun its annual upheaval. The asphalt softens, breaks against the pressure of the giant mushrooms that push their way through like nobody's business. The mushrooms have thick, wide caps, three to four inches in diameter. Here, it all comes down to who is the strongest. Perhaps it is this way everywhere. Do you think?

I went to elementary school with a girl named Amanda Ruth. In kindergarten, our sleeping mats were right next to each other. Mine was red, hers blue. We had just learned to print the letters of the alphabet. We printed our names on our mats with magic markers in thick, ungraceful letters. And like this, we claimed them as our own.

The girls slept on one side of the room, the boys on the other. The boys' sleeping mats lay beside the windows. They would lie on their backs, eyes open, looking out, I thought, at everything green. I envied this vision. I wanted to know who was walking in the courtyard, what the sun was doing in the sky.

Amanda Ruth would never go to sleep at nap time. She stayed awake, lying on her side, trying to get me to talk to her. "I'm scared," she would whisper. "Don't go to sleep." So I would whisper back to her, lying in the shadows, and I don't know what we talked about but I know it was delicious, to be such intimate friends, to talk so quietly, knowing the danger. When Ms. Grimes heard us talking she would call us up to the front of the room and slap our wrists hard with a plastic ruler. Afterwards, I would finger the rectangular red welt on my wrist, write my initials on the welt with my fingernail.

We went to chapel every morning and prayed the prayers they taught us, rhymed prayers that made no sense. We wore navy jumpers with navy button-downs underneath, navy knee socks and saddle shoes. Once a month we had hem check, and we never knew when it was coming. All the girls lined up in front of the room, kneeling. Ms. Grimes went down the row with a measuring tape and made sure our dresses came at least two inches below our knees. Twice in one year, my hem was too short. I lined up single file behind Ms. Grimes with the other girls whose uniforms exposed some soft-haired slice of little girl leg, and we marched to the office. Then the football coach took us into the office one by one, and we held down the backs of our skirts while he gave us three whops with the paddling board.

There, in your navy jumper and knee socks, you never thought to question any of it.

In Mobile it has been raining for weeks now, but it doesn't thunder.
I send these letters to Ivan in Saudi Arabia, and I tell him only the barest and safest details of my life. His letters to me are brief, filled with numerical references: 164 cases of sanitary napkins buried in the sand because things are coming to an end and there is no way his unit can bring home all the supplies they've accumulated; 32 days since the war ended and no telling when he'll get to come home; 16 weeks since he saw me sitting alone in a corner booth at Sabrina's; 7 days of quiet rain outside his apartment building in Al Khubar; 129 high school math students back in Riverdale, New

York awaiting his return. He says that numbers are his strong suit and words never add up right. I will have to imagine the rest.

Looking out my window at the rain that doesn't stop. I know that this is how it is in Saudi Arabia—deep, thunderless rains. There the orange earth whips up in clouds and comes at you like a monster, until the rain comes and soothes the rage.

Now, the rain hits the sun lamp on the ceiling like pebbles, beats the grass with an incessant thud, hammers the house into the soft earth. We created the house and the house creates the wound and the rain drives the wound in deeper.

It is something to think about, the orange earth rising in a fury of particles, rising and subsiding in the place where everything but the earth is white. The apartment buildings are white. Americans there for the war sunbathe on top of them when there is nothing else to do. There is often nothing else to do. Inside, just Nintendo, and books and magazines sent from home, sent from students in New York who beg, *Come home sooooon! Why are they keeping you there?*

The mosque sits on the edge, tempts the sea, and the mosque is white.

I have moved in with my family while I decide what to do with my life. It's nice being home, settling into the old routines. In this house, I become a child again.

We have just had our evening meal, sat around the big, rectangular table like the family that we are. We held hands and said the blessing. "Dear God, thank you for our food, thank you for everything you have given us, please take care of Gran-Gran and Grandmother and Granddaddy and everybody we love, in Jesus' name we pray, Amen." I say the entire prayer in one breath. I have been saying the same prayer since I was six.

Everyone has his or her turn to pray. Mostly "her," because the only "he" is our father. He is outnumbered. His prayer always begins, "Lord, bless this food that we are about to eat." Each of us has one prayer that we have been repeating for years at the dinner table. Except the youngest sister. She's fifteen. She gets creative. Sometimes she says, "Dear God, please help me not to get fat, since Mom put a ton of butter in these beans." I think we are all a bit envious of the way she talks to God.

There are five hundred churches in the city of Mobile. That's 500. *I have only been to three of them.*

Just lately we have begun fragmenting. I told my family I was moving to New York. I'm not sure why. I have an older sister who is in love and wants to marry and live in Atlanta. The youngest one is going to be a missionary, live in the jungle and eat roots and berries. She also would like a house by the ocean, and a mountain chalet. "You can't buy anything on a missionary's salary," I tell her.

My mother is proud of her, but worried. She sits at the table and listens to our plans, drinks her coffee black. She traces the scars on the Formica tabletop with her fingers. There was a time, when the table was new, that she guarded it like her own children. She kept it safe from our childhood scissors and markers, protected it with place mats when we ate. For my mother, things have always been hard to come by. I think she is resigned now to their inevitable disintegration, to the way her children, unthinking, destroy the things she has acquired. She traces the scars we have made—slowly, thoughtfully—and I notice her hands are getting older. The veins are thick, bulky. I look at them how they are pumping life through her body, pumping life through us all.

She used to be a nurse and got strong from squeezing the little black rubber bags on the ends of the blood pressure gauges. When I was small I used to get her to take my blood pressure. I remember the wide band around my arm that fastened with a Velcro strip, the way it went on loose and then she started working that rubber pump, and the band got fat with air around my arm, tingling. My mother no longer nurses, she hasn't touched a blood pressure pump in years, but even now she can open any jar you give her. She holds the jar tight under the left arm, and with her right hand gives the lid an unholy twist. She is beautiful, with hazel eyes that none of us got. My father's eyes are brown. Sometimes she seems like the happiest person on earth, like when she jiggles her hips and cups my face in her hand and sings, "You're still my little baby, even if you're going off to New York to live with all the crazies."

Sometimes this fact crosses my mind and I don't know what to do with it; we are all leaving her.

With the letters, Ivan sends rolls of film which he asks me to develop. In the one-hour photomat, the man behind the counter issues orders to his wife, who is small and wears a yellow smock. I recognize them from my parents' church. He is a deacon; she teaches children's choir. They have the look of salvation about them, the resigned faces of people who understand that they have been pressed eternally into the service of the Lord.

"Our son didn't get to go," the woman says, sliding the envelope across the counter to me. "He's stuck in Fort Bragg. Your man's the lucky one."

Driving home, I think of the sealed envelope beside me on the seat, the images concealed there. I expect to see pictures of soldiers horsing around in Saudi shops, playing backgammon inside the white rooms of their apartment buildings. In my old bedroom of my old house I open the envelope, remove the glossy photos from their plastic sleeve, lean my back against the pillow. For a moment, the walls of my bedroom disappear and I enter this foreign landscape; for a moment I believe that I am there:

I am walking. It is dusk. The road from Kuwait. Telephone lines slope from pole to pole, cable-sure in the clear sky. Nothing breathes beside the cleared road. The buses rest on their sides, windows gone in February's dry heat. The bodies have been covered, the charred messes swept over with sand.

This desert valley, stunned by death, sinks below the shadows of sand hills at dusk. The tanks lie side to side like dominoes. I overturn a fender with my boot and find an arm in its brown sleeve, intact, leaving its isolated imprint in the sand.

This is the truth. The solid things remain: a looted yellow tricycle with one twisted wheel, small refrigerators, two brown throw pillows gathering grit. I reach destruction's end, leave the stolen goods behind-the diaries, the missile scraps with their magic marker dedications. I am stunned at dusk by the ease of death, the way a gutted truck, upturned, lifts its unharmed tires toward this clarity of sky.

There are no rivers, no cool mirages. The moon dusts its dull reflection over the valley.

There is more to tell about Amanda Ruth. When I was a sophomore in high school I learned that she had been raped behind the skating rink in Tillman's Corner, right across the street from my parents' church. The church is huge and white, with a steeple so high it seems like it is punching a hole in the sky. When I was a child the steeple terrified me, the way it reached so high above the telephone lines and traffic lights, so high above the skating rink. Everything around the church looked insignificant in comparison. On clear nights when the moon shone brightly, the steeple cast its long, pointed shadow over the parking lot. The girls going into the skating rink, in their tight jeans and soft, pastel-colored sweaters made a game of walking straight down the middle of the shadow.

The skating rink is a rectangular building with aluminum siding, alternating yellow and blue panels. I used to go there with my older sister on weekends. I stopped going the summer before my eighth grade year. So did most of my friends. But not Amanda Ruth. By the time I was in the tenth grade, Amanda Ruth was a year behind me in school. The rape happened in February. *February is the coldest month in Mobile. Everyone freezes because no one owns winter coats, just denim jackets and windbreakers. The winter always takes us by surprise, so suddenly it comes, as if from nowhere.* I guess Amanda Ruth was probably chilled to the bone the night she went behind the skating rink with one of the referees to smoke a cigarette. He knocked her around with his fists before he did it, slammed her head against the aluminum siding. He got her pregnant. She had the baby.

Sometimes, still, I see the tires, turning, upturned in the night, beside the black road, and no one has found him yet. The other driver goes on, swerves his way into the darkness. The wheels turn, and slow, and no more. The hubcaps, in the moonlight, cast a metallic glow.

A cat emerges from the woods across the road. He sees a jeep, ascends, stands upon a tire. He arches momentarily, a hiss to no one. He settles, declaring it home.

And underneath it all, Mr. Carlisle, in his silent contortion, unfound.

Americans there for the war are wondering when they will get to come home. They sign their names on a piece of white paper that is stuck to a clipboard. The clipboard has a chewed, army-issue pencil tied to it with string. After they sign they are allowed to take the video camera with them. They have to return it in four hours, but that is enough time to ride around Al Khubar in the back of an Army truck. They make wide turns, and the Saudis in their white cars smile and wave their white-sleeved arms at the Americans.

There is a tall American with dark hair whose fatigues are loose from the weight he has lost on his six-month diet of Ramen noodles and saltines. He points to the sign of the Phuk-Et Restaurant and makes crude, quiet jokes about the name. It is not the Ivan I thought I knew, the one I was attracted to that first night at Sabrina's; I wonder if in so short a time, five months, this place has changed him. There is laughter in the background, from behind the camera.

A woman in a long black robe crosses the street, slowly and with her head bowed. Her hair and face are covered, her wrists and ankles. She walks behind a man in his white robe and a child, a boy, who smiles and waves at the Americans. Soon this man and this boy and this woman in her life-long mourners' clothes will bow toward Mecca. They will sing-chant a prayer, high-pitched and broken, and it will remind you of charred arms and sand-dune graves, but it will be a prayer of praise, not suffering. This woman will hold the edges of her black robe and feel something like love for the boy and the man. The boy and the man will be yards away, facing the same direction, their white robes bright in the sun. The child will think of his mother and look to her, and see her bent and black and formless, and the father will not think of her or look to her or remember what has been.

I noticed last night for the first time how crooked the bedroom is, the angles all wrong, the whole room sinking and slanting toward the big white door with its tiny thumbtack scars. *My biggest flaw: I am never satisfied with the state of things.*

The decorations on that door change weekly. Last week, it was a silk scarf with a Picasso print on it, something I bought from a tall skinny man outside a bookstore in Manhattan. He wanted thirty for it. I bartered him down to ten. The picture is of a woman. Half of her face is green, half hot pink. Her breasts are pink with black nipples. One arm is bright yellow and shaped like a banana. She sits in a green chair. Thick black lines break her body into pieces. I admire Picasso for his understanding of what womanhood is—always being broken apart, then trying to put yourself back together, nothing ever fitting quite right. But he angers me by making her face into a series of vaginal slits. Her eyes, her ears, are like vaginas splitting. As if this is what we are at the core.

This week, a print of a Spanish lady dancing in a long peach dress in a courtyard. People sit around her clapping and bobbing their heads to the music. When I close my eyes, I can hear her feet tapping on the brick. One hand is raised up behind her, the long fingers reaching, as if she is touching the fingertips of God himself. I want to be a Spanish dancer in a courtyard full of strangers. I long for romance, that lusty Old World love.

Sometimes at night when I lie awake, thinking, my mother comes into my room and sits on the edge of my bed. She tucks one foot underneath her, wraps her arms around a throw pillow, and like this we talk. Her face is shiny from night cream. She surveys the scars I have made on the walls of my bedroom where I have tacked up photographs, strange Picasso prints. They are from when he was younger, images clear and lucid, nothing disintegrating. A woman bends gauntly over an ironing board, her black hair hanging toward her hands. Her days are filled with ironing, warm fabrics beneath her fingertips, steam curling in hot wisps, entering her throat.

"You should go to New York with me," I say, and mean it. I would like to have her there with me, this beautiful Southern woman in a strange and alien place. I would like for Ivan to meet her. She says New York is dangerous. I say Mobile is dangerous too. I tell her the water in Mobile will give her cancer. I tell her everything nasty from the whole country floats down to Mobile Bay. I tell her that these things I am saying are true, that I learned them in college.

Here, too, is what I know. I know that my mother will never leave this place, and I am beginning to understand why. She is not in love with the city itself, but with the house where her children grew up. The children that she knew, and are gone, somehow inhabit these beloved rooms. Somehow they are here, and they are not elsewhere. She is the only one in the world who truly knows these children. We, changed, do not know them. Our father does not know them.

I think of Ivan in the place where he is now, the place it seems he will always be, and I wonder what sounds, somehow, may reach him. Does he hear the long, enraptured wail of Ramadan?

I say the word and it sounds like this:

Ramadan.

And again.

I do not want to be there in this strange place, where the women cast their impassioned prayers toward Mecca. They are shadows, bent and black, against the whitest landscape.

Ramadan, I say. And my body feels bloated and gone, like a lost prayer, like a thing unanswered.

I admire you for your focus, for knowing what you want. Perhaps you are like this because of your affinity for numbers. Everything for you is so defined. Everything has set parameters. I wonder if we will ever master the differences between us, make sense of what separates us.

I don't tell him that two cats are going at it on the driveway. With cats it is always a struggle, always like rape. I want to pull the male cat off the female, but there are some things you cannot interfere with. It is not my business to throw this moment on a hot driveway with the cats screaming and the asphalt splitting into chaos.

In Ivan's letters he writes of alien things. Of theorems and theories, of the way my shoulders, bared to the cold, moved him those two nights at Sabrina's. He speaks of the angles my body makes, as if my body were a definitive structure, a mathematical thing. I want to say to him, *Numbers will not save you.* I want to say to him, *They will not save the world.* But I choose my words too carefully. I tell him such small things.

Mary Louise Robison

Baby in the Cold Frame

Itta Oka Massapeka Gillum chanted planting songs as she crumbled and raked leaf mold through the soil with her redbone fingers, the palmsides pale as walnuts. On a cool Alabama morning in 1949, Itta squatted in the sand next to the cold frame with its earthen floor. She had cobbled the glass box together herself, making a lid from a window begged from Judge Talmadge when he razed the old servant's quarters where Itta had lived as a child.

"Miss Sara! Baby, come on and run your fingers round in this dirt," said Itta. "Can't you just feel the aliveness pumping through it? My Chickasauga grandmother taught me that God's in the ground and breathes the seeds into life."

The small blonde girl slid her hands into the fragrant soil up to her wrists, moving her fingers like earthworms in its coolness. She imitated Itta's combing motions. Itta resumed her song. Her voice twined like honeysuckle around Sara who crouched companionably against her hipbone. A doll, Marguerite, sprawled in Sara's lap, warming her canvas torso between Sara's legs and chest. Sara hummed along with Itta, pretending to follow the words. Itta was preparing the soil for lettuce seeds. Six year-old Sara Jane Talmadge was praying for a baby.

Itta's daughter, Julia Johnson, the Talmadge's cook, had a brown baby boy that she let Sara hold. Sara's parents had looked at each other and laughed when Sara told them she wanted a baby girl, just like her favorite baby-doll, Marguerite, only alive: a soft warm baby all her own to sleep next to her bed in Marguerite's bassinet. Or maybe right in the bed with her under the covers. Sometimes she brought Marguerite into her bed, but the doll's molded head and limbs hurt her when she rolled over and seemed to crowd her out of the narrow bed. Marguerite had sculpted hair, a blunt nose and real eyelashes. Her brown eyes closed when Sara kissed her goodnight and tucked her in, and opened when Sara got her up in the morning.

Itta said, "The moon's in just the right phase for planting. If we can get these seeds in the ground now, every one of them will come up. Dirt this rich would grow just about anything."

Sara held Marguerite's wrist and smoothed the fine surface with the stiffly curled fingers. She walked Marguerite a few steps across, leaving small footprints in the floor of the cold frame.

"It feels good," she said. "Marguerite likes it too. Itta, is this dirt rich enough to grow a baby?"

Itta's astringent gaze touched Sara's face. "I don't reckon so," she said. "I've helped to birth many a baby in my time. This birthing business is always taken care of inside the house, with a knife under the bed or tucked under the pallet to cut the pain."

"Did you help my mama to birth me?"

"No, child, your mama went to the hospital."

"Is that how Julia got her new baby, at the hospital?"

"I pulled my grandbaby, Julia's little Punkin, out myself. The birthing's only the last part of it. My Chickasauga grandmother told me, and I told Julia: if you want a man or a baby to come to you, you got to bury a charm that they can't resist, attract them to you like a magnet."

Sara had an idea. "Itta, would you help me plant a baby? She could grow right in this cold frame along with the lettuce."

"What you want with a baby, child? You're not much more than a baby yourself. If Itta's still around when you grown, we'll see what we can do. Come on, let's walk across the pasture and see if Polly's done with her chores." Polly was Itta's eleven year-old granddaughter, who lived with her parents and baby brother in a two-room cabin that belonged to Judge Talmadge. Mrs. Talmadge paid Polly a dime a week to look after Sara every morning except Sunday.

Itta went on, "Her daddy, C.C. Johnson, wants her to put in a little garden of her own this year. Maybe you can help her. When they were boys together, C.C. Johnson and your daddy used to roam all over Cockrell County, from one end of Lubbub Creek to the other. They spent more time together than you and Polly. I already told you that Punkin's named after your daddy—his real name is Bonn Talmadge Johnson. You two girls can play with him for awhile."

Polly and Punkin were waiting on the shady porch. He kicked and laughed on a quilt pallet. They carried him and the pallet to the chinquapin oak where they liked to play house. Sara held Punkin on her lap and pretended that he was her own sweet baby. When Punkin fell asleep, she and Polly played with Marguerite.

Sara said, "Polly, do you know how to charm up a baby?"

"Granny says that like attracts like. If you want sweetness in your life, you bury cinnamon and sugar. If you want a man, you make a man-doll and bury it with a new penny. If you can write, you write down his qualities, and bury the paper wrapped around a buffalo nickel. As soon as the paper melts into the ground, he'll be on your doorstep. If you can't write, you whisper his picture into the buffalo's ear. You've got to give the dirt something you cherish to get what you want."

"I want a brown-eyed baby that looks just like Marguerite. What can we do to get me one?"

"I'll have to study on it, see what we might do. Want me to carry you for a ride on my bicycle?"

Sara's father had painted an old bicycle silver, put new tires on it, squirted oil into the sprockets and presented it to Polly so she could ride Sara and Marguerite around the small town. Sara liked to wrap her arms around Polly's waist, lean into her ribby back and listen to her heart beat as they rode from one end of Jemison to the other. Mrs. Talmadge had an account at the drugstore. The druggist added a nickel to the bill for an ice cream cone. Sara felt grown up when she placed the orders. She and Polly sat on the curb in the sun and licked vanilla ice cream from pointed cones. When Sara and her mother went to the drugstore for a Coca-Cola, her mother did the ordering. They sat on curly wire chairs next to the soda fountain, inside, where it was cool.

In the kitchen that night, without asking permission, Sara hid a paring knife in Marguerite's underpants, wrapping it in a dishrag so the doll wouldn't get hurt. After her mother had kissed her goodnight, Sara placed the knife carefully on the floor under her bed. In the glow of the nightlight, she pulled the doll's pink dress over her composition head and threaded her stiff arms into a nightgown. Rocking the bassinet to help Marguerite fall asleep, Sara sang, "Hush little baby, don't say a word, Mamma's gonna buy you a mockingbird."

Sara knelt down beside her junior bed, folded her hands, squinched her blue eyes and promised God anything His heart desired if only He would breathe Marguerite into life like He did Adam and Eve. Sara expected to be awakened the next morning by a wriggling, gurgling baby girl.

Sara dreamed that she was lost in the woods. She was running and stumbling in the dark, miles away from anybody who could help her. A red-eyed wolf was chasing her, snuffling and panting at the back of her neck. Just when he was about to bite her head off at the neck, she woke up, shaking and breathing hard. She needed to go to the bathroom, but didn't dare hang her foot over the side of the bed, much less put her feet on the floor and walk to the bathroom. The wolf or something with men's hands lived under her bed at night.

The next morning she opened her eyes, sure that she heard a baby calling for her, but Marguerite lay motionless in her bassinet. Although disappointed that God hadn't breathed her alive, Sara felt a familiar upsurge of love when she looked at her doll. She picked her up, kissed her and dressed her. Sara hid the knife under her pillow.

Marguerite didn't wake up alive in spite of Sara's putting the knife under the bed every night for three weeks. One night, the moon was full outside her window as well as in her dream. Exhausted and frantic, she ran into a clearing just as the wolf's lips touched her neck.

"Enough," commanded a tall woman who stepped into the moonlight and scooped Sara into her strong arms. Sara leaned against the woman's soft buckskin bosom and played with the fringe, bathed in the scent of violets. The wolf somersaulted around them as they flew to a sunny meadow filled with laughing babies of every color and size. Sara sat in the redbone woman's lap as they played in turn with every one of the babies. The sun was shining hot, yet rain streamed gently through the sunlight, cooling them. In the light of a triple rainbow, Sara finally found her baby, the one she had been looking for, lying in a bed of wild violets.

"Tell Polly to help you get ready for the next full moon. Trade me something you love, if you want your wish to come true," said the tall redbone woman, speaking with Itta's voice.

For the next four weeks, hidden by a wall of growing corn, the girls dug in Polly's garden, adding leaf mold they brought from the woods near Lubbub Creek, until the dirt was as rich and smooth as the dirt in Itta's cold frame. They drew pictures of the baby and buried them with cinnamon sugar. They went about their usual business of riding the bicycle and playing with Punkin, so nobody would suspect that they were conjuring up a baby.

"You've got to bury something valuable," said Polly. "You can't dig it up or even think about looking at it for three whole days. If you can wait that long, Granny says your heart's desire will come to you."

Sara mulled over what to bury, but really, she knew all along it had to be Marguerite. She knew she'd miss her doll, but she wouldn't need her anyway if there was a real baby sleeping in the bassinet. She felt sad, but she knew there was no other way to draw the baby to her. Marguerite would understand.

The day before the full moon was the hottest one yet. Mrs. Talmadge asked Polly to ride Sara to the town's only swimming pool, so Sara could cool off. The back of Polly's dress was wet from the effort of peddling up MacShan Road to the pool, so on this trip Sara didn't rest her cheek on it to listen to the heart beat. Polly wasn't allowed to dip even one toe in water. While Sara splashed with the other white children, Polly waited outside the fence with Marguerite. Sara was afraid that the doll's face and limbs would dissolve if she ever got any water on her skin, so she counted on Polly to keep her safe and dry.

Sara played in the water for about an hour. Polly waited under a pecan tree. When Sara climbed into her place on the back of the bicycle, she noticed that Polly was in a bad mood. "Sulling," Mrs. Talmadge called it. Polly acted that way sometimes when she and Sara went into town. Sara pressed her wet front against the back of Polly's thin cotton dress. Polly's heart was beating faster than usual. Sara made her stop at the drugstore. Polly seemed to feel better after she drank some ice water and finished her vanilla cone. They whispered about their upcoming night's work.

"I'll come and get you tonight, as soon as the moon comes up," said Polly. "I'll whistle like a whippoorwill and tap at your window."

Sara was excited as she prepared to go to sleep. She cried a little as she tucked Marguerite into her bassinet for the last time. She finally fell asleep and dreamed of the wolf. Just when he was about to catch her, he changed into a friendly white dog and barked, "Wake up!"

She got up, put on her clothes and dressed Marguerite in a lace-trimmed dress, Sara's own christening gown that her mother kept wrapped in tissue paper in the cedar chest. Sara slipped out the back door, being careful not to wake her parents. She couldn't wait to show them her new baby. It would be such a good surprise for them.

It was a clear full moon night. Polly wasn't there yet. Sara hugged Marguerite and caressed her face as they squatted under the window. The moon moved across the sky. Polly still didn't come. Sara's heart pounded when she heard rustling at the corner of the house. It was the neighbor's cat. She waited a while longer.

Her parents did not allow her to walk across the pasture by herself, even in daylight. She was afraid to try it, but even more afraid to miss her chance to get a real baby. Praying she wouldn't step on a rattlesnake, run into the wolf or a booger man, Sara hurried across the pasture, hugging Marguerite. They arrived safely. She gently laid Marguerite in the hole that she and Polly had prepared. Marguerite closed her eyes and reclined on her back in the soft loamy bed. Anticipation mixed with tears as Sara sifted dirt around Marguerite's head and over her long white dress. She jumped when Polly stepped through the wall of rustling corn stalks. Polly knelt down to help her fill the hole.

"Where were you?" said Sara. "Don't get dirt in her eyes and nose! She's got to be able to breathe."

Polly put a dime on Marguerite's throat. "So your baby girl will have a golden voice," she said.

After they were done, Marguerite's pale face gleamed in the moonlight, as did her fingers, her dimpled knees and toes. The dress and the rest of her were buried in the rich, dark soil. Polly lightly covered Marguerite with a layer of pine straw, then fragrant pine boughs. Taking her hand, Polly walked Sara home, their warm hands stuck together with pine resin.

The minute she woke up the next morning, Sara looked in the bassinet. It was empty. No gurgling baby was waiting there for her. She hurried through her breakfast of grits and scrambled eggs so she could play with Polly and Punkin under the chinquapin tree. Sara wanted to check to see if Marguerite was comfortable in the ground, but Polly reminded her that they'd break the spell if they looked. Sara talked about how much fun they'd have playing with her baby when she came, wondering if she'd turn up alive in the bassinet or in the cold frame or if she'd come crawling out of the garden. Polly seemed tired.

"I've decided to name my baby Marguerite Itta Oka Talmadge," said Sara.

"That's my Granny's name," said Polly. "You can't have it. I'm going to call my own little girl Itta Oka. Why don't you name that baby for some of your own kinpeople?"

"It's not fair. Y'all named Punkin after my daddy. What if I get me a boy next time? What can I call him?" Turning to pick up Punkin, Sara ignored Polly. Sara figured she could give her baby any name she liked. Itta didn't belong only to Polly. Sometimes Sara wished that Itta was her granny too. Maybe she'd call the baby "Margher Itta," rather than "Marguerite." That would make Polly really mad.

Both girls were sulling as Polly walked Sara home across the pasture. Sara's anger turned to sadness, so she moved closer to Polly and slipped her hand into hers. "I'm sorry, Polly," she said. "I won't take your granny's name for my baby. You can name your own little girl, when you get one, after her."

"All right," said Polly. "I hope your baby comes to you real soon. Not me though. I've got enough to do looking after you and Punkin."

That night, Sara snuck the knife back into the kitchen drawer. Fretful, afraid to close her eyes, she couldn't find a cool spot anywhere in bed. She worried about Marguerite. What if a snake crawled over her face or a wild dog dug her up and tore off her arms? Only by holding Marguerite's blanket to her cheek, singing the mockingbird song over and over again and pretending she was leaning into the soft sweet bosom of the redbone woman, was Sara finally able to sleep.

She woke up with great excitement the next morning. She hoped to find the baby bouncing in the bassinet, holding her arms out, wanting to be picked up. The bassinet was empty, but it was only the first day. Sara and Polly spent the morning riding around on the bicycle. They ate ice cream. They lay on the pallet, making up stories about the cloud shapes they saw through the chinquapin leaves. Sara talked about her new baby. Polly was quiet and polite.

Only one more night to wait. Again, Sara had trouble falling asleep. Thunder and lightning woke her up about two o'clock. She sat straight up in her bed. "Oh, no!" Marguerite would be terrified out in the open garden. What if it starts raining? Wouldn't Marguerite's face slide off? Would the sawdust solidify in her body, the canvas turn black and rot like the old ropes and sacks in the barn? Sara knew that if she even looked at Marguerite, her real baby would be lost to her forever. But if she waited any longer, Marguerite would die. She couldn't stand the idea of abandoning Marguerite, but the thought of losing the love of her baby constricted Sara's chest and burst open a vault of unshed tears.

High winds whipped the trees outside her window. Lightning exploded in the sky. Thunder shook her bed. What if lightning struck and killed her as she ran across the pasture to rescue Marguerite? What if the real baby was already waiting for her in the garden, lost and crying inconsolably? Sara sat sobbing in the middle of her bed. She got out of bed, ignoring her terror of the men's hands that lived under it, and began pulling on her clothes. She knew what she had to do.

She heard the sound of windows being slammed shut all over the house. Her father rushed into Sara's room and closed the window with a bang. "Are you all right, Sara? Were you having a bad dream? What are you doing out of bed? Close your eyes for a minute, I'm going to turn on the overhead light."

Sara's father sat on the edge of the bed and put his arms around her. She sobbed uncontrollably, burrowing her face into the familiar daddy smell of his chest under the blue striped pajama top. "Daddy, Daddy, Daddy. Poor Marguerite, my baby, buried alive. We've got to help my baby with the golden voice, cold and lost in the rain. We can't leave them out in the storm, alone. The wolves will eat them. They'll be ruined."

"Whose baby are you talking about? Where is your doll? Where is Marguerite?"

"In Polly's garden. Let's go, Daddy. Please, let's go now. We can't wait any longer."

"It's too dangerous to go out in an electrical storm. I'd be like a lightning rod in the open pasture. I'll buy you another doll."

"I don't want another doll, I want Marguerite. I want my baby."

Her mother came into the room.

"She won't stop crying," he said. "I think she forgot and left her doll up at C.C. Johnson's garden. The way she's carrying on, you'd think she'd lost a real baby."

"Sara's just like you, you've both got an overactive imagination. We can't give in to her, she's already spoiled rotten."

"Rotten or not, I can't stand to hear her crying. She's frantic. There's a lull in the storm."

"I think it's a big mistake, giving in to her every whim. But I guess one more time won't make that big of a difference," she said, buttoning Sara into her red raincoat.

"Come on, Miss Sara, I'll carry you piggyback. We'll run over to the garden and see if we can find your baby. Just promise me you'll never pull a stunt like this again."

Sara snuffled against her father's neck, her legs tight around his waist as they hurried across the pasture, his galoshes clomping. The wind died down, the darkened garden was quiet. Sara listened with every drop of water in her being for the sound of a baby crying. Nothing moved, not even the cornstalks. Bonn Talmadge shone his big black flashlight between the rows of corn. A pale face gleamed near his right foot.

Sara heard a rustle; Polly and her father appeared. The men shook hands.

"Sara," said Polly. "Your baby's not here. We looked everywhere."

The flashlight shone on Marguerite's grave. Even though she was still lying on her back, now her brown eyes were wide open. Her hands and legs stuck out of the dirt, as it she were getting ready to run away. Sara knew then that the spell was broken. She had broken the spell. She had missed her chance for a real baby because she wanted one so bad that she couldn't wait long enough, because she couldn't bear to lose Marguerite. She hadn't been able to steel herself against the thought of Marguerite missing her in the night; terrified, melting, rotting, and crying. Her baby was gone forever.

After the garden had dried out somewhat, Sara and Polly squatted against each other, side-by-side, sadly sifting throught the dirt they had so carefully prepared. They found the dime. "Her golden voice," sighed Polly, pressing the dime to her own throat for a moment.

"We did the best we could," said Sara, putting her arm around Polly's waist, resting her cheek against Polly's shoulder. Marguerite warmed her torso between Sara's legs and chest.

"I know," said Polly. A redbird called from the chinquapin.

Marguerite never closed her brown eyes again, the wires inside had rusted. Her nose was scuffed, making her face more like the sphinx than ever. The color was gone from her cheeks and lips.

Sara's mother had to Clorox the christening gown twice. Then she sprinkled it with lemon juice and laid it in the sun on a patch of clean grass to bleach it out completely. Sara leaned against her and helped fold the snowy dress and wrap it in tissue paper to wait in the cedar chest for the next Talmadge baby to come along.

The following spring, Polly's garden was over-run with wild purple violets that seemed to come from nowhere. Every once in a while she and Sara found surprises when they least expected them. Sara unearthed a small china cup and saucer, sprinkled with painted violets. Polly dug up a silver dollar dated 1888, the year of Itta's birth. Sara's little sister, whom her parents named Marguerite after Grandmother Talmadge, was born later that summer, exactly one lunar year from the full moon night when Sara Jane Talmadge buried her doll.

Scarlett Saavedra

excerpted from Living in the River

Asheville, 1979

When I ran away from home the year I turned sixteen, I should have taken my brother Alex with me. Seven years later, he brought me home.

It was July. I was living then in the Outer Banks of North Carolina, where two brothers had learned to fly. The wind off the Atlantic delivered a desolate yet comforting music above the boom of the sea, and periodically the ocean washed upon the shore a bone, a long fin, the ear of some animal, as if piecing together all that she had destroyed long ago.

If the ocean reminds me of a mother, yet it is children, children only, that the waves imply. Running and laughing, the waves slacken for a moment in the wet sand, then lie listening on the colorless shore, until—dissatisfied, frightened—they draw back into the bosom of the horizon.

I had stayed in the Outer Banks awhile. Almost two years in Ocracoke. When the book store closed, I moved to Calabash where tourists go for fried fish. In Calabash I worked evenings waitressing at Bonney and Read's, a restaurant named for two female pirates who had taken refuge in the Outer Banks.

The summer trespass of tourists in 1978 brought money, more money than I'd ever made, but they interfered with the music of the wind. Hundreds of tourists glided in over the Pamlico Sound bridge. Above the twang of the country music and the clatter of plates, the noise of the surf was lost. It seemed like bad luck to make more noise than the ocean, in whose treacherous shifting sands scores of ships had wrecked. Even Blackbeard, who had lived a long life as a hellion, had died in these feared islands. So one day I hitched a ride on a fish truck bound for Asheville. I had the jones for a river anyway.

I found a river, but I didn't make it to the mountains. The truck driver was going to Asheville, and the plain poetry of its name hooked me. I also liked the name of its river—the French Broad. Walking down the gray streets of Asheville, North Carolina, was like entering a photograph from 1932. It seemed simple, honest as a woman pulling laundry from a front-porch washer. I didn't look long enough to see the sly, silent "e's" lurking in its name—

Asheville. By the time I discovered it, I was busted. Someone had broken into my room, found the money I'd stashed in my sock. But as soon as I could rub two hundred-dollar bills together, I would try Arden. Flat Rock, maybe, if they had a couple of diners.

In Asheville, I took a shine to a Victorian boarding house on Wolfe Street. I liked the name of the street. Also it was three blocks from the YMCA, which could always be counted on for having a 25-meter indoor pool. When I saw the third-story turret room, I knew it would be my room for awhile. I often dream of the varied rooms in which I have lived. I would have lived in more if I could have. A new room gives you a starting-over point in your life. In its emptiness and dust, dreams have space. And I especially liked this room: its marble fireplace, its single-pedestal lavatory, its old black bed. I envisioned myself propped up against it, reading away the hot Carolina afternoons. Many a night later I wished I had tried that bed out before signing up for it: at heart, its mattress was iron, too.

With the exception of the venerable landlady, I was the only female inhabitant in a house of about twenty men, most retired from the L and N Railroad, and each one tired and grizzled, each body rusted in the same way from the same kind of work. They even coughed alike. The coughs were not synchronized like the scratching of crickets. Rather, one hack from the second floor called up another from the fourth, just as one dog's bark sets off a whole mountain of barking dogs. The house itself rasped for breath.

In the dark, in a constellation of strangers, it occurred to me how alone I am. Orphaned and solitary as a star. Wasn't born that way. I am a twin; I have a twin brother, Alex. If no one else knows where I am, he always does.

Even though we were both Buck and Carmina's children, both born at the same time, our lives were turned in different directions. I was born with the sandy, freckled complexion of my Irish father and the small strong legs of my Puerto Rican mother; Alex is tall and slender like Buck, but stronger—his chest like dark carved marble. I am chatty as a creek; Alex is quiet as a river. I have dark brown eyes and they are nice, but the gaze of my left eye is cast slightly off and frozen, a defect; Alex's dark eyes are Spanish-beautiful, though they always look sad. Alex could have taken that Greyhound bus out of Columbus, Georgia, out of the chaos of Buck and Carmina's house, but he stayed because he is their beloved prince. He gets all the love. I would be jealous except that he is my prince, too. Upon his mighty wingspan, I pin my possibilities for flight.

If he were here now, I would not have to worry about the man who tries to break into my room. He will come at 2 a.m. when the bars close.

I stared at my doorknob until—this time at 1:56—the creaking of the stairs stopped and, in the light filtering in from the street, I saw the porcelain knob of the door glint with movement. I jumped out of bed and grabbed the small Coke bottle I kept handy. "Go away," I whispered in the crack at the door.

"Lemme in," he said, his voice low and slurred.

"Get out," I said louder. "Get out of here." I cracked the bottle over the marble door handle. Glass sprayed around my feet. I held the gleaming bottom half of the Coke bottle at the keyhole hoping he could glimpse its jagged curve. "I'll kill you. I've killed a better man than you," I snarled, my lips against the crack in the door.

Eventually he went away. After a while, in the cool of the dim gray morning, transient as a creek, I slept.

In the afternoons, I lingered at the Y. The landlady would phone me if the manager rang from the Sizzler steakhouse where I worked. I took comfort in the anonymity of water-streaked tiled walls in familiar shades of blue and yellow. Even the iron creak of old shower faucets was soothing. Despite a natural shyness, I blithely peeled off my clothes in the company of older women, who swam every day, and I strutted around the locker room naked, before snapping on my racing suit.

I had just completed the somersault of my eleventh lap, flip-turning off the back wall, when someone touched my ankle. A human touch is startling and intrusive in the underworld of the solitary swimmer, moving in dreams, blue water cut with light. It was the lifeguard, tall and plain as a stalk of corn. I swam back to the wall where he knelt in his faded red shorts.

He glanced down at a scrap of paper in his hand, then looked up at me. I think he was saying my name. I thought I heard the word "Alabama." I peeled the yellow cap off, shook water from my ears.

"Yeah. I'm Ava."

"A lady telephoned from," he glanced down at something scrawled on a YMCA calendar, "the Wolfe Street House. Said someone was trying to reach you. Do you know a Robert Elden Livingstone?"

Though I'd seen it on plenty of bills, I'd never heard anyone use Buck's real name. It startled me. I locked my arms on the edge of the pool and vaulted out of the water. I stood there trembling, near naked. Because my swimsuit was so worn, I held my arms around my chest, and while he talked, I studied the old women, ones who came every day, who pulled heavy-handedly through the water, their arm muscles anchored in arthritis, their faces drawn with anguish, as if they had been pulling themselves down these solitary lanes all their lives.

The lifeguard ran his fingers through his yellow hair. He said, "I'm just delivering a message, okay? All right?" He seemed to need a good joke.

"He said to tell you that an Alexander Livingstone is dead," the lifeguard told me. He said it like a question, the last words rising thin. "Do you know who I'm talking about?"

I looked at the idiot. "That's my brother, you big fuck. That's not funny."

He wet his lips, "I'm sorry, Miss. That's the name he told me to give you."

I could easily have slung him into the water by grabbing the gold cross dangling from his hairless chest. My toes nudged the cool cement edge of the pool. "You big fuck," I repeated and knifed back into the warm blue water. I swam underwater, my legs propelling me past the lifeguard chair, back to where the water lost its depth and shimmered against the blue walls like the shadows of children playing. I took a deep breath, reached the other side where I flipped, kicked off hard and came back for the twelfth lap with a butterfly, circling my strong arms, lifting high out of the water and surging forward with a great pull of my shoulders. I glared at the guard each time I surfaced; each time I filled my lungs, I glared at that skinny son-of-a-bitch still on his haunches at the opposite side of the pool, his hands hanging off his knees.

I am strong, and Alex—my twin brother—has always been stronger, always more beautiful. We were born together, we would die together. And I knew *I* was too damn tough to die. I'd even tried to a couple of times. I've tried to hold myself down at the bottom of the pool. It was impossible to stay down. God-damned Buck had to tell a better lie than that to get me home. I kept swimming, determined to finish my usual mile. I had thirty more laps to go. I switched to freestyle so that I would be submerged as much as possible, immune to the violence of sound, the heartbeats and exhalations of the swimmers smoothed into one near-silent murmur.

When I finished, I didn't look back at the guard or thank him as is my custom. Tingling from the workout, I soaped myself twice in the maypole of showers in which strangers with imperfect bodies turned themselves round slowly, rinsing, turning rosy, angelic, in the steam.

I cursed Buck Livingstone all the way home. I cursed him from the Boeing 707, six miles above the earth. I cursed the morning breaking like fire over the Smoky Mountains. Below the Nantahala River glinted like a machete. I cursed him over Altuna Dam. I cursed him over the whole town of Atlanta while a storm brewed black, and I dropped down out of the sky, mad as the devil. It was mid-morning. No way Buck Livingstone was even awake, much less at this airport to pick me up. I stuck the foil package of honey-roasted peanuts in my jeans' pocket. I'd be starving before Buck arrived or found the keys so that Tomás or Alex could pick me up. In 1969 Buck established a personal best by making it to work on time three days straight.

I marched down the steel ramp watching disdainfully as the other passengers embraced their families. The rain had started. It was beating furiously, turning the windows and the terminal the same color gray. I strode through the Atlanta terminal, intent on going downstairs to find a safe place to curl up. There, straight in front of me, was Buck, my father, as punctual as a railroad clerk. For the first time in his life, he looked neither young nor handsome. Yet, for the first time, he seemed dignified, tragic.

The packet of roasted peanuts fell and skated across the waxed floor and came to a standstill inches from Buck's scuffed cowboy boots. Buck took off his hat and a lick of hair fell over his forehead. He stood hunched forward as if another big man, stronger than him, had just driven a fist through his stomach.

"Mama's dead, isn't she?" I whispered.

He shook his head from one side to the other.

"Elena?"

He shook his head no.

"Tomás," I said, my chest heaving, afraid. "Tomás?"

He shook his head, tossing the tears from his eyes.

"No," I whispered at him. I took both his wrists and shook them downward. "No." The echo of my footsteps chased me as I ran down the long terminal. I ran, hunched to one side, as if paralyzed by a stroke.

Buck said Alex was found at the swimming pool where he worked, the night of July Fourth, when everyone was at the river for the fireworks display. The coroner's report said he blew a hole straight through his heart. In the morning, another lifeguard, opening the Riverside Pool and Park, found him leaned against the picnic bench; Alex's eyes were open as if he were still looking out over the river. The coroner ruled it a suicide. Afterwards, the police shipped the body to Auburn for the required autopsy. The owners, who had loved my brother, shut down the pool for three days, even though it was summer vacation week for the millworkers and those who didn't go to Panama City or to the river would have brought their children to the pool. I wanted to go there, but Buck wouldn't take me. So I took a taxi.

The cab driver waited while I crossed the yellow police tape from the pines to the lifeguard chair to the picnic bench. It had happened two nights ago. No one had had the time to clean up, not thoroughly, at least. So if I needed proof, there was proof. A puddle of blood, hard and plastic, stained the table. I stood there a moment, but realized that Buck and Carmina would come here tomorrow if not tonight,—they might even be on their way now. I moved forward toward it. I told myself it was just blood.

God knows I had seen enough of Alex's blood. When he was seven, his nose bleeds started. The second grade teacher, a gray-haired veteran of St. Andrew's School, thought he had been picking his nose. She said this while I held a wad of wet paper towels against his nostrils. I saw his eyes widen with anger, but she had his head back and he couldn't say a word. He wouldn't have anyway. He was quieter than most. He never stopped bleeding. In fifth grade, when Mr. Donelly called him to the board to subtract fractions; the problem stood in giant white letters. When he turned around, a thin crimson line curved from his nose. Same thing happened in tenth grade when he didn't make the swim team.

I drew cold water from a hand pump. It took a long time for the bucket to fill. My hands were shaking. I made them into two fists and held them underwater to drown the shakiness. I drenched the table until no pink welled up from the dark, wet wood. The stain was deep, and I believe it is there at the Riverside Pool to this day, though I have never gone back to see. Still, something was caught in between the broad pieces of pine. I loosened it with a stick and held it up to the light. It was a piece of bone, tender pink on one side, innocent and small as a child's tooth. My fist closed over it. Finally, it was not the blood at all, but that piece, a shard of his breastbone, that was more convincing than the blood. I held it like a treasure, standing there with it in my fist, unable to let go of it. If I could understand this fragment of bone being there, I would understand the conundrum of Alex's absence. When I looked up, the sky had let go of the sun. I could hear only the slight hum of the cab and the slight lapping of the pool. I hurled the light bone at the lake and fled toward the yellow lights of the taxi.

CAROLYNNE SCOTT

Dancing in the Basement

The old lady lived in a corner of her room. Her black cat. A large, ornate desk of cherry wood. Her dishes at the other end of the room reflecting sunlight as it streamed through a narrow window. Her clothes and linens in the adjacent bedroom.

For days now, she had been planning an excursion into the big world, the outside. There was a short trip she needed to make. She fingered the portrait of a young man on her desk. He had black, wavy hair with a central part and a tightly buttoned shirt with a rounded collar showing its whiteness out of the black suit he wore. The portrait was small, framed in gold, and always sat on her desk. She picked up a newspaper clipping beside it and examined it once again. A couple stood at the edge of a balcony peering down into a living room she knew well.

The light-skinned young woman wore her hair in a twist or a French braid and somehow looked determined, yet kind. The man looked rigid, as a deer caught in the hunter's spotlight might. He, too, had on a dark suit. She wondered about them, their relationship. The article mentioned no children. It was all about the old house with its three eerie stories, two-story living room, ship's rib ceiling and cavernous basement.

"And have you seen any ghosts here?"

"There does seem to be some presence."

Mrs. Johnson gathered her purse and fluffed her hair one last time in the foyer mirror. She made her way to the elevator on her hall and down to the street. The doorman, Frank, hailed a cab for her and went out to the street with her to help her in. She rewarded him with some loose coins from the pocket of her navy coat.

"Where to, ma'am?" asked the cabby, a short, fat little man who reminded her of Danny DeVito.

"To Hanover Circle, sir," she said with a little lilt in her voice.

"You got friends over there?" he asked as he turned sharply and sailed down Nineteenth street.

Mrs. Johnson held to the back of the seat in front of her as the cabby braked and turned again. "Hmm. Could be."

"It's a beautiful Sunday afternoon, ain't it?"

"Beautiful," she agreed as he turned up Twentieth and soon whirled onto

Highland Avenue. At Twenty-seventh, her heart began to race a little as he turned left and passed the old brick apartment buildings on each side.

Soon she heard the familiar whir as the cabby turned onto the circle with its deeply embedded ridges in the pavement. She adjusted her lace collar and took hold of her purse. From the depths of her pocket, she found a bill to pay him with.

"This old street puzzles me with these funny grooves in it," the cabby said.

"They were made for the Model A," she said. "Stop at the next house, please."

"Now ain't that one a dilly," he said, taking her money and reaching across the seat to open the door for her.

A curving brick sidewalk led up to the tall, narrow, stucco house with a front window embedded with points of stained glass. Mrs. Johnson paused for a moment to enjoy its features, the dark green trim and putty colored stucco that looked as if it needed a wash job here and there. She stepped up onto the red tile porch and paused before the double glass doors to smile at her own image—a tall woman, rather thin with wisps of white hair sticking out around the edge of her dark cloche of a hat. The bell gave a familiar ding-a-ling as she pressed the ivory button.

"Come in," said a young woman as the French doors opened.

"How do you do," said her husband extending a large hand with a rather rough palm. "We've been expecting you."

"My goodness, everything looks so tasteful. Have you a decorator?"

They both laughed and looked at one another. "No, ma'am, I'm afraid we're it."

Mrs. Johnson paused to take in the beauty of red Oriental rugs on the floors, antique furniture, old, old lamps. A pedestal in the adjoining dining room held a profusion of colorful paper zinnias. A magnificent etagere with many curlicues filled one wall. The painted walls were a pleasant cream color. "Did you choose these colors?" she asked.

"No, we pretty much left the wood and the old plastered walls in their original state," said the young woman, who raised her arms and then stifled a yawn. "You'll have to forgive me, I lost a little sleep last night. Our ghost was up to no good."

Frowning at his wife, the husband asked, "Wouldn't you like to have a seat?"

"Well, I'd really rather look around if you don't mind. This ghost, what was he doing?"

"Turning the balcony light on and off every five minutes."

"Oh dear!" She heard herself giggle like a young girl. "I'll bet that interrupts quite a bit." She couldn't tell them of course, but she remembered when Hartley was spending a week with them once to see to some detail of the unfinished wooden ceiling in the living room. He had slept on a day bed on the balcony and every time Ferris wanted to touch her, the lights would go on and off.

She looked at the distraught reddish face of the young husband and laughed again.

They led her into the downstairs bedroom, and she noticed a mural of an ancient bridge in the mist had been painted over the mantel there. "How lovely. Who's the artist?"

"We're not sure."

"It just happened," said the husband, "between closing on the house and moving in."

"Perfectly charming. A real addition to the feeling of the place—old world, you know."

They went back through a narrow hallway, and the young woman stopped. "We've always wondered about this little cubby hole here. It looks like it was sealed, then someone unsealed it and left this flimsy little curtain over it. We just park the vacuum cleaner in there."

"Good idea," said Mrs. Johnson, feeling a shiver run up her arms.

"Won't you have a seat here in the living room?" the young man asked.

"Why, yes, thank you."

"And what is your interest in this place?"

Interest? She couldn't fashion an answer. All of it rushed back, the selection of the wood for the paneling, the search for just the proper lighting, the handrail on the stairway, the stucco color outside, Ferris and Hartley being childhood buddies, then together assuming the task of getting her house raised. The hope for children on the stairs, the accident. . . . She coughed delicately, then said: "Why, it was my house, of course."

"You mean you had it built?"

"Then you had to know the architect," said the young man. "We've been trying to find out about him."

"Yes," said the wife excitedly. "Did he do other houses?"

"Oh definitely, and the cathedral, of course."

"Show her the print, Honey," said the man. The woman plucked a small print off the wall in the dining room. It was of a farmer plowing with steel mills behind him. A lovely lithograph. Number 3 of 10.

"This is Hartley's, unmistakably," said Mrs. Johnson.

"Oh we hoped so!" The young woman did a small pirouette before she took the picture back to its nail.

"I wanted to ask the builder of this house about the garage in the basement. It's so small," said the man.

"Oh yes, we had it built to accommodate our Rio." She smiled, then paused to remember some of the excursions the three of them had in the Rio —particularly the one to Niagara Falls. Hartley was possessed by the Rainbow Bridge to Canada, and she and Ferris had a bit of privacy at the old English inn. But when Hartley was through making his sketches, the three of them would dine or walk to the foot of the falls together. It was a wonderful week.

"How long did you and your husband live here, Mrs. Johnson?" asked the young woman. "And by the way, please call me Claire and my husband Neal."

"Why certainly. Let's see, we were here two years, I think, when Ferris developed tuberculosis. He left for a sanitarium in Colorado Springs and was gone several years. I kept things going with Hartley's help, of course. Then after Ferris' lung collapsed, I sold the place. It broke my heart to leave it."

"Of course, we know just how you feel. Do you have any children?"

"No. I lost one, you know, a precious little boy about five months along."

"Oh, I'm sorry," said the young woman looking uneasily at her husband. "We're hoping for a child someday ourselves. Wouldn't this be a grand place to raise one with the window seats and stair rail and the secret basement rooms."

"Yes, oh yes!"

"Sometimes we imagine we hear a baby crying here. It is so faint—like a kitten mewing almost," said Neal.

"Where do you hear this, young man?" asked the old lady.

"Near that small opening in the wall we showed you. The one with the curtain."

"But the nursery was meant to be upstairs, behind the balcony." The old lady got to her feet weakly and started toward the stairs. "I must see the second floor," she said.

"Oh course," said Claire. "By the way, where did you ever find the lamp for this newel post?"

"Oh Hartley found that. Mobile or somewhere. It was when he was bringing it back that I had my accident."

"Really?"

"Yes. I ran to the car to greet him as he opened the door. He leaned out, handed me the box, and forgot to pull up the brake, or perhaps it failed. Anyway, I was knocked down by the door, the box flew over into the grass, and Hartley managed to stop the car down in front of the house next door." She started up the steps as she spoke, admiring the red Oriental runner against the soft oak floors.

"And were you all right?"

"Well, I had a hairline fracture of the pelvis and had to stay abed a bit. And that was when I delivered prematurely."

"My goodness," the young woman said, taking a bony elbow in her young soft palm.

"I'll bet Hartley felt pretty bad about that," said Neal.

"Oh, he liked to have never gotten over his mortification. Ferris teased him about trying to wipe out his best customer. He stayed at our house all one Christmas to wait on me. We drank egg nog and milk punch until we were silly."

"Sounds like this old house has seen some good times."

"Yes, yes, it certainly has!"

As she reached the top step, she noticed the rocking chair in motion as if someone were enjoying it. Then it stopped.

"What did you have in mind for this room?" Claire asked.

"Oh, the upstairs balcony was just a place to read and relax before an open fire. Ferris kept his large desk there in front of the window, and I liked to crochet or knit on winter nights. "May I try this rocker?"

"Surely," said Claire.

The couple settled on a blue damask French sofa and watched as the old lady began to rock gently with a beatific smile on her face. "Was anyone up here before we arrived?" she asked.

"Not unless it was the cat."

"Oh, what kind of cat do you have?"

"An orange Persian. We got him as a wee kitten, now he weighs ten pounds as least," said Claire.

"Charming," said the old lady. "I have a precious cat. He's black as velvet." As she held onto the rocker's arms, the chair began to move faster, then she settled down in it, smiling broadly.

"That little room there behind the French doors was intended for a nursery."

"I thought so," said Claire. "I have my ballet bar in there and a stationary bicycle, but they could come out." She looked wistfully at her husband, who patted her shoulder.

"What line of work are you in?" she asked Neal.

"Photography. Commercial, mostly."

"He has his studio in the basement," said Claire. "It's real convenient, except when clients drop by at odd hours. One night I was sick, and he carried an advertising man and his mother through at about eleven o'clock. I could have croaked."

"Well, they wanted to see the house."

The young woman shrugged, and Mrs. Johnson stood up, then gave the seat of the rocker a pat. "Since I'm here, I'd like to see the basement. And then I must call a taxi."

"Sure," the couple answered in unison.

As they moved down the stairs and through the hallway, Mrs. Johnson felt goose bumps break out. Following the young couple, she paused momentarily to glance into the veiled closet, but sure enough saw only an old Hoover. A faint mew shocked her. Then an orange cat stretched and came from behind the vacuum cleaner. "My goodness, what a beautiful animal!" She leaned over to pet the cat and ascertained that there was nothing else in the old enclosure. She wondered what had happened to the large wicker basket she and Hartley sealed up there once after a Bastille Day picnic.

"Watch your step," said Neal, as he turned to give her his hand. She took hold of his upper arm and stepped delicately onto the top wooden stair. Claire, who had gone before them, screamed.

"Oh my God!" Neal said in answer.

"What is it, Children?" asked Mrs. Johnson.

"It's a river, mostly," said Claire.

As she and Neal hurried down the stairs, Mrs. Johnson paused to view the concrete basement floor rushing with waters, seemingly from nowhere. She paused and giggled to herself for she remembered when Hartley conducted his experiment once to check for the tightness of the house. Ferris came home and found them wading in the waters there.

"Where could it have come from?" asked Claire.

In answer, Neal rushed back past her and stepped over onto the dirt part where the hot water tank sat. He bent down and lit a match to read the gauge. "My word, it's been pushed up to 180 degrees."

"The water's flowing from this pipe over here," Claire said.

"We always waded when this happened," said the old lady. Both residents of the place turned to stare at her, then Claire laughed—a delightful tinkle just like a bell.

"Let's do it," she said, removing her tennis shoes.

Mrs. Johnson leaned forward to untie her oxfords, anticipating the feel of the swirling waters when Neal warned, "Are you two daffy? The stuff is 180 degrees."

"Oh, it'll cool down, Darling, and feel like a wonderful foot bath. Come on, Mrs. Johnson, let's try it." Claire came back up to where the old lady sat on the stairway removing her shoes and thigh-high stockings. Claire took her thin, wrinkled arm and guided her to the bottom step.

"Let me test it first," she said softly. Suddenly the cat was between them rubbing on both their legs. His fur felt like the finest silk. He stayed behind as they splashed down into the waters. There was not a doubt in Mrs. Johnson's mind where Hartley's spirit dwelled. She held out her arms to him and waltzed all over the dark floor with its buoyant waters.

Claire, caught up in the merriment, took her arms and laughed at Neal who had a pipe wrench and was working away at the plumbing. He glared at them, shook his head, and eventually went upstairs where they could faintly hear him dialing a plumber. He reminded Mrs. Johnson so much of her redhead, Ferris, with his busyness and his scowl.

"Promise me, young lady, that you will never leave my house," Mrs. Johnson said to her lithe dancing partner.

"I won't if you'll promise to come back, too."

"That's a given, my dear."

The following Sunday, Claire was sprawled across the olive velvet sofa in the living room reading the paper. The sun, winking through the stained glass fell on a small item on page ten. It told all about an elderly lady from the Plaza Apartments stepping in front of a taxi and being run down.

"I didn't see her from nuthin'," the cabby was quoted. *"One minute there was nobody, and the next minute I saw her goin' under the wheels."*

The lady had no family or next of kin. None of her neighbors had noticed her seeming depressed. Someone did say she had given away her black cat.

Millie Anton Skinner

A Bully and His Victim

All the students walked to and from the old Drummond School house. Most of the children in the small farming community were our cousins.

Those who lived at the far end of the fields would leave their homes in the chill of the early morning, stopping at each house along the way. Children would pour out of the door of each farmhouse. With loud shrieks, squeals, whistles, singing of songs, and jests, they would join friends and kin for the walk to school.

Before the group of youngsters reached our family's door, our red-headed brother would be outside, standing by the fence, or sitting on the gate post. As always, he would be reading a book, while he waited the arrival of the noisy group.

As the cousins and friends approached, a resounding chant would be heard, "Red-headed Peckerwood, sittin' on a fence, trying to peck a dollar out of fifteen cents."

"Red," as he was called, was forever being teased about his carrot-colored mop of wavy hair. He usually ignored the teasing.

Mama's long established custom was that if any of her children got into a fight away from home, she would finish the fight when he returned home. Her method of "finishing a fight" was by the application of hands to certain tender portions of the anatomy.

Red had determined that it was less painful to ignore being compared to a peckerwood than to fight over it. Besides, family members assured him that being teased was proof of his being well liked. He never believed that.

It is sad to acknowledge, but it's true: one of our cousins was a bully. He wasn't just a plain, simple, regular, good old boy, farm-yard variety, garden-hoeing type of bully. He was a hard-down, low-life, black-hearted, back-stabbing, mean-mouthed, donkey-braying, bam-boozleing, rip-snortin', dare-deviling, mad-dog-yelping, rattle-snake-lying-in-the-grass watching-and-waiting for a bare foot to bite, kind of bully.

Every day that the sun rose, Cooter, the bully, beat up one or the other of the children from the area as they walked to school or home from school. However, the boy was fair minded.

He took turn about with his brutality. He practiced equal opportunity abusing.

Cooter was never greedy. He aspired to maim, mutilate, and pulverize only one human body per day.

One afternoon in late September Red and our other brothers, along with our cousins who lived across the road, were pulling corn in the bottoms. They talked long and earnestly about the problem of cousin Cooter, the bully.

Red said, "Our daddy has a theory—"

Cousin Lee interrupted him with "Your daddy's always got a theory about everything. I bet you don't even know what a theory is."

"Do so," Red answered.

"Well, then what is it?"

"I ain't gonna tell you."

"Oh, of course you ain't gonna tell what you don't know," Lee spit out.

"I ain't a gonna tell 'cause I aim to see if you know what a theory is," Red retaliated.

"Oh, shut up, both a' you dim wits," brother Charlie said.

"Red, which one of Daddy's theories are you talking about?"

Red answered, "You 'member how Daddy always says that nine out of ten bullies are cowards? That if just one person will stand up in a bully's face, nine times out of ten the bully will back down?"

Odis said, "Old Cooter is the tenth one. He ain't a gonna back down, back up, or go sideways. He's a gonna kill one of us if we don't stop him."

"How we ever gonna stop him?" asked cousin Roy.

Brother Jim, the brain, entered the discussion. "We got to stick together, that's what. Dadgum it, whenever the Cooter starts in to beating up on somebody, all the rest of us just stand and watch. Nobody tries to help. We got to help each other. If we stick together he can't kill all of us."

"He'll kill most of us," said cousin Johnny.

"Wonder what makes him so mean?" Roy asked.

"It's cause his ma fed him rusty nails when he was little, and he still eats 'em every day," said Lee. "They say rusty nails causes poison in your stomach that makes you real evil.

"You'll turn into a mad dog and foam out of your mouth. Then you'll grow long shaggy hair all over your body."

Joe said, "I heard my folks talking about Cooter. They said he was real smart. They said he has a big brain."

"Wonder where at he keeps it hid?" asked Red.

"Wonder why he don't take it out of hiding and use it sometimes," said Joe.

After agonizing over the problem and much discussion, they reached a decision and formed a plan. They all agreed that the very next time cousin Cooter attacked any one of the children on the way to or from school, they would all jump on top of the big bully.

Positions were assigned and rehearsed. First, Charlie, the biggest one, would land a killer blow straight into his stomach.

This always worked when he was trying to settle a dispute with one of his younger brothers.

Odis would get his attention, while Jim grabbed his right leg. Cousin John would take his left leg. Together they would stretch his legs one to the east and one to the west, and hang on for dear life.

Red would hold Cooter's right arm, Odis would hold his left. Cousin Lee would straddle his back and pull his hair. Dick would jump in wherever there was a body part not flapping.

The other boys would pound on top of his head, and Sam would kick him in the ribs. They would all give Cousin Cooter a dose of his own black-hearted bees wax.

That night the autumn rains set in. Next morning, when the children gathered to walk to school, the country dirt road was a sea of black mud.

When Cousin Attie Bell joined the group she was holding her sweater clutched tightly around her body. She had sniffled, sneezed, and snuffled all the way down the path that led from her house to the country road. She joined the group and walked quietly.

Red said, "Attie Bell, why ain't you singing with us this morning? It's your favorite, 'The Church in the Wildwood.' What's the matter with you?"

"I'm sick with a cold. It's pouring down rain. My shoes are soggy. I don't know my spelling words, so just leave me alone," she said.

Cooter stepped up beside Attie Bell and poked her in the ribs. "Now, now, Attie Bell, that ain't nothing for you to be a bad-mouthing about. Come on now, let's see a itty bitty ole smiley wiley."

"Leave me alone, Cooter, you hear me? I'm plum sick and plum wore out. I ain't had no sleep cause I coughed and sneezed all night. I got a cold. I got a chill. I got a fever. I got my dander up, too, so you'd just better not bother me."

Like music to Cooter's ears was this taunt from a mere girl. It had been a while since he had beat up on a girl. This seemed like a good reason and a timely occasion.

He pushed Attie Bell. She turned and looked straight into his eyes. The rain splattered down on her shoulders. She brushed back her hair and quietly said, "Cooter, I told you, leave me alone."

She turned on her heels and walked away from all of the group and hurried into the school house to get out of the rain.

Throughout the day Cooter meditated on Attie Bell's behavior. He couldn't quite put his finger on the reason for it, but somewhere, in the back of his mind, there was a strange nagging feeling. Something just didn't feel right.

He re-played the early morning scene over and over in his mind. About lunch time he grasped the idea that this tiny, mere wisp of a girl had displayed a lack of respect for him. He had suffered an insult. From a girl. A five-foot tall, ninety-pound girl. Can you beat that? This could not be allowed to pass unchallenged.

All that day Attie Bell's face burned with fever. Her body was near freezing, shaking with chills. She should have gone home. She wanted to, and would have, except for the fact that she had maintained perfect attendance and straight A's for four years. If she completed this year without being absent, she would receive not only a five year certificate for perfect attendance, but also a five dollar bill. No simple common cold was going to stand in the way of her reward.

When the three o'clock bell rang Attie Bell was in a hurry to get home, swallow a B.C. Headache Powder, and go to bed.

There was nothing else on her mind.

She walked out of the school yard, and was soon joined by about a dozen of the students who regularly walked together. It had rained intermittently during the day. The cool air hung heavy with moisture, signaling the onset of winter. The leaves hung gold, scarlet and brown. They fluttered lazily in the breeze. Attie Bell rejoiced in the lovely colors.

The road was filled with deep rain puddles and black mud.

Attie Bell picked up a short heavy stick from beside the road. With the stick she tested the depths of the mud holes before each step. She would have no other shoes until the new Sears-Roebuck catalog arrived in the spring.

She was lost in thoughts of lovely falling leaves and drifting snow flakes, when Cooter fell into step beside her.

"You got a itty bitty ol' fever?" He spoke in a high falsetto voice.

"Leave me alone, Cooter," she said.

Cooter screwed his face up so that his bottom lip appeared to be covering the end of his nose. He waved his hands from side to side in front of his chest, and mockingly said, "Oou leabe be awone, dow, Cooter."

Attie Bell ignored him and walked quickly on ahead of the group.

Cooter caught up to her, placed his hand on her shoulder and turned her around facing him. "Hey!" he screamed into her face. "I'm talking to you."

Attie Bell stood perfectly still. She stared into Cooter's face. All of the group fell silent and moved into a semicircle around the two. The silence stretched out for a seeming eternity.

With a movement so subtle and swift as to be almost imperceptible, Attie Bell brought the stick up and whacked it savagely across the bridge of Cooter's nose. Blood spurted.

He made the mistake of raising his hands to his face. With lightning speed she kicked his shin with brutal force. As she pulled her leg back she stomped the instep of his foot with the entire weight of her body.

His body bent downward, and "Crack!" She slammed the stick across the top of his head. Cooter fell face first into a very large and very black mud hole.

Attie Bell instantly leaped onto his back. This position proved delightfully springy, so she enjoyed bouncing up and down several times.

She stood on top of Cooter's back without moving or speaking. Cooter tried to raise his head out of the mud. Attie Bell stepped off his back and knelt beside him. She fastened her hand firmly into his hair and jerked his head up.

He spluttered and spit black mud. He gasped for breath.

His clothes were soaked and stained. Blood from his nose mingled with the mud clinging to his clothing.

She pulled his hair once more, for good measure. She looked at the black hair clasped in her hand. She opened her fingers and watched the hair fall from her hand onto the ground.

She raised his head and craddled it against her. She lifted the hem of her skirt and with it she gently wiped mud from his lips.

"Cousin Cooter, honey," she said, "I told you to leave me alone. You see what happens when you don't listen? Poor baby. Fall down, get all dirty."

B. K. Smith

Calling Up the Moon

Spiraling downward toward stardom,
she pauses to hold the old Druid's
sword between her teeth.
Lips once red and pulsing with ballads
of the North now lie dead locked
on the unholy spectre of selfhood,
banging his knees on the rocks of Ulro.
Instincts sure once upon a time
crumble with the old watchtower in the West.
And from the East there is
promise of passion, an offer
of songs that will heal,
bringing rebellious rebirth
to Morgan le Fay,
a Venus on
the half shell.

Our lady of the lake, your salvation
began the night you died,
protected by salt and tears
as you knelt before the water
to call up the moon.
Remember this night, and the East,
and the anvil forging sweet
music in the North.
First you go up, then down,
then side to side,
circling, fleeing.
Cast your sights on Albion and Avalon
before the tumble
costs you
our lives.

First she goes north; then she goes south. From the watchtower in the West to passion in the East, Morgan Shelley moves like a shark. She feeds on chemicals and turns a deaf eye to her pain. Only Doppler radar can find her, and that's when she calls up a storm. I know where she is by the small red blurb on an otherwise clear weather map of Alabama.

I have known Morgan for years, before her meteoric rise to stardom. My brother, a musician himself, even kissed her once when we were drunk just to see how her lips would feel. He never did that again because the raw energy pulsing through her veins knocked him flat as if from 50,000 volts of untamed electricity. Touching her hand after that was more than enough.

Morgan is a shape shifter. Sometimes she's a big cat, clad in tight black jeans, striding across the stage. She screams into the microphone a call to the wild to join her magic show. Other times she's a kitten, purring and cuddling before she draws back her head quickly in a teasing gesture. Thick, black wavy hair falls across her face to frame green eyes that narrow as she smiles wide like a Cheshire.

We used to talk until the early morning hours while we drank Coronas with limes or dark German beers. She never tired, never wound down even when the moon melted into sunrise. It was then she became Morgan le Fay, Queen of the Faeries, who would tell me bedtime stories of Arthurian legend to keep me awake one more hour. Then we would sleep until noon, or past, to awake drowsy and grumpy before caffeine.

I watched her shows, mesmerized along with the rest of the crowds as she banged her black leathered legs with an electric guitar, her voice clear and loud within the music. But the best time to watch was when her slender, white fingers stroked a classical Fender in search of a new song. She caressed the strings like an artist playing with light and shadows. And her voice, like quicksilver, crystallized common language into myth. She had written 200 songs by the time I met her when she was 25. The first ones were folky melodies and ballads. Later came punk rock, but all were powerful. Her talent amazed those who knew her.

Morgan danced through men like a hard rock ballerina. She loved artists and intellectuals but mostly musicians, who knocked her around a bit emotionally. But if she decided to tame any man, including a musician, she could, especially after her transition. That was to be the most frightening and exciting period of her life, and mine.

I remember the exact date that her odyssey into transformation began: June 24, 1997. She had been calling me all weekend—sometimes at one o'clock in the morning and then at six o'clock, only five hours later. She was doing battle with her fiancé of two years, and she was combating some demon by spreading salt all over the kitchen while she talked to me. I heard David in the background, telling her he was not carrying that gummy blob of something in the floor out in the rain for her. It could wait until tomorrow. I kept telling her it was probably just an innocent clump of bubblegum, but she insisted to David and me that it contained an evil spirit that had to go. I got David on the phone and told him to take her to bed, hold her, and make her feel safe. She was definitely not her usual self, all business and in control of most situations. That Saturday night was a long one on the phone. She could not rest.

On Sunday, Morgan came to my apartment to sleep. I didn't recognize her when she stood in the doorway. Her face was as pale as dawn, and heavy black circles were all that supported her tired green eyes. I hugged her thin frame to feel sharp shoulder blades protruding from her back like stoney wings.

"You look like you've been in a fight," I said.

"I have, with the devil."

"David?" I asked.

"No. I don't know where he is. He left last night. He thinks I'm crazy."

"Well, you weren't yourself," I said, noticing how she resembled the gaunt knight from "La Belle Dame Sans Merci." I asked her when she had last eaten anything, and she couldn't remember. I gave her something to eat and put her to bed after listening to an hour of paranoid, disconnected babble about how "they" were out to get her, or frenetic lapses into Arthurian legend. She assured me she was Morgan le Fay and that she had to hide for awhile, somewhere safe, to rest.

After she finally settled into sleep, I washed her clothes. They smelled odd—earthy and musky—an almost inexplicable scent—not dirty—but ancient, old, like from another time. I had never smelled anything like it. When she awakened six hours later, I gave her a dinner of vegetables. She refused any meat. She seemed better, with a little pink back in her cheeks. So, I figured she had just needed sleep and food. I let her drive back to Muscle Shoals where she and her band were cutting their first CD. I assumed she had just been really over tired and strung out from many hours on the headphones, so I let it go.

On Monday night the calls began again, and the salt, and the rounds with David. He was sinister, she said, and had locked himself in his study to commune with his computer and to read books by Aleister Crowley. It didn't sound like David, a second-year law student. But I listened to that and to her ramblings about how the four cats were afraid of her, and how the old Druids in Muscle Shoals were playing games with her. She seemed to be afraid of one guy in particular who had told her he was the devil and would take her soon enough. I assumed they were playing myths, legends, and demons again to make the hours and rigors of recording easier. They had done this before. By two o'clock the next morning, I concluded that someone had drugged her during one of the practice sessions. It seemed a clear case of L.S.D. This was not my friend.

I had to hang up, so I could get some sleep before work the next morning. But I told Morgan to call if she was scared or needed to talk. She did, four hours later. "Can I come over?" she asked.

"Morgan, I have to go to work today," I said.

"I can't stay in this house. It's scary," she pleaded, but I ignored her, much to my regret later.

"I want you to do two things," I said. "Go over to your mother's house, what is it, only four blocks away? Take a shower, eat some breakfast, and go straight to your doctor. Ask him to test you for drugs. I believe someone has slipped you something. Will you do that? Then call me later?"

"That's what I need to do?" she asked.

"Yes," I answered, feeling like a mother directing her child. So, that was the end of phone calls for awhile. Later, I would've given anything to have heard my friend's old voice—laughing, joking, or planning her musical career and success. Actually, I would've been happy to hear any of her voices by eleven o'clock that night. David had been calling all of her friends that day, worried sick after reading crazy notes of goodbye she had left around the house. Her mom, whose storm door had been locked at 6:30 a.m., had seen her daughter drive away before she could answer the knock. "She has a key," Margaret Shelley said, frantically, and almost in tears, "but the storm door was locked. I saw her driving away before I could get to her. What are we going to do? My baby needed me, and I wasn't here for her."

I felt the same, and so did a sheepish David who had spilled the story to Morgan's brother about her apparent onset of dementia. Everyone was looking for Morgan and trying to contact her by cellular phone. Before midnight, her mother had connected with her for a few moments. Morgan said she had been driving and had gotten lost in the lake area near my apartment, that she was trying to find me. Just after midnight, I called her car phone and heard her voice for only a few seconds amid the crackling static. "Hello! Hello!" she screamed, her voice sounding almost frantic, and very frightened.

"Morgan, are you okay? Where are you? Tell me. I'll come get . . ." The phone went dead for a second; then a recording apologized to say that the person I was trying to reach was now out of the calling area.

After midnight no one heard from her again. She seemed to disappear into thin air. I kept looking for her, listening for her car, and then finally fell asleep at 3:00 a.m. I had never gone to work that day after all because David and Morgan's mom had begun calling by 7:45. I felt low and ashamed that I had not been there for my best friend. I fell asleep worrying, wondering where she was, and wishing to hear her voice, safe at my door.

I slept fitfully and had strange dreams. I saw an arid, barren land with gnarled old oaks—dead and stark beneath a relentless sun—which seemed to hold no brightness, only deadening heat. Demons began to emerge from the trees. They were chasing a woman in a white, almost transparent gown. Suddenly she changed to a huge panther, whose cold stare dared them to advance. Reflections of falling stars danced in the cat's eyes as this magnificent animal grabbed the demons and spectres one by one and shook them in her powerful teeth, their swords breaking in half and their bodies strewn about, writhing in agony.

Next, the panther sprouted wings, and her countenance seemed to distort, changing to the face of a gargoyle as she flew by what looked to be a watchtower. It crumbled under her fiery glance. She flew upward into a cool, airy space where Orion pointed her in the direction of the creator in the North. He was banging out words on an anvil. They spread across the sky to read, "IMAGINATION."

Her features began to change, and the woman returned in the flowing white gown as she floated toward the East. Music began to play, and a host of angels with rosy lips and fluttering wings sang to the woman. They surrounded her as her feet softly touched land near a small lake. She knelt to pray, and a great hand waved itself across the water, bringing an enormous wind to cause white caps on the lake. And clouds rolled away in the sky, revealing a brilliantly placid full moon.

I awoke feeling more relaxed than before. The clock read 4:00 a.m. I was no longer worried about Morgan. Somehow I knew she was safe, and I knew the direction she had headed: north toward Florence, Alabama, and on toward Tennessee. This didn't bother me. I drank a glass of cool water and went back to sleep. However, Morgan's family did not have a good night, nor a good morning. By 9:00 a.m. the next day, they were really scared and had friends from the state police place an all-points bulletin. They also sent a helicopter to search in the Muscle Shoals area, hoping she would head for the recording studio. Morgan's mother and aunt had already begun to drive in that direction when the call came at noon. State police had found Morgan's car and her, sitting in a driveway of a home near the Tennessee line. She said she was trying to find a friend who used to live there. I heard later that Morgan gave the police a hard time, demanding a glass of water and some salt. She wouldn't answer their questions but, instead, sat glaring silently at them and her surroundings. The mention of salt made me remember a cup she had left by my bed on Sunday. There was a chalky residue at the bottom. It had appeared to be salt.

Morgan was glad to see her mom and her aunt, but she was not so happy to see David when she returned home. He had been driving in the wrong directions all night. "It's over. You didn't protect me," was all she said to him as her mother took her straight to a Birmingham hospital for numerous tests and psychological evaluations. There were no drugs, no injuries, just many bruises and unusual marks on her body. She came back to her parents' home by evening, exhausted and dehydrated, but fairly healthy.

After a week of recuperating and more doctors, Morgan's mom finally let her visit me, with a promise to call home when she arrived. Morgan stood in my doorway, and she looked completely different again. She seemed taller, and her shoulders were broader, her arms more muscular. And her darker skin seemed to glisten as the sun danced on her forearms. Her hair was blacker and her eyes a clear, intense green. After we settled in with a glass of wine, I asked Morgan, "Are you going to tell me about it, your odyssey?"

"I like that," she said and laughed. "That's a good name for it."

"So were you afraid of success or failure? Isn't that why you ran away from your music, the CD?"

"Maybe. Or maybe too many hours in a glass cage with headphones. Couldn't take that repetitive torture any longer or those guys. Talk about torment. Sing it again, lower your voice, drink more vodka—it makes you sound sexier. They almost killed me. And those stupid mythological characters and games," she said, with a tear just balanced and ready to roll onto her cheek.

"But it's good, right?" I asked.

"Damn good. Gold record, I'd wager. I think I'm going to be a star."

"Oh, a star is born. Was it worth almost losing your soul?" I asked, and noticed that Morgan's eyes had darkened to almost black as she leaned toward me.

"It isn't funny, you know. I did die that night," she said.

"What? Are you sure it wasn't delusions caused by drinking salt water? I realized you were doing that, you know. Why on earth?"

"Why indeed?" she questioned. "I left the earth. And I will tell you exactly what happened, but it can never go beyond this room."

"I promise," I said as I held up my right hand. Then Morgan began to tell me of her journey into darkness. Her eyes turned a strange shade of green, and her face became almost trancelike. Her voice was deeper, lower, than I had ever heard it.

At first I just drove around all day. I had planned to hang out at the lake and drive to your house later. Then, somehow, I got lost. When night fell, I thought I was headed back toward your apartment, but I was turned around apparently. I don't know how it happened. The roads just kept winding around until everything got darker and darker. The trees took on strange shapes, and they seemed to be closing in on me. Their limbs reached out for me, all gnarled and knotted like huge bony fingers trying to grab me. Then I don't know where I was. One moment I was driving, and the next thing I knew I was pulled out of the car onto the ground. Druids were chasing me, on me, fighting me, pulling me under into this dry, hot wasteland. I couldn't breathe. I was moving downward into hell. Demons were snarling and snapping at me. Somehow I think I changed because I was stronger and was clawing my way out past them, trying to get up again. I don't think I was in my body.

Then I seemed to be moving upward toward the stars. I caught a glimpse of Hercules, Jesus, and a blacksmith working at his anvil. They were beckoning me to come up toward them. Everything was cooler farther up. I saw a lighthouse in the West and was momentarily transported inside. I saw a portrait of a woman with her hair pulled back in a bun. She smiled and shook her head up and down as if she were telling me yes to some question I hadn't asked. Then hell broke loose again when Norse gods stormed the lighthouse. It began to shake and fall apart. I was catapulted down again toward the mouth of hell. I saw the Norse gods as I fell. They were biting their nails, shivering, and I could sense jealousy and rage in their angry faces.

I took off my engagement ring and tossed it into hell. Hounds were barking and chanting, "Lord of the rings!" Hands were pulling me downward again. Later, I saw myself get into my car, lie down, and ask to die. Insects were crawling all over me. And a giant, white Easter bunny banged on the window, his ears huge and long. He was yelling that he was the devil come to steal my eggs. I lost all thought. I know that Morgan Shelley died in that moment. But, I heard a voice. It was my grandmother, gently speaking to me at first, then loudly calling me to come back. I heard another voice and another. One was yours, pulling me back. I saw goddesses and light all around me, and I gained strength to sit up, open the door, and walk down to a lake a few feet in front of my car.

I dropped to my knees, crying, and I prayed. The mist on the lake was beautiful. I saw the barge of Avalon and faeries dancing across the water. I closed my eyes and blessed the lake. I felt so safe and surrounded by goodness. A comet shot across the sky, and a great spirit swept across the water, causing it to lap against my knees. And a strong wind blew the clouds away as I called for the moon to allow me to see more. Everything became brighter as a full moon spread its light across the water. Fish jumped, and birds began to sing in the brilliant night. Small brown rabbits hopped from the woods to drink from the lake. And the good trees bent down to caress me and to whisper many secrets that I may reveal, or conceal, later in my music.

Morgan continued and said, "All I can remember after that is waking up in my car. There was a small green grasshopper on my right index finger. And there was black fur all over the car, my clothes, and on my arms. That scared me. I hoped I hadn't hurt anything. Somehow I drove to what I thought was my friend Ellen's house. When I remembered she was living in Mobile, I just sat and stared for I don't know how long before the state police pulled me in to the courthouse and jail in some little town on the Tennessee line. You know the rest. I believe you were with me that night somehow, and you helped me to live again. Do you understand?"

"I know I was there," I said, and I think I understand. I am so glad you are alive—in any form."

After Morgan's odyssey, no moon was sighted in the sky for weeks. I suppose the moon goddess had spent most of the watts revving up Morgan to become one more star. Morgan finished her CD recording in spite of all the rumors and tales of alcohol problems or a nervous breakdown. Some people said she had been on drugs or abducted by aliens; others said she was raped by a musician in her band. But most attributed her flight to extreme stress and exhaustion from too much loud music blaring through headphones, pressure from the band, and lack of sleep. And despite all of this, her recording won her a gold record. The music was hauntingly beautiful, mesmerizing, and the most unique sound heard in years. And it wasn't the last. She did become a star, with several gold records and numerous hits topping the charts.

Only Morgan and I will ever know what took place during her odyssey. And, possibly, others who have struggled to reach the top may know that painful journey as well. Did Morgan truly have to battle the old Druids and Norse gods and Satan himself to reach the bright light of success? So few ever know that battle. Is there is a rite of passage to fame? Maybe, maybe not.

>I called you Orion
>in a dark bar
>where the band's
>name doesn't
>matter,
>and the smoke shifts
>like constellations
>hit by hail
>or bop
>or beer.
>But you are a Venus twin
>in your black leather jacket,
>a biker chick
>for the night,
>hot tight pants
>hugging long legs
>moving across
>the floor,
>easy,
>like a big cat.
>You are a sister
>to the gods,
>green orbed planets
>taking in the room,
>angel's voice with
>a devil's mischief
>on the side,
>brushing away the legended suitors
>in scuffed jeans and boots
>not fit for Morgan le Fay.
>A faerie's breath against
>my ear, the secrets
>mine for a moment
>before dawn bleaches
>white the mourning,
>and ends
>a comet's tale.

Patricia Lou Taylor

Sex on the Beach

"Have you had a drink called Sex on the Beach?" Cheryl asked me as we rolled Dave towards her so I could rub his back with coconut lotion. She'd just gotten back from vacation on St. Simon's island and was talking about her experiences there. We were leaning over either side of Dave's hospital bed and finishing up his bath. He hadn't said a word in several days and we'd forgotten the rule to assume your patient can hear you even when he isn't speaking.

"Sex on the beach? When did we have sex on the beach?" Dave piped up. Cheryl and I laughed.

"Dave, Sex on the Beach is the name of a drink. It's like a tequila sunrise. Have you ever had one?" I asked, happy to have him talking to us again. Hope rose in me that this was somehow a sign of recovery. But it wasn't to be.

"When did we have sex on the beach?" was his only reply.

* * *

Dave had been admitted to our cancer unit with complications of the AIDS virus six weeks before that discussion. He was among a number of young men admitted with the same diagnosis over the last couple of years since the virus had been identified. We saw more than our share of the disease, more than a lot of cancer units around the country because our hospital was located downtown in a large metropolitan area with a very high gay population.

And we saw a lot of deaths, as this was before there were drugs that enable people to live with AIDS as they do any chronic illness. Then, patients reported to us that their entire social structure was dying of AIDS: most of their friends and neighbors were vanishing in a very short time period. Even our head nurse at the time, who was gay, had lost his lover and then his own life within a year.

When I first met Dave I was impressed with his demeanor. He didn't look sick, but like he was just there to visit someone. His clothes were casual but expensive and he carried a briefcase. He was well built and had dark wavy hair neatly cut around his neck line. His chocolate eyes bore into me like he was really seeing me, and he had one of those smiles that made me want to tell him everything. I found out why right away: Dave's admission papers said he was a psychiatrist. I introduced myself and led him to his single room. With his soft, musical, Southern accent he told me to call him Dave. I said "Sure" and wondered if I could marry him too. I told him to get settled and I would be back to formally admit him soon.

When I came back and started my admission questionnaire I decided to try to get to know him a little before starting on all the routine questions. I was sitting on a chair that I had pulled up at an angle by the right side of his bed, and I held a clipboard with papers and pen on my lap. He was leaning up against the head board and a pillow, and his long muscular legs stretched out over the still-made hospital bed. He had all of his clothes on as if he wasn't planning on staying long. Papers were scattered over the bed-side table that was pulled near him on the other side of the bed.

I looked down at my admission form and read the basic information that Dave had already given the admission clerk. His name was David William Faulkner. I liked the ring to that, and it sounded familiar. "I see that you are a psychiatrist. Are you new around here, or just new to me?" I certainly wasn't an expert on physicians in the area, much less psychiatrists, but I'd never heard of him before, and I thought I would have remembered that name.

"Yes, as far as my practice goes. I finished my residency in general psychiatry at Penn State last year and I just moved back home and am establishing my own clinic. I have an office over on Bay street. I'm getting a lot of referrals so I'm hopeful that it will go well." He gazed toward the window, which happened to face Bay street, though we were eight blocks above it. He looked like he would fly over there if he could.

I started to warm up to him and relaxed. "I kinda thought with a name like William Faulkner, and your accent, that you must be from somewhere around here."

"Yeah. I was raised here, but I don't have any family here any more. Both of my parents are dead and my sister is out west. But it still feels like home."

Instead of picking up on that fact that he had no family, which would have been the helpful thing to do, I just blurted out, "Well, now I know who to call when I start having problems coping, not that I ever do." We both laughed at that. I could really be a card.

"Anyway, now I need to ask some nurse-type questions. Do you mind?" This was my standard way of starting to ask those questions that could be embarrassing but were necessary to get the whole clinical picture. (Questions like: *How often do you urinate?; Is your sex life satisfactory?; What financial concerns do you have?; Have you passed gas through your rectum today?; Are you spiritually content?*)

"Go ahead."

"What brought you here today?"

"I've been having some problems breathing when I exert myself and so I'm going to be evaluated for pneumonia. I'm probably run down as I've been so busy moving and starting a new practice." He said this casually like he really didn't think this would be a problem for him; then he looked longingly at his paper work. I got the hint, but forged ahead anyway.

"Any other symptoms?"

"No that's it. I just need a few days of antibiotics and some rest, and then I need to get out of here because I don't have anyone to fill in for me right now. I called my patients and cancelled till next week."

I forced a smile and said something inane about caring for yourself before you could care for others, as if I, as a cancer nurse, knew anything about that. I mean, does any cancer nurse? I think we do this because we have such a need to be needed by and to take care of others.

I continued my initial interview cheerfully like I believed that Dave just needed a few days' rest, but I thought about how difficult this was going to be. Dave's admission paper work stated that he had 'Rule-out Pneumocystis carinii' which is a type of pneumonia common to people with the AIDS virus. "Rule out" meant that they were not sure. But Dave must have been told about this possible diagnosis by his physician, who had a reputation for being very direct and for caring for people with AIDS.

Dave apparently was choosing not to deal with it then. And I at least knew enough not to push the information on him. I played along with his fantasy that he would be better and back to life-as-normal soon.

Walking back to the nurses' station, I wondered if Dave was gay. Most of the men we saw with AIDS back then were gay, especially the single ones like Dave. But he didn't seem like most of the men who came in with a designated male lover and a multitude of male friends to offer support.

It was a few days later when I noticed that Dave didn't have visitors at all. His sister lived in another state. And I never saw any friends. He said that he hadn't had time to keep up with a lot of friends over the last few years. But I thought it strange that no one came in with him when he was admitted and no one came in to visit later either, although he did talk on the phone from time to time. That happened mostly at night when I wasn't there, according to the night nurses. I thought that if he wasn't gay he would surely have a girlfriend, but that didn't seem to be the case either.

Because Dave didn't have visitors I spent a lot of time with him. I was assigned as his primary nurse, which meant that I always took care of him when I was on duty, and I also started to stay after work occasionally. It wasn't a sexual thing, honestly; it was just that I felt safe somehow and better about myself when I was with him. I brought him little gifts like candy and nice-smelling lotions because he didn't get those things from any one else.

We found out that we had a lot in common. We both collected antique furniture, enjoyed opera and ballet, and read classical literature. I loaned him novels, and on his good days we would discuss them.

I also brought him a book on "wellness." The author wrote about how to improve your immune system with nutrition, positive thinking, meditation and visualization of the good cells multiplying and fighting any bad cells. Dave read it in bits and pieces; I could see that the bookmark was slowly moving to the back of the book. He didn't talk about it, though.

He did have Pneumocystis and had gotten very sick with it. And then, when he partially recovered from that, he developed purple sores on his legs that were also related to the AIDS virus; he was diagnosed with Karposi's Sarcoma. He still talked about getting out soon, and not at all about the seriousness of his diagnoses or his prognosis. It was as if he'd never heard the word "AIDS."

* * *

On one of Dave's good days, he asked me to wheel him in a chair up to the roof. It was really a screened-in area on the tenth and top floor of the hospital which was open to patients and visitors. He used to walk up there by himself every day during the first week when he was still feeling pretty well. Our unit census was low, so I had the luxury to take him up. Slow days were very rare and considered a real blessing because you could actually have quality time with your patients, which was the reason most of us went into nursing in the first place.

Dave and I could see the city from there which stretched for miles. It was early in the day and misty, and the auburn colors of fall were everywhere. It was quiet, too, compared to its usual hustle, because it was Sunday and most people had stayed in the suburbs. There were some children playing in the screened-in area. The were laughing happily. Dave sat in his wheelchair and looked at the scenery for a long time. I sat back beside him on a plastic chair, took a deep breath and let myself relax a little bit from the usual constant hectic pace.

Finally, he spoke. "How could anyone see a day like today and not believe that there is a God?"

Well, it wasn't too hard for me. Usually on a day like that I was running from room to room filled with people who were sick and dying. "I'm not sure. . ." I started, while looking down.

Dave turned his now-familiar dark eyes on me. "I have to believe that there is a God who cares. Otherwise what is the point?"

I faced him and wondered if he was thinking about his own life and imminent death, but he didn't mention that. "I'm not sure that I can believe there is a reason for all of this but I'd like to."

Dave looked back out over the city. "St. Augustine said that if we take a leap toward faith that God will illuminate the soul and give us a knowledge of his existence. And he said that 1300 years before Kierkegaard was conceived."

My eyes widened. I didn't realize that Dave was *that* deep.

"That's why my practice is so important to me. I think that God wants me to love people and try to help them find some quality of life for themselves. And it seems like the least I can do for a God who created me and loves me."

Never at a loss for words, I tried an answer: "Well I believe that it's important to help people too. I'm not happy unless I think I'm really working hard and making a difference in people's lives. I'm just not sure about the God part."

He smiled at me, and I said that I should probably get back downstairs. We never had that discussion again, but I thought about it. And years later I realized that he had planted a seed for me that was to change my life.

* * *

Dave had lost a lot of weight and had no interest in trying to drink milkshakes, which is the nurse's answer to all appetite problems. (This is probably because we wish so badly someone would tell us that *we* had to drink several chocolate milkshakes a day.) He was having to spend almost all of his time in bed. With an occasional burst of new energy he'd make it to the chair with help. He'd spent a lot of time reading case files until he finally was forced to refer his patients "temporarily" to another psychiatrist.

One afternoon about a month after he'd come in, we finally had a breakthrough of sorts. We had been laughing over Graham Greene's *Our Man In Havana*. Dave was starting to have problems seeing, but he had read it before and I quoted some of the funny parts to him. When I bent to give him a hug and say goodbye for the day, he hugged me back and then asked me to stay a little longer.

"Sure, Dave, what is it?"

"I'm not going to live, am I?"

I couldn't think of one comforting, therapeutic thing to say. I just looked at him hopelessly. He continued, "You don't have to say it. I know what this disease is doing to me. And really it is almost a relief, because I don't want to live like this."

"Dave, have you read that book I bought you? You have to fight it. You have to eat better and meditate and visualize!"

"I'll try. I really will."

Later, I realized that I cut him off when he was finally ready and needed to talk. I would not let him talk about what it was like to be dying. I'd worried about him being in denial about his illness, but it ended up that I had the hardest time accepting the situation. It didn't seem possible that this beautiful, loving person would actually die. He'd just started a new practice and he was going to make such a positive difference in so many people's lives. Why couldn't someone else die? Someone who didn't care about making the world a better place? I couldn't believe that Dave could even suggest that there could be a loving God!

* * *

The next week Dave became very confused and agitated and was diagnosed with meningitis, which is also typical with AIDS. He had to go to the intensive care unit. And it just so happened that the day he went to the unit was Halloween and all the nurses on my floor had decided it would be fun to dress up for the holiday. So I had to help transport Dave to the unit dressed in a white apron over a red puffy-sleeved dress, with pigtails and red ribbons sticking out from the sides of my head, and my cheeks painted with big red dots, brown spots over my nose, and bright red enlarged lips. I'm not sure what I was supposed to "be" but I know that being it was one of the more humiliating moments of my life. If was as if I didn't have a clue as to how serious this was for Dave. Luckily for me, Dave smiled at my get-up and even let one of the other nurses get a picture of us together. It's the only picture I have of him.

He stayed in ICU for a few days, and then returned to our unit with a "No Code" order. This meant that if he stopped breathing we were not to do anything "heroic," but were just to let him go. Apparently the physician had talked to Dave's sister on the phone and decided that this was best. We would just be trying to keep him as comfortable as possible.

He was what is called semi-comatose, meaning he would moan out when we turned him or did anything else painful, but he did not respond to us in any other way. We fed him through a tube and let his urine come out through a tube. We gave him oxygen through a mask over his face, we changed his position often, and we cleaned him up after his bowel movements. It seemed like he was already gone. Then came that day when Cheryl and I turned him and he asked, "When did we have sex on the beach?"

I was excited. But, other than asking this twice, he said nothing. Those were the last words that Dave spoke: "Sex on the beach. When did we have sex on the beach?"

* * *

I was surprised to find the chapel packed for the funeral. I found a seat near the back. Where were all of these people while Dave was is the hospital? Most were men who looked his age. A few introduced themselves and told me that I had meant a lot to Dave. Did he tell his friends about me? Did he tell them not to come to the hospital so that no one would suspect that he was gay?

Several of the men stood up during the service and talked about what a good friend and colleague Dave had been to them. One young woman stood and said, "Dr. Faulkner was my doctor and he was great. He helped me to get my act together and get back to school and become a better mother. I'll miss him a lot." I wanted to say how comforting Dave had been to me, but I was too shy to stand in front of all those people.

Finally, another woman stood to give her farewell. She looked like she was in her 40's; she was probably about 10 years older than Dave. She had on a conservative brown dress and her hair looked like a helmet, from too much hairspray. She introduced herself as Ellie Watts, Dave's sister.

"We are here to celebrate that Davy, my baby brother, has gone to be with the Lord. He told me the last time we talked on the phone that he had accepted Jesus as his savior, so I know that he is in heaven now. I want to encourage all of you to accept Jesus like Davy did."

A Christian? I thought about this while she talked. I knew that Dave believed in a loving God, but I didn't realize that he had become a Christian. Despite his talking about St. Augustine, he had also talked about Buddha, Hindu gods, and American Indian gods. I was glad that he had found something that had given him peace throughout his illness, although it definitely surpassed my understanding at the time.

I woke up from my reverie to hear her end with: "God took him on home. I'm so grateful to know that he is finished with his sinful, disgusting lifestyle. His life was a total waste here until he repented."

Someone behind me gasped. I slunk down in my seat, as if guilty for listening. A man in front of me sat up straighter in protest.

As she sat down, the silence in the church was stifling until the organ started for the final time. What she said, I thought much later, made about as much sense as Dave asking when we'd had sex on the beach. Even less. A lot less.

Tammy Townsend

Piano Lessons

"*E*ar bobs!" Uncle Kay shouts, staring at the gold studs in my ear lobes.

I stand my ground, digging dirty white tennis shoes into the grass at his feet.

"What do you mean?" I ask.

"Jezebel wore such," he thunders before turning his back to walk away. He heads out toward the orchard, muttering and grumbling.

Rooted with surprise at the unexpected reaction, I watch him retreat.

"I'm growing up, in case you haven't noticed!" I yell at his back.

Walking around the corner of the house, I take a savage kick at an unsuspecting dandelion growing in a clump beside the sidewalk. Grandmother insisted on having a cement sidewalk, just like people have in town. The community of Vinemont is far away from town. I sulk under the oak tree by the road. Sitting by myself on what Grandpa calls "the liar's bench," I shuffle the wooden shavings on the ground around with my feet. A bunch of old men usually sit out here across from the store to whittle, spit, and tell stories.

Across the expanse of gravel that serves as a parking lot, Grandpa's store looks as countrified as Gomer Pyle's filling station. A white box-like building, stacked together with cinderblocks, decorated by two barred windows that don't open, stands behind two old pumps. The prices aren't marked on the pumps like they are in town, because nobody cares. Grandpa gives them a fair deal, they think, and there's not another choice of a station for at least ten or twelve miles.

I wish Grandpa Morrison had more business. Sometimes an hour or two passes between customers. The only person I can count on to come by with regularity is the Merita bread man, and he only comes on Tuesdays. Plus, I hate his guts.

Morrison's Store doesn't even have a cash register I can play with. Grandpa keeps the money in his pocket. He's so far behind the times that even President Lincoln could have run the store if he were to come back from the dead like Jesus. Not that Jesus would have wanted to. If he rose from the dead today, he'd have to do it somewhere besides Vinemont, or there wouldn't be any use rising at all—Vinemont is dead as a doorknob.

Today is so dead, I'm even glad for it to be a Tuesday, which is the worst day of the week. Piano lesson day. Maybe even this day wouldn't have been so horrible, if it hadn't followed my birthday. Yesterday I was twelve on the twenty-eighth of July—a red-letter day on my calendar, because Mother had taken me to town and had my ears pierced. I'd waited on earrings since I was eight, because Mother had somehow decided that twelve would be an appropriate age. I had given up trying to figure out the mystery of Mother's mind long ago. Now I was just glad I had earrings. Except for the fact that nobody could see them but crazy Kay, and he wouldn't look. He still treated me like a baby. When the blue and yellow Merita bread truck pulled up by the pumps, I was glad to see it, so I skipped through the store's side door, beating Ray Parker inside and jumping up onto the slick wooden counter to wait for him, trying to look casual and bored. The bored wasn't too hard. Grandpa was asleep in the black Naugahyde chair against the wall.

Ray bumped his bread trays into the doorjamb when he came through the door backward with a load of fresh bread.

Grandpa shuffled his feet in the chair, stifled a yawn, and moved around like he was about to rise.

"No, don't bother getting up, Mr. Morrison," Ray said pleasantly, checking the colored wire ties to find stale bread masquerading for fresh on the shelf.

Grandpa settled back in the chair, grinning at Ray, pleased to have such a polite young man notice that he made the effort to be professional. "How you doin' boy?" he bellowed from the depths of the dark armchair.

"Can't complain," Ray replied. After a pause he added, "I guess I would, if I could get anybody to listen to me."

"Wait'll you get old," Grandpa snorts. "When you complain then, they just call you senile. Won't nobody give a damn."

"I do Grandpa!" I protest from the counter.

Hoisting himself from the chair with the help of his walking stick, Grandpa makes his way to where I perch. Ruffling my short blonde hair, he says, "Only because you wouldn't have nobody to buy you dolls."

I'm tempted to say I could taper off on the dolls. They just sit on the bed, and it's getting to be a real pain to make the bed and prop their butts up there every day.

"That's not true," I offer. "I don't want no more dolls, I want a watch. And you probably wouldn't get me one anyway." Smiling a wicked little smile, I know the watch is as good as on my wrist. He can't resist a statement like that. I should be ashamed, playing my old grandpa like a banjo.

Grandpa thumps me hard on the head, while Ray Parker goes about his idiotic little game.

"Let me see your feet," he demands.

"No." I draw my feet up under me, sitting on the soles of both my dirty tennis shoes.

"Come on, Sis," he wheedles.

Just to get it over with, I stick my feet out. Ray Parker jerks my left foot under his arm and wrestles the tennis shoe off. He holds tight to my ankle while he reaches inside his pants pocket for his nail clippers.

"I'm going to cut your toes off!" he yells, pressing the clippers together over and over in the air above my foot so that they snap loudly.

That routine used to scare the crap out of me when I was ten. When I was eight, I'd run for the barn and hide when I saw the bread truck coming. Now that I am older, it just makes me tired.

Ray Parker drops my foot when I don't squeal. Then he starts talking about what kind of rolls Grandpa ought to start carrying. Brown and serve in a box or a tin?

"Damn," I say to the gas pump on my way out, kicking the black hose curled in the gravel. "Damn."

I sit out under the oak again, thinking of playing mummbly peg, but since I'm not talking to Kay, that's out. I can't borrow his knife to play it with. So I'm sitting out under the tree, the weather is stifling hot, I have nobody to play with or talk to, and Mother will be coming down the road to take me to piano lessons in a little while. Things can't get much worse. Just as I'm about to give up and go into Grandpa and Grandma's house up the hill, a car drives up.

The Rickinbackers start climbing out of their old yellow station wagon. The little ones come bailing out of the very back of the wagon first, not even bothering to open the door. They just jump out the window. Three snotty little boys hit the ground running.

The two girl Rickinbackers come out of the middle of the car, one on each side. They look around and smirk. Because they're from Ohio, they think they know everything.

Mrs. Rickinbacker takes off into the store, sandals flapping, while Mr. Rickinbacker leans against the back of the car to smoke. He props his leg up on the bumper, lights a Camel, and says something to the girls, who walk over to me under the tree. Because we've never spoken before, we all eye each other cautiously.

"I'm Melinda," the biggest one says. She has on a short pink jumper. Taking her sister by the arm, she informs me, "And this is Theresa. You can call her Tee."

"Like you drink?" I ask.

"Maybe you do," she says, "but we don't. That stuff's gross. We drink pop."

The only "pop" I knew about was how the weasel went.

Before I could say another word, Mother came rolling up alongside the store in the Ford, honking her horn like a wild goose.

"Jolene! Get over here and get in this car, young lady," she hollers out the window, beating her fist on the outside of the brown door to get my attention.

Mortified, I walk to the passenger's door, which creaks as loudly as Dracula's casket.

Mother is chewing gum and smoking a cigarette at the same time. She puffs and pops as she pulls out of the parking lot, gravel crunching under the wheels.

I roll my window down, sticking my head part way out the window so I can't hear her if she tries to talk to me. She can't possible have anything interesting to say. All she's been doing all day is hoeing in the garden and sewing a dress from a Butterick pattern. I know I should have helped her hoe, but I just hate it when the Forsythe boys drive by and see me hoeing the garden. They hang out of the windows of their Mustang and yell "Hoe-er!" It's obscene.

Mother, of course, is oblivious, concentrating only on keeping the Ford between the ditches. I hate this car. It is so ugly. Just like a big hearse.

"Well," Mother says, "What's got you so down in the mouth?"

I pretend I don't hear, fluffing my hair in the hot wind blowing up from the road.

After a moment, I know she's going to drop the conversation if I don't reply. So I say, "You just have to embarrass me to death, that's what's wrong with me."

Mama really looks surprised. "What are you talking about? I drove up to get you for piano lessons. What's so embarrassing about that?"

"The Rickinbackers were standing right there," I reply.

"So?"

"They just think we're hicks, is all."

"Now hold on, Missy. You're swelling up like a toad frog because those trashy Rickinbackers know you're going to piano lessons? Haven't you ever heard of culture?"

"Culture!" I hoot. "Going to Vinemont High School on Tuesdays all summer long to sit with seedy old Mr. Gilbert? All in the world he does is talk to me about crap, breathe his smelly old Sucrets breath down the back of my neck, and sit beside me on the piano bench. Don't you see I'm not learning anything?"

"That's because you never practice, you ungrateful heathen." She sucks furiously on the last drag of her cigarette for a second, and I pray the worst is over. But it isn't.

"You know he does the best he can. He's the music teacher at the high school! Don't you think he could teach one scrawny little girl to play a song if she wanted to learn?" Thumping her cigarette out the triangular vent window beside her, she leans forward to the steering wheel, intently guiding our big brown piece of crap down the road. Her eyes bore into the windshield, her hands grip the steering wheel, and she's driving for all she's worth.

"I do practice!" I protest, even though I know I don't practice much. If I ever learn anything new, Mr. Gilbert gives me a great big bear hug, so I spend most of my time trying to make mistakes. I love the look on his face when I've played "Spring Song" down to the very last bar. On the next to the last stroke, I play a flat. I try for a B flat if I can get it. It's my favorite wrong note. Mr. Gilbert's ears shoot straight up about three inches and his neck contracts the same amount into his collar the second I hammer that B flat.

But he gets himself together to say, "From the top once more!"

That old coot is just wasting Mother's money.

Mother knows when I'm right. She rides along in silence for a few miles, rooting around in the black patent leather purse beside her without looking. Snapping the lighter under her cigarette, she takes a long drag.

"You know those pink butterfly earrings we saw yesterday at the dime store?"

"Yeah," I say, apprehensive because she may have me here.

She's got something I want, and she knows it. Lifting first one thigh, then the other, I check out the pattern the brown vinyl seat is leaving on the underside of my bare leg below my denim shorts.

"I'll buy them for you if you will just try a little harder to learn something."

Now, I'm no fool. And I do want those earrings.

"Okay. If you'll get them first, before we go to the lesson. It'll make me want to try harder," I negotiate.

Mother considers. I could weasel out of the deal after she's already bought the earrings. But then, I might want the earrings so badly I'd actually learn a song I could play when my grandparents come over next week to watch the astronauts on television. Neal Armstrong is going to walk on the moon, even though Kay says people have no cause to go fooling around up there. That up there is the Lord's business, Kay says.

"You can't wear them until your earlobes heal," she warns. "Sure," I agree.

After the stop at Elmore's Five and Ten, I hold the tiny gold box in my hand as we drive two blocks over to the high school.

"You got the best of me on this deal," I say.

Mother smiles, pulling the car to the curb in front of the school. The windows are open in the main hall, and a summertime maintenance worker is buffing the floors. We can hear the dull hum of the machine echoing in the hall. She slams the gearshifter into park before rolling down her window.

"It's a job, listening to that old man rattle," I continue. Mother frowns, but I have to convince her she got the best end of this bargain, that I'm really sacrificing for these earrings.

"Last week all he wanted to do was talk about some book called *A Clockwork Orange*. It's a story about all these rotten kids doing I don't know what all after the world ends."

"Why was he telling you about that?" Mother asks.

"Don't know." I fiddle with the earring box, taking the lid off and on.

"Were you being a brat?" Mama is getting touchy, and I wish I could get off this subject. Her throat is breaking out in red blotches. I don't know if it's me or the heat that's causing it.

"No," I yelp, wondering how things got so bad so fast.

"Well, I bet you were. That book is probably something you need to know." If Mama never heard of it, she thinks it's something important.

"I don't think so," I reply, remembering the way Mr. Gilbert smiled as he showed me the book.

"Even if it is," I say, "it's something I don't want to learn."

"Ah ha! Now we're getting somewhere! You've admitted it!"

"Admitted what?"

"That you're not trying to learn anything." Mother grabs the little gold earring box from my hands. Because I know my mother well, I start figuring out where the box will land.

Sure enough, the box flies out the window like a golden bird.

"I am going to make you learn something if I have to write it on a rock and beat it in your head." Mother vows beside me.

Climbing out of Dracula's brown casket, I step onto the grass. I am so embarrassed to be crawling on the front lawn of Vinemont High School searching through the clover for an earring box.

Locating the lid just as Mr. Gilbert comes out the double doors to beckon for me, I reach for the box, which landed a few feet farther away. The soft green fake velvet pad is empty as a bird's nest at Christmas. I can't believe Mama actually threw away my pink enameled earrings with fourteen carat gold posts. I'll never find them in all this clover.

As I walk down the hall beside Mr. Gilbert, I feel so sad I'll probably forget to mess up and play the whole song correctly. The old coot takes his Sucrets box out and flips the tin top up as we turn left into his classroom. He ushers me to the piano with his hand on the small of my back. Positioning my fingers alongside middle C, I wish Mother would find my earrings while I'm taking my lesson. I daydream that she will give them back to me, and say, "I'm sorry, honey. I just didn't understand." As my hands move along the keys, touching them in secret places, Mr. Gilbert leans toward me and smiles.

I wish Mama would come in here to get me, but I know she won't. I've been too bad for that.

Betty Jean Tucker

The Dog That Wasn't a Dog

Before the dog came, when I was fourteen, I needed no one. There was just Joe and me, growing up together in the old Smith house just outside the city limits.

We got along all right, Joe and me. We didn't know any better than to be alone, ever since that morning I woke up and She was gone. I remember the welfare lady had a word for it—desertion. I didn't know what it meant then, but it didn't matter much, except that Joe was so little he didn't know better than to love Her. I didn't know much, so I let him cry at first, but I learned and we got along all right by ourselves.

I didn't even need Joe. I could have got along all right without him. Even better, maybe. He was just a little boy, always in the way when I was at Mrs. Kinnard's cleaning or at the café washing dishes. But when they came to get him, after She left, he cried and begged, "Neldy, Neldy, my Neldy." And they didn't take him after all. I don't know why they didn't, unless it was just hot and the woman in her white starched dress didn't want to get mussed from him being dirty and crying. Sometimes now I wish they had taken him on then; I didn't need him no more than I needed Her, and maybe I would not have got so mixed up after the dog came.

But he stayed with me, and I got him clothes, fixed him toys, and washed him. I never did really touch him though, and soon he understood the not touching. He was so pretty and so soft, sometimes it made me want to cry, but I couldn't kiss him and hug on him like some folks would've. From the very first, I meant for him not to love me. I weaned him to need nobody, like I weaned myself, and that's the way I knew it had to be.

That's the way it was before the dog. As Joe grew up, I liked him for that part of him that was like me, and I was proud of him. We lived by ourselves, alone together and yet apart.

You didn't see that part of us that was alike when you looked at us. I was tall and bony with splotched skin and stiff, smooty-looking hair, and I had purplish eye pouches that made me look like an old woman. It seems to me that I must have been born with sores on my legs because even after the time when other girls—the clean, soft, giggling girls with nickels for recess and brassieres to wear even before they needed them—were shaving their legs, I was picking scabs off boils. I was so ugly I didn't even like myself. So I didn't blame them, but I cringed before the beauty of pretty faces and white hands twined together swinging down the street in laughing, whispering intimacy. The hot, sweet deliciousness of shared secrets was never mine, and I wouldn't let myself hunger for it. I didn't really need it anyway. No more than I needed Her or Joe.

It wasn't hard for me to be unloved or for people to leave me alone, but with Joe it was different. He was beautiful, with a man and little boy and womanness all mixed up in a way that made people want to touch him. Only they never did, because he was like me in that special way. I watched him grow up and always the smooth darkness of him hurt me. All of him was dark. His silky, straight hair was night black, and his skin was rich brown like the underside of a magnolia leaf. Sometimes at night, after he was asleep and could not know, I would reach out and stroke the soft, warm skin of his back. I didn't do it often because it made me sad and afterwards hollow inside.

After She left, I taught Joe to be a man before he was a boy, taught him to live without before he lived with, and he almost learned.

It was like the time they pushed him in the town water trough when we were coming home from school. I don't remember what the fuss was about. The reason didn't matter anyway. The thing was that I had always wanted to see somebody in that trough. I was glad in a way it was Joe because he was beautiful, and the thing was nasty, and I guess I might have thought it would make him ugly. I don't know why I could have wanted that, but I might have. It was a gray oblong stone trough across from the jail, and the bottom and sides were lined with a green slime, the water gurgling with rotted stuff. They threw him in and smeared his face with the slime, and I watched.

When they turned him loose, he stood up in the trough, his clothes dripping darkly, and flung his wet hair back from his face. Without taking his eyes off the boys, he wiped his face with his shirttail, and his mouth didn't move and his eyes didn't cry. At first they laughed, but because he didn't cry, it became unfunny and they went away. I was the only one who ever saw Joe cry, but that was after the dog came.

The evening of the water trough, we went home together, and he said why didn't you help me. You can take care of yourself, I said, not wanting him to know I knew he didn't want my help. I'd a kilt you if you'd said anything, he said, and I was proud of him. We went on home, liking each other.

But that was the last time like that. Because the dog came, and the first time I kicked it. I don't know why, or even whether or not I meant to. Maybe it was because she was dirty and pregnant, and you could see the fleas running in and out of the greasy-looking brown and white spots on her. Maybe it wasn't that at all, but rather that she was like somebody, like us or like Her. That first time, I was sorry. Not for the dog, I didn't care that she was hurt. I don't know, but I think I was sorry.

It wasn't right that the dog's eyes should be so like Joe's, so large and richly dark. Maybe that's why he wanted her. Because he saw the eyes when he bent over to feel the brittle ribs where I had kicked. And then the dog twisted her heavy body around and licked his hand. I remember thinking then, standing in the kitchen door watching them, that it would be all right. I could feel Joe shiver, knowing it made his flesh creep to be touched. He sat down on the porch step and looked at the dog. She didn't approach or tuck her tail and slink away. Just faced him, admitting a mistake and promising that it wouldn't happen again. I was ashamed for watching them watch each other. So I was glad the night was coming in fast and the dog would go away.

That was in the prelude to darkness when it's hard to tell light from dark. That was when I thought the dog was a dog.

But it didn't go away. It was there all the time, growing bigger and bigger and making a fool of me. I hated it for being a mama dog, and I hated Joe for being the way I wanted him not to be, for having a stupid heart, a little boy heart that let a dog slobber on it.

At first Joe was ashamed before me about the dog. We can't let the mutt starve, he'd say, with his dark, soft eyes looking past me. And I wouldn't say anything. I never did say anything, but he knew. He knew something else too, something about the dog that I should have known.

He learned everything about her in the few weeks before she got sick. He knew her better even than he knew himself, or me, and he talked to her with silly love when he thought I could not hear. She would stretch out at his feet in the dust with her tongue hassling in the heat, and he would sit for hours talking low to her and picking and killing the ticks and fleas off her.

One time he almost got killed for her. He acted that way about her, like she was Jesus Christ or something. It was when Mr. Reen caught her sucking the eggs in his hen house. She'd been doing it a long time, he said, and so he got his shotgun and waited for her one evening. It was about the time Joe was coming along the road from school, and when he heard the first shot, he began to run without really knowing what it was about, and yet in that funny way seeming to know too. When he saw the dog come limping and howling out of the chicken house, he ran for her like mad and grabbed her. He was holding her and both of them were yelling and wailing with the dog bleeding all over him. It happened so quickly, Mr. Reen couldn't stop his shooting, but the shot missed them. The old man had a heart attack from coming so close to killing Joe, and when he got over it and Joe went to see him about working after school to make up for the eggs the dog had sucked, Mr. Reen wouldn't hear to it at all. Said he had already been paid in full. We didn't know what he meant by that. It didn't matter anyway. He was old and sick, and I knew he had not learned much in his life.

Then the dog was sick, a gut-splitting sick, for three days, and the burlap sack bed under the house smelled of greasy shed hair and vomit. Every time Joe crawled to her, I told myself thank God she will die and he will be the same again. He crawled in and out, in and out, and the third night he slept all night with her. When he came out, I saw the saliva wet on the blackness of his hair, and I shivered.

That was the day he had to cut grass for the Fentons. I ought not to leave her, he said, but he didn't look at me, and I knew he would go. He got ready, slow-like, and went again to look at her. Come here a minute, he said, and I went and squatted and looked at the dog. She's trying to have her pups, ain't she, he asked, like he knew already, but wanted me to say it. Yeah, I said, squatting and watching. She was stretched out, her head limp on the ground and the specks in her eyes mingling muddily. Her bones stuck out and her shriveled tits were sucked up into the big bloated belly that jerked and strained. She didn't see us, but her blue-streaked tongue gave a tired lick when Joe put his hand on her head. Something's wrong, I know, he said then. Let's get the vet. Something's wrong. I knew something was wrong, but I didn't let on. What do you know about having puppies, I said. They all act like that. Go on now.

I got up and went into the kitchen hearing him call all right now, you watch her. If she gets worse, get Dr. Morton. You better do it now. I'll work and pay him for it. I think you better do it now.

When he was out of sight, I went back to the edge of the house and watched. She was whimpering then, and the side of her mouth on the ground was caked with dirt. For a long time I watched her—her with a belly full of life that never would be life. When the blood started out of her mouth and the birth hole, I said bitch, bitch, bitch, until she looked at me and saw me saying it. It wasn't long until her sides were still and the gray ground was dark purple, and I was glad, only I didn't feel good because she had seen me, and I wished she hadn't.

I stayed squatted down there a long time in the hot, white death air and the gladness oozed out of me, so I could smell myself sweat. I went inside and it was even hotter. I couldn't breathe and finally I vomited. I didn't like myself then, and I shook to think of the dead thing under the house. I shook, and I thought of Joe and the dog that was something other than a dog and I was afraid.

I felt him coming home fast and knew that his dark, pretty eyes would be old with his worrying. I saw him stoop down to look under the house, and then nothing showed but his hands—long, strong, clean hands holding to the floor. At first they were very still, like held breath in a spasm of fear; then they jerked and scratched the plank so that the gray porch splinters stuck under his fingernails and made the blood ease out. And still his hands scratched. Then they dropped to the ground, and he rocked and moaned hurting moans with the flies swarming around, and the ants crawling greedily.

I wanted to hold him like when he was a baby and blow the silky blackness away from his forehead, but I couldn't, and it hurt so bad. I couldn't because I felt dirty and ugly, like sin. It was the dog, that dirty damn bitch of a dog.

Suddenly the heat exploded in a dry, crying gust of wind. The bright whiteness of the sun died like an electric light turned off, and the daylight was dark. Joe staggered from under the house, his little boy arms filled with the dog and her great sagging load. He was crying, and when he laid his head against the dog's, a big blotch of blood from her mouth smeared across his face. He put her down just a little way from the house and got a pick. He dug her grave, propelled by silent, jerking sobs, while the streaked lightning made his hair blue-white, and the wind hurled the dirt back into his face.

The rain waited for him. When he was through with the mound, and the cross was in place, it came plunging down, slicing through the heavy air. Then he was at the bottom of the high porch steps, looking at me. He looked, and he was not crying anymore, and his soft eyes were not soft. Then he was like me, like me the morning I woke up and She was gone. He was like me then, and I thought thank God, it's over and he'll be the same again. He didn't really need the dog.

But then I could see the storm in him, and when he started talking, it was like the thunder was churning up his insides. You killed my dog. You killed her just the same as you'd a picked up the ax and hit her in the head. I knowed you wouldn't get the doctor. I knowed it.

He started walking fast toward the road. Once he looked back and then started running like he was racing with the hot rain. He became legs, shining legs, then nothing.

It's been a long time now. I can remember him running, running away in the rain, and my heart runs after him sometimes, but he is always ahead of me. Sometimes I can feel that I'll catch him because I almost know what it was about the dog. But then it eludes me—that thing that Joe knew and I didn't—and I can't remember anything except that before the dog came I needed no one. But the dog did come—that dirty, damn bitch that wasn't a dog.

Biographical Notes

Robyn Allers listens to the blues in Birmingham, where she is a freelance writer, actor and theatre director. As a contributing writer for *Black & White*, she has written restaurant reviews, features on the arts, and profiles on photographer Spider Martin, writer David Sedaris, and local activist Marie Jemison. Her stories have appeared in *Apalachee Quarterly, Sundog: the Southeast Review*, and *Crosscurrents*. Her directing credits include *Oleanna, Alabama Rain*, and *Three Tall Women*, which she co-directed with her husband, Roger Casey, all at Birmingham Festival Theatre. A Florida native, she received her MA in creative writing from Florida State University, where she studied under Janet Burroway and the late Jerome Stern.

Emma Bolden, a native of Birmingham, graduated from the Alabama School of Fine Arts after five years of study in creative writing. She recently moved to Bronxville, New York, where she studies writing at Sarah Lawrence College. She is currently working on her first book of poetry.

Wendy Reed Bruce, a native of Birmingham, currently teaches reading and composition at the University of Alabama at Birmingham and Jefferson State Junior College, while also teaching first grade Sunday School and struggling through her Master's Thesis for UAB's creative writing program. Her stories, essays and poetry have appeared in *The Atlantic Monthly, New Letters, Aura, Analecta*, and *277 Things Everyone Should Know About Arthritis*. She is also the mother of three, ages 12, 10, and 5.

Marian Carcache is a native of Russell County, Alabama. She holds a Master's degree in Hispanic Studies and a Ph.D. in Literature from Auburn University. Her short fiction and critical articles have appeared in such journals as *Shenandoah, Mississippi Quarterly, The Chattahoochee Review, Bronte Society Transactions* and *National Forum*. An opera based on her short story, "Under the Arbor," premiered in 1992 and was televised on PBS in 1993. The opera was nominated for a regional Emmy in 1994 and was a finalist at the International Festival of Film and Television in 1995. She lives in Auburn with her son, John-David, and their dog, Frank. She is an instructor at Auburn University.

Loretta Cobb considers herself an Alabama writer because she grew up in Birmingham during the Civil Rights struggles, making notes in her heart. Her family was the first generation off the farm in the foothills of Appalachia. Since her marriage to William Cobb, a novelist from Demopolis, Alabama, in 1965, she has been listening to and telling Alabama stories about enduring and prevailing. "Seeing It Through" is dedicated to Don Pippen.

Sandra King Conroy is the author of a novel, *Making Waves in Zion*, published in 1995 by Black Belt Press. "Fig Picking" is an excerpt from her second novel, *The St. John Show*, publication pending. A native of the Wiregrass area of L.A. (Lower Alabama), she is currently a resident of South Carolina Low Country and is working on a third novel, *Rise To Worlds Unknown*, also set in the Florida Panhandle.

Linda Elliott of Meadowbrook, Alabama, gained inspiration for her work by a notation in genealogical records. She believes this story of a woman's morbidly freakish end, like her life, is brief, a single glimpse, and so being is all the more poignant.

Anita Miller Garner received an MFA in creative writing from the University of Alabama. She has taught creative writing at Virginia Commonwealth University and served as poetry editor of *The New Virginia Review*. Currently, she teaches English at the University of North Alabama. She lives in Florence, Alabama.

Anne George is the author of the *Southern Sisters Mysteries* published by Avon. Some 30,000 of them are currently in print. The first in the series, *Murder on a Girls' Night Out*, was awarded the Agatha Award for best first mystery, and is in its sixth printing. *Murder Gets A Life* (hardback May 1998) is already in a third printing. The sixth book in the series, *Murder Shoots the Bull*, will be published in May 1999. A literary novel *This One and Magic Life* will also be out in 1999.

A native Alabamian, Anne George received an Individual Fellowship award from the State Arts Council in 1992. She was named Poet of the Year in 1994 by the Alabama State Poetry Society and in 1998 received the Silver Bowl Award from the Birmingham Festival of Arts for outstanding contribution to literature. She is the recipient of three Hackney Awards. *Some of It is True*, her fourth book of poetry, was nominated for the Pulitzer Prize by *Elk River Review*.

Aileen Kilgore Henderson, a native of Tuscaloosa County, was educated in Alabama schools including the University of Alabama where she earned BS and MA degrees. She has taught in Alabama, Texas and Minnesota. For twenty years, Henderson freelanced articles and photographs for adult markets such as *Dynamic Maturity*, *Mature Living*, *Christian Science Monitor*, *Southern Review* and others. In the 1990s, she began writing for children. Her stories have been published in *Children's Digest*, *Odyssey*, and *Nature Friend*.

The Summer of the Bonepile Monster (1995) received the Milkweed prize for Children's Literature and the Alabama Library Association Award. It was also a finalist for the Maud Hart Lovelace Award in Minnesota and is a current nominee for the Connecticut Nutmeg Award and the Utah Book Award, both to be announced in 1999. Another work, *The Monkey Thief* was chosen by the New York Public Library for their list of the best books for teenagers in 1998. Henderson is a member of the Society of Children's Book Writers and Illustrators and the Alabama Writers' Forum.

Laura Hunter, a native of Cordova, Alabama, graduated from the University of Alabama with an Educational Specialist degree in Secondary Education and English. A retired high school teacher and college instructor, she lives in Tuscaloosa with her husband, Tom, and their two cocker spaniels. Her work has been published in *Marrs Field Journal* and *Beyond Doggerel*. She has received the Birmingham Southern Hackney Award, first place in the Scott & Zelda Fitzgerald Museum Association Literary Contest (1998), and first place in the West Alabama State Fair for metered verse. Hunter is the mother of twins, the grandmother of one, and has been a kitty-sitter for her son's cat for the past eleven years.

Cindy Jones, a native Alabamian, graduated from the University of Montevallo. Recently returning to her home state, she lives in Montgomery with her husband, Guy, and their children, Lane and Nancy.

Tina Naremore Jones, a native of Bessemer, Alabama, is co-director of Livingston Press and teaches at the University of West Alabama. She is currently pursuing a Ph.D. in American Literature at the University of Southern Mississippi. She resides in Demopolis, Alabama, with her husband, Britt, and their two dogs, Bo and Chelsea.

Janet Mauney, a native Alabamian, is currently completing a Ph.D. in creative writing at Florida State University. She is completing work on her novel, *Tattoo*.

Patricia Mayer, a native of Mobile, is a registered nurse, wife of a nurse anesthetist, and mother of five sons, including two sets of twins. After training as a psychiatric nurse in Florida's infamous ward for the criminally insane, she decided that the publishing business was not so scary after all, so she drew on her experience to create the personalities inhabiting the fictional Southern railroad town of *Terminal Bend*, her first novel. Mayer currently resides in Mobile where she works as the school nurse for a small parochial school. It's a safe, sane, and quiet job.

Julia Oliver lives in Montgomery, Alabama. Her 1994 novel, *Goodbye to the Buttermilk Sky,* became a Quality Paperback Book Club selection, and subsequently was published in Dutton/Plume and German language editions. She is also the author of a 1993 collection of short fiction, *Seventeen Times as High as the Moon*, and is working on another novel.

Ann Vaughan Richards was born in 1940 in Elba, Alabama, into a family whose ancestors on all sides flocked to that one area when Alabama became a territory. Why they came and why they stayed are questions Richards ponders when she has nothing better to do, which is seldom. She stays busy living her life pretty much on her own terms. Richards has been married for a very long time to a very patient scientist. She is the mother of two independent, strong and sassy daughters. According to Richards she is reclusive, unconventional and quirky — all of which are the more positive of her inherited family traits.

Judith Richards spent her early life in the tri-state area of Missouri, Arkansas, and Illinois until 1961 when she left home and traveled on a tent show, Bisbee's Comedians. She married a performer from the show, but when they separated she moved to Alabama. Her encounter with an aspiring writer changed her life. In 1977, her first novel, *Sounds of Silence*, was published and followed by *Summer Lightning*, *After the Storm*, *Triple Indemnity*, and recently, *Too Blue To Fly*. Richards is married to author C. Terry Cline, Jr., and they live in Fairhope, Alabama.

Michelle Richmond, a native of Mobile, Alabama, earned a BA degree from the University of Alabama. Since graduating six years ago, she has lived in Tennessee, Georgia, Arkansas, Florida, and New York, but she still claims Alabama as her home. She currently teaches creative writing at the University of Miami. Richmond is the recipient of a James Michener Creative Writing Fellowship and two first place Hackney Literary Awards for fiction. Her stories have appeared in *Fish Stories*, *Fiction Collective Two*, *Gulf Coast* and *Alabama Bound*.

Mary Louise Robison was born in Tuscaloosa, raised in Florence, and lives in Cleveland Heights, Ohio, where she writes about growing up in Alabama. The award-winning short story, "Baby in the Cold Frame," is taken from her novel-in-progress, *Bones in the Gingerbread*. She recently obtained an MA in Creative Writing at Cleveland State University. In addition to teaching writing, she coordinates research in psychiatric genetics.

Scarlett Robinson Saavedra owns a house in a community called McElderry, Alabama, between Talledega and Anniston, and she still calls the blue-gray hills of Cheaha home. She currently teaches at Florida A&M and lives in northern Florida with her two daughters. She received an MFA in creative writing from the University of Alabama.

Carolynne Scott has been an Alabama writer all of her life. She has been a newspaper reporter, publicist, non-fiction book author (*Country Roads: A Journey Through Rustic Alabama*) and author of short fiction (*The Green and The Burning Alike*). In the course of her life, she has won the Faux Flannery Award given by Georgia College, an NEA grant for fiction writing, and five Hackney Literary Awards. Her stories have been published in about 15 journals, the most current of which is *Noccalula*.

Millie Anton Skinner, a resident of Jasper, Alabama, has been writing since the age of twelve in spiral bound notebooks kept hidden under the mattress because her big brothers made fun of her. The youngest of eight children and the only girl, Skinner grew up hearing family stories she hopes to preserve for her two children and six grandchildren.

B.K. (Karen) Smith is an instructor of composition and literature at Bevill State Community College, where she is also editor of *Beginnings*, a freshmen sampler of essays, and poetry editor for the college's literary magazine, *Equinox*. Several of Smith's poems and short stories have been published in literary magazines, and her first collection of short stories, *Sideshows*, was published by Livingston Press in 1994. Her book received many favorable reviews, including a starred review in *Publisher's Weekly*. In May 1998, *Prince of Personality*, a biography of Alabama philanthropist Earl McDonald, was published by Bevill State Community College in conjunction with Birmingham Printing and Publishing.

Smith has given fiction readings, served on panels, and directed writing workshops in colleges and universities throughout Alabama and in Florida. Her works and readings have been featured at writing conferences and festivals and several of her stories have been taught in college classrooms. Three current works under consideration for publication include a novel, *Something Down The Road*; a collaborative collection of short stories, *Sassy Cats*; and a collection of poetry, *From 2000 Feet*.

Joe Taylor published a novel, *Old Cat and Ms. Puss: A Book of Days For You and Me*, last year, and has a second novel forthcoming from Black Belt Press entitled *The Once and Future Bunion*. He is co-director of Livingston Press and teaches at the University of West Alabama.

Patricia Lou Taylor worked ten years as a cancer nurse and now teaches psychiatric nursing at the University of West Alabama. She is completing a collection of stories centered around nursing. "Sex on the Beach" is her second published work of short fiction.

Tammy Townsend is the mother of Karissa Hilliard and Alexander McNees. She teaches at UAB Walker College, where she teaches English Composition and American Literature. She is also co-editor of *Voices and Visions*, UAB Walker College literary magazine. Townsend received a BA from Mississippi University for Women and an MA in English with a concentration in creative writing from the University of Alabama. She plans to matriculate to the University of Southern Mississippi to work on her Ph.D. and a collection of stories.

Betty Jean Tucker, with the exception of a two-year stint in Birmingham as a reporter for the *Birmingham Post Herald*, has lived all of her life in the Alabama Black Belt town of Linden. She holds a BA degree from Alabama College, an M.Ed. from the University of West Alabama (formerly Livingston University), and a Ph.D. from the University of Alabama. She is now retired after twenty years as a professor and chairperson in the Division of Languages and Literature at Livingston University. Her writing career began at the age of nineteen with the publication of the story, "Callie," which was included in Foley's list of Distinguished American Short Stories. Her short stories have appeared in such publications as the *Montevallo Review*, *Ball State Forum*, *Alalitcom*, *Alabama Prize Stories – 1970*, and *Alabama Bound*.